THE SPEED OF DARK

BY BARBARA QUINN

PublishAmerica
Baltimore

First printing

ISBN: 1-4137-4308-0
PUBLISHED BY PUBLISHAMERICA, LLLP
www.publishamerica.com
Baltimore

Printed in the United States of America

My heartfelt thanks go out to Cesar Garza, Meredith Morganstern, Eric Giere, Leslie Longstreet, Jerry McCarty, and Sharon Schafer who work with me at *The Rose & Thorn Literary E-zine* (www.theroseandthornezine.com), and who graciously and diligently lent their time to help with the editing and nurturing of this book, and so much more. Thanks also to Janet Matz for her encouragement, to Angela Bongiorno for her unflagging support, and to Sandy Folb, Joan Smith and Kris Occhicone for our daily cleansing walks and talks. A kiss and a hug go out to Tom and Bret, and to Mom and Dad, for their belief in me and for allowing me to follow this dream. Without you there would be no words.

There is in God, some say,
A deep but dazzling darkness.

– Henry Vaughan

CHAPTER ONE

I was bent over the sink, opening the buttons on Pamela Wilcox's blouse with my teeth, stroking her thigh, when my mother's voice intruded.

"Luke! Don't stack the dishes in the sink like that or everything is going to fall. Pay attention to what you're doing!" Mom reached over and shut off the water. "Go get the rest of the silverware from the table."

I sheepishly did as my mother asked, thoughts of Pamela draining away with the soapy dishwater. I heard the familiar put-putt of the town's DDT truck, and quickly placed the remaining flatware on the counter. Without catching my mother's eye, I wheeled and headed across the room.

"Back soon!"

The screen door banged shut behind me and I raced past my mother's new 1964 Grand Prix. As I mounted my bike, my mother's voice rang in my ears, "Don't stay in that cloud too long, Luke D'Angelo. Who knows what it might do to you!"

Most neighborhood parents were saying the same thing to their children, many tacking on, "Don't forget to come home when the streetlights come on!" We welcomed the arrival of the truck, riding to it willingly, drawing in the sweet scent, trusting that no harm could ever come to us.

The sound of windows slamming shut followed me that evening as I fell in behind the white truck, pedaling blind, deep in the spray of poison where you couldn't keep your eyes open for long. I lingered in the gas as long as I could, Lord of the DDT Flies, dropping back and coming up for clean air now and then. Though I had never done more than sit near her in eighth grade English, Pamela Wilcox and I hotly groped one another in the fog.

The voices and shouts of the other kids faded in the distance as they fell back, letting the truck continue on its route while they awaited the next arrival of the evening: the Bungalow Bar ice cream man. But I pressed on. After a bit, I slowed to get my bearings; being recently transplanted to Faith Junction, nothing was familiar in this part of town.

Out of nowhere in that dense haze someone laughed near me, a laugh that tinkled melodically. I looked left, then right, but the fog hung too thickly to make out who rode there. All I could tell was that someone female inhabited the cloud. My heart raced and my imagination flew. I increased my pedaling and thought I could see a slim shape ahead, arms extended to the sides, riding without hands. A daredevil girl. No one I knew.

She laughed again and I realized she was laughing for the pure joy of the ride; she had no idea I was watching her. I resolved to get her attention. Perhaps I could sneak up on her, shout above the noise of the truck, give her a scare.

I saw sparks near her front wheel and thought the DDT truck might be on fire. I slowed a bit. "Watch out!" I yelled, but she didn't acknowledge me. Before I could yell again, the sparks moved upward and gathered over her head. I held tight to my handlebars to keep my balance, watching as the sparks grew into a shiny ball with a dark core. Bright rings circled the outside of the globe. I pedaled hard again and watched as the ball settled a few inches above the front fender of the girl's bike. She held her arms wide.

As I drew nearer, I thought I felt something tugging my bike. I wasn't sure what drew me forward, but it was as though my Schwinn had been caught by a magnet. Now I rode alongside her, holding tight, trying to gain control of my front wheel. The ball was wider than the back of the

DDT truck, a silvery sparkling object with a dark center that frightened me. Overhead the sky was dark now, and I wondered if the moon had somehow fallen from the heavens. In spite of my fear, I reached one hand out toward the pulsing mass. As my fingers passed through the object, which felt neither hot nor cold, the dark at the core suddenly glowed blue, then dispersed and faded into the night. The remaining glow pulsed and formed into a sparkling tornado that moved back and forth in front of us and threw off a mesmerizing swirl of shards of black light. I tried to focus on the shape, but the more I stared the less I could see. The image faded. I felt cool air. And I heard her laugh again, just before my wheel hit a huge hole.

I launched over my handlebars into the air. My bike clattered to the ground and I landed hard on the asphalt, tumbling to the curb. The DDT truck moved away, taking the girl, and the light show, with it in its wake.

I watched her recede as I rubbed a skinned knee. The poisonous fog dissipated slightly, but the aromatic remains of the gas stayed. To my surprise, the girl fell back from the truck, turned her bike in my direction and rode toward me. My pulse beat hard at the sight of her slender shape, and I felt a stirring inside as she pulled up next to me and planted her pink sneakers on the pavement.

"You all right?" she asked.

I blinked twice. This was no ordinary girl. She possessed the most beautiful skin I had ever seen, even more beautiful than Pamela Wilcox's. She wore white short-shorts that exposed tan and taut legs, and above the shorts, a red and white checkered top was tied at her waist, Ann-Margret style, exposing a flat belly. Blonde and trim, she was as near perfection as I could ever imagine. She had to be about my age, yet our paths had not crossed. How could that be?

"You have to stay focused to ride in that fog. It's not much different from a real fog," she said softly.

I nodded at her, not able to find my tongue, angry at my ineptitude, embarrassed by what was occurring in my shorts. She hooked her thumbs in her front pockets and my eyes lingered on the curve of her hips.

"I've never been in a real fog," I replied finally. "I only moved here a few weeks ago." As if "real" fog didn't exist anywhere else. I stopped myself from staring and knew I was as crimson as her shirt.

She tilted her head at me. A golden wave of hair caressed a heart-shaped face.

"What was that?" I asked. "That ball...." I didn't know how to describe what I had seen. "Those sparks, and lights...." I pointed to the sky.

"It's time for me to go get some chores done at the farm. The animals need feeding."

"Wait a second...."

Her eyes held mine for an instant. She was radiant. There was no other word to describe her that evening in the fading light. I wished I had put on a clean T-shirt and pants instead of the faded madras shorts and stained white shirt that hung on me. I tried to think of some words that would keep her from leaving, but nothing came to mind.

She laughed that high tinkling laugh again and dug into her pocket. Shyly, she handed me a small jar with a metal cap. I let her drop the container into my palm. The glass was cool and comforting in the summer heat. I held it up to the light and found my voice. "What is it?"

She pursed her lips. "Something I think you could use."

The jar appeared empty. I began to unscrew the cap and she placed her hand over mine. Oh, that touch. It was like a butterfly coming to rest. I tried to stay still, but to my dismay her hand alighted in an instant.

Her voice was gentle but firm. "Not now."

"Don't open it?"

She shook her head. "Save it."

Her blonde hair fell in waves past her shoulders. She pushed a strand behind her ear, an ear as delicate and translucent as a seashell. I thought about how good it would feel to nuzzle her, to bury my face in her neck and draw in her scent. I was sure that she would smell as good as she looked. She peered through the clear side of the container and smiled.

"It's really quite a good specimen. One of these days you'll appreciate it."

"Looks like an empty baby food jar," I said, shaking the container.

"Appearances are deceiving. Didn't anyone ever tell you that?" She giggled and as she pushed off and began pedaling away, I could swear that the cicadas stopped their thrumming for an instant.

I realized with a start that I didn't know her name. I wanted to yell, "Don't go!" But I had learned long before I was fourteen that you didn't try to control a girl like that. I was saddened for I didn't know if I would ever see her again. That thought was unbearable.

I watched her round the corner. As she turned onto the main road out of town, she raised her hand to the sky in what I thought was a wave. The air suddenly grew cooler; then from the junction of the two streets, a bank of fog rolled toward me, softer and cleaner than that spewed by the DDT truck. The girl faded as great whorls of mist enshrouded me. I tried to track her, but she was gone, lost in the distance, in the fog. She left me wishing for more time with her and broader shoulders with which to impress her.

Thinking about it now, I can see that I raced toward her the way I raced to the DDT truck, with a sense of joy and an undercurrent of danger, incapable of understanding that there could ever be any negative consequences to my actions. At fourteen, why shouldn't every bright light on the horizon turn into a rosy sunset?

After a time, I headed for home where my mother's kitchen radio blared something about unseasonable fog scattered throughout our area. I climbed the stairs to my room and fell on the bed studying the jar. Something silver ran in my veins.

The phone rang and I gently placed the jar on my desktop. The voice of my buddy, Joshua Weingrad, squawked at me.

"Twice in one hour. Do you think I'm going to go blind?"

I sighed. Josh enjoyed detailing his solo sexual exploits. He assumed I didn't mind listening as I didn't generally switch the subject, but tonight I had my own agenda.

"I just saw the most incredible girl, Josh. Blonde. About fourteen or fifteen. With blue eyes and an unbelievable shape."

"Go, Lukie!" he cried.

"I'm wondering if you know her name."

"Guess that's a no. How many quarts of this stuff do you think I can accumulate over the course of the summer?"

I glanced at the jar on my desk. If Josh got his hands on it, he would no doubt try to fill it the way he did most things these days. I made a mental note not to tell him about the receptacle and to keep it hidden.

"She's about five-foot-two, Josh."

"I bet if I keep it in the fridge it would stay longer. I'm a goddamn machine."

"Josh!"

"Sorry. Big bazookas?"

"She's gorgeous, Josh. I want to know who she is."

"Deanna's having a party tomorrow night. Maybe your mystery bazooms will show up there."

"I haven't seen her anywhere before." I was too embarrassed to mention her wonderful laugh.

He let out a low whistle. "I bet I know who she is."

I held my breath.

"She gets out now and then when her father's not looking. Not stacked but not bad at all."

"What's her name?"

"Celeste. Celeste Carey."

Though I'd never heard it, the name sent shock waves into my groin.

"She's too weird, man. Ask Alec if you don't believe me. Only reason I know anything about her is 'cause he dated her."

Alec was our third musketeer. Unlike Josh and me, Alec had had an occasional girlfriend.

My mother's voice rang out from below. "Luke, I need you to help me move the table. Could you come downstairs?"

With my father absent, as usual, on a business trip, Mom relied on me to help her with her constant organizing. I wished my father would spend more time with us and lately wondered if there was more to his absence than selling paper products. Beneath the domestic sea of tranquility that my mother liked to pretend existed, I sensed turbulent waters.

"I have to go, Josh. Catch you tomorrow."

"Tomorrow, douchebag. I'm working on filling a peanut butter jar. Wanna lay odds on how long that takes me?"

CREO

Later that night I lay restless in bed in the June heat. I switched off my transistor radio in the middle of a story about three new cases of flipper-like arms on Thalidomide babies. As I tossed and turned trying to induce sleep, something caught my eye, something glinting on my desk. I raised up on one elbow and studied the pile of things scattered on the green felt blotter. Next to a Silver Surfer comic book, I saw a half-finished model of a Corvette, my ticket stub from the 1964 NY World's Fair, some loose S&H green stamps, two 45 rpm's and that little jar of Celeste's.

Again there was a soft light. My window was open and outside a full moon cast an eerie light in the backyard. Surely, something had caught the moonlight coming through the window and reflected it toward me. I held my breath.

There it was again.

This time I saw it was the empty baby food jar that glinted. I stared hard at the glass, but the light disappeared under my gaze. I lowered my head to try a different angle. Nothing. I lay back on my pillow and thought about the exotic girl who had given me the gift.

The light started again. For the next few minutes, the jar twinkled off and on in the moonlight. Was there a pattern to the flashes? I tried to find one, but eventually I gave up and let the jar be. There was space enough for both of us in my room.

Sleep blanketed me and when I awoke in the morning the jar sat empty and still, nothing more than a baby food jar. I reached over to remove its cap, but as I twisted the cool metal, I heard her voice in my head.

"Save it."

The pull in my chest was unmistakable.

I sighed and buried the jar in the depths of my underwear drawer, away from the prying eyes of my family and from Josh's sticky fingers, and bounded down the stairs to face the day.

CHAPTER TWO

I next encountered Celeste on a full-throated, screaming hot, stinker of a day. Josh, Alec and I had sought out the coolness of Ben's diner, a silver bullet-shaped place on Main Street. We dropped our bikes, their wheels lined with clothes-pinned playing cards for maximum noise, at the curb. The heat rose in waves from the street, reminding me of the way heat radiated from my mom's electric stove burners. The asphalt oozed beneath our feet. But it wasn't the scent of warm asphalt that assaulted me.

"What the hell is that stink?" I said. "I've been smelling it ever since we moved here. But never this bad." I held my hand to my nose.

Josh chuckled and looked at Alec. "I don't smell nothin'. How 'bout you, Alec?"

Alec shrugged.

I said, "Yeah right. It smells like dead fish, or worse."

Alec said, "Wind's from the north. They must be cooking today."

"Who?" I asked, my eyes watering.

"The plant," said Alec.

Josh grinned. "You'll get used to it. The rest of us don't even notice it anymore, right, Al?"

Alec nodded. "It's the Spi-Sea plant. Shrimp cocktail in a glass cup with cocktail sauce." He patted his belly.

Josh chimed in, "They're cooking up a big mess of shrimp today. Later on it'll be the sauce."

"Gross," I said. "My mom sometimes buys that stuff. I'm never going to eat it again if that's what it smells like." I pulled my shirt over my nose, trying to ward off my gag reflex. We made our way to the diner door.

Alec said, "Wait till August. Even I can smell the damn place then."

"Yeah, nothing like August in Spi-Sea land," said Josh. "The stink brings in mosquitoes the size of pickup trucks." He snorted loudly. "And it's too hot to wear a long-sleeved shirt so you wind up eaten alive and scratching like mad."

Alec grinned. "Something to look forward to." He clapped me on the back and we crossed into the air-conditioned coolness of Ben's.

"Let me guess," said Ben. "An eggcreme for Josh, a rootbeer float for Alec and a black and white soda for the new kid."

Alec and I nodded in agreement, and Josh spoke up. "I think I'll have a vanilla malted. And bring us some fries too, okay, Ben?"

Ben wiped his hands on his apron and headed toward the grill area. "Coming right up."

I watched as he pulled down a silver can that matched the shiny shell of his diner. Soon the malted was whirring on its spindle. It would yield Josh two glasses full. In no time Ben had served our order. Talk turned to girls and Celeste's name came up.

"She's cold as ice if you touch her," said Alec between gulps of his rootbeer float. He passed the plate of fries to me and I helped myself.

"When did she ever let you touch her?" asked Josh. "Now I bet I could score with her."

"In your wet dreams, dirtbag. The only thing soft you'll ever get to touch is hanging between your legs," said Alec, the disdain in his voice evident. "Oh, and I sure as hell did touch her, and it's none of your business when, and I'm not saying more than that so don't bother asking."

Josh dumped catsup in a pool on the corner of the plate; an action I knew was intended to irritate Alec, a catsup polka-dotting-all aficionado. Alec glared at Josh and grabbed the bottle of Heinz.

"I should make you go wash those paws before you go fishing around in these fries," said Alec. "How's the latest jar caper going?"

I had known the two of them for five weeks, ever since my family had moved to bucolic and boring Faith Junction, some 117 miles north of our previous home in the Bronx. I was not used to their constant bickering and shifted uncomfortably in my seat as in my experience direct confrontation of this sort usually led to flying fists.

But Alec was not in a belligerent mood and we were not in the Bronx. He dotted a few fries with catsup then leaned back against the red vinyl bench and wiped his mouth on his sleeve. He fixed his heavy-lidded eyes first on Josh and then on me. I could imagine what that look would do to girls our age. His eyes drew you into them. The pale blue color, not that different from my own, seemed to change depending on the light or what he was wearing. Today he was wearing a blue polo shirt with one beige stripe stretched taut across the chest. His clothes always arranged themselves respectfully over his ranginess as though they were in awe. Mine hung in shame.

"I'm telling you, she's a strange one, Looner," he told me. That's what Alec called me. He had dubbed me loony the first time they saw me. I had been singing and collecting dead cicada shells, unaware anyone watched. The fact that my given name was Luke cemented the moniker. I became Loony Luke, or Looner. "I don't think I've ever met anyone like Celeste," he continued. "One day she's hot, the next...."

"I thought you said she was cold as ice," Josh said. "Now she's hot?" He smirked at me trying to get me to take his side, and threw a French fry into his mouth. I stared at the plate and avoided speaking. Josh started dumping salt on the fries.

Alec sighed and smacked the salt shaker out of Josh's hand. "She can be hot, cold, whatever she wants."

I wished I had just a little of whatever it was that poured off him. A scrawny 5' 4", I envied his tall, filled-out athletic body with ability to match. He narrowed his eyes to slits and pushed a blond shock out of the way. My hand went to my wiry brown hair that I knew shot out in too many directions. More than a little dab of Brylcreem did not do me no matter how long I spent in front of the mirror.

"Most people have moods, don't they?" asked Josh. "That's what you're talkin' about I'd bet." He spoke rapidly, slurring his words. He poured a second glass of vanilla malted from his canister. Compact and athletic, with a wrestler's build, black hair and flashing green eyes, he seemed to be moving fast even when he was seated in the diner. He threw a potato into his mouth.

"Moods. Yes. But..." Alec waved his hand in the air, conducting with a French fry, "Celeste isn't moody. She's molten lava and the core of the earth. She's the polar ice caps." He lowered his head. "I don't know what the hell she is, but she's strange and she really can burn you." He dropped a French fry onto the plate. "Ask Deanna if you don't believe me."

Deanna. This was a name familiar to me. An attractive redhead, she owned a big house not far from mine and liked to give parties. I had already been to several where the liquor flowed freely.

Josh screwed up his face and looked at me. "Shit. I hate it when Alec gets poetic. What football player talks like that?" He held Alec's gaze. "But you're only the backup quarterback so I suppose it makes sense." He let out a rapid-fire laugh.

"Why don't you go play one on one with yourself, dirtbag," said Alec. "Seems to be what you do best."

Josh, who only had me by an inch in height, had played benchwarmer for the Faith High Rollers JV basketball team, a fact that rankled.

I chuckled. It sounded to me like Alec had a major crush on this girl and perhaps Josh did also. After my brief encounter with her, I could understand why.

I watched Josh and Alec as they ate and reflected on their differences. Alec was the brooding, poetic quarterback. Storm clouds could gather in his eyes at any time. Josh was our comic relief, always mischievous, sometimes foolish enough to taunt Alec, and though he often said things that got him into trouble, he would do anything to avoid a fight. Me, I was the quiet observer. The two of them were such strongly drawn characters that they made me feel like a faded cartoon. I felt honored to have such friends.

The bell over the diner door tinkled. Beside me, Josh looked up and I followed his gaze. His lips turned up slightly at the corners and I took in the object of his attention.

Celeste.

Trim and compact, dressed in plaid shorts and a white blouse that had tiers of ruffles all round, from the waist up she looked like a wedding cake. A white headband pushed her blonde hair off her sweaty brow. Tanned legs jutted out of shorts and made me want to run off with her for the rest of the afternoon. I looked outside and saw a pink bike leaning neatly against the rack where ours lay spilled in silent worship. Josh nudged me hard in the ribs, and I jumped, sending a silver metal napkin holder clattering to the floor.

"It's her," Josh said in a loud whisper.

At this pronouncement, Alec turned his head and stared. That made three of us.

She ignored us and everyone else in the diner. She placed her order and in a few moments the waitress returned with a double-decker vanilla cone.

We watched, salivating, as she licked at the drips on the sugar wafer and paid the waitress. As she left the diner, she glanced our way. Her eyes found mine for an instant and my heart leapt into my throat. I blinked and tried to look cool. Then those intense golden eyes were fixed somewhere else above my head and, ruffles jiggling, she turned and stepped out the door. She climbed on her pink bike and pedaled away. I watched the bottom of her tight shorts move across the leather bicycle seat and felt my blood pumping madly.

"We should have said hi or somethin'," said Josh whose eyes were fixed where mine were. "She is such a piece."

"She didn't want to talk to us or she would have, dirtbag," said Alec, poking at the fries. "Dream on, Josh. The only date you're ever going to get is your left hand, doofus."

"I just wanna be that ice cream cone of hers and then I could die happy," said Josh. "You think you could stick your dick in a quart of ice cream and cum?"

Alec steamed across the table at Josh. I didn't say anything. I wanted to run the moment of Celeste's and my eyes meeting over and over in my head till it was etched in my brain. There was something electric in her gaze, something I was drawn to on a primitive level. I wished she had acknowledged me.

"Do you think she's worth going after, Looner?" asked Alec.

Josh said excitedly, his words running together, "If she wasn't so weird I'd put the moves on her inna minute."

Alec said, "You'd put the moves on an alien if one let you close. You'd be lucky if Celeste so much as looked at you, you loser."

Ben brought our check.

I never answered Alec's question. But I knew the answer.

Seeing her for the second time only increased my certainty that Celeste Carey was the most fascinating girl in the world. I knew I had to get to know her. I was once again totally under her spell. Something burned in my chest.

We paid our bill and headed outside to our bikes. The heat of the day had built to a late afternoon crescendo that intensified the smell of the shrimp cocktail plant. Dead fish and tomato sauce assaulted me and made me want to run back inside the diner. I covered my nose with my hand. Josh and Alec gave no indication that the foul smell existed. I wondered if I would ever be able to stomach the scent like they did.

Josh said, "Want to sneak into the McCaffrey's pool? Or play some baseball? Or wack off to Playboy in my basement?"

I shook my head.

Alec said, "I have to get home early today. My aunt's coming over and I have to spend time with the twerpy cousins."

Josh said, "Boss. We still have time for a swim. And don't forget we're supposed to go to Deanna's tonight for a party."

They both looked at me. My eyes were on the road that Celeste had taken. I could not stop thinking about her.

I asked, "Where do you think she went?"

"Who?" asked Alec.

"Celeste."

Josh nudged Alec in the ribs. "Uh oh. She's left another one high and dry."

The two of them guffawed, though I thought that Alec's laughter was forced.

Alec said, "She lives out that way. She probably headed home. There's a shortcut in back of the bird sanctuary that goes to her family's orchards."

Josh said, "Bet Looner is thinking how nice it would be to get his sticky hands on Celeste." He moaned, "Ooooooh, oooooooh."

I shook my head and scuffed a sneaker in the dirt.

I was grateful to Alec when he slapped Josh hard on the shoulder and sent him reeling. Alec turned to me, his fists still clenched.

"She's a loner. Her dad's scary and doesn't like company. I think he'd keep her at home if he could. You'll see them in church on Sundays."

Josh said, "Once we tried to take some apples from his orchard and he came after us with his shotgun."

"You're kidding," I said.

"I wish he came to my temple 'cause it's so boring. Alec says he does this weird thing at Mass with his leg."

Alec smacked him again before he could continue and said, "Let's get out of here and catch that swim. You coming, Looner?"

I swung my leg over the center bar and sat back on my seat. "I've got to mow the lawn before my dad gets home."

Before either one could say another word, I pushed off and began pedaling. My reasons for going home went beyond what I said, but I was not about to discuss them. I had to be home to call my sister, a dinnertime ritual that never varied and that I dreaded and looked forward to at the same time. With my father out of town, I knew my mother relied on me more than ever to be there for the call.

"We'll see you later at Deanna's," Alec's voice rang out behind me. "Eight-thirty."

I waved without looking back and pedaled faster.

Soon, the silver half moon of Ben's roof faded into the distance behind me. I rode on, farther from the main part of town than I'd been before, until my bike crested a hill and before me lay hundreds of apple trees. I applied my brakes and stopped on the side of the road. The sight of so many trees was dizzying. Only a few weeks ago I had been on the streets of the Bronx, in a neighborhood where trees grew only at the Botanical Garden. The scene before me was too hard to digest. Plus, the smell of the shrimp plant hung heavy in the air, overwhelming the pleasant fruit scent that occasionally wafted to me. "Christ, it stinks," I called out and pulled my shirt up over my nose.

The thrum of cicadas assaulted my ears as I studied the orchard. Which way had she gone? The strip of land that abutted the orchard marked the beginning of the bird sanctuary that Alec had mentioned and a dirt road ran between them. I ran my eyes all the way down the road. At the very end was an outcropping of brown and orange rock that led up a hillside, and moving away from me toward the rocks was a pink bike.

I let my shirt fall back to my chest and began pedaling down the rutted dirt path toward Celeste. Her bike was heading slowly up the last hill of the orchard toward the stone outcropping.

I acted purely on instinct and that instinct told me to follow Celeste Carey to the ends of the earth if necessary. I had had crushes on girls before, but never of this magnitude. I knew I was acting like an idiot and a part of me wanted to turn around and head home and shoot some hoops. But a larger part of me did not. And so I pressed on.

Rather than close the gap between us, I decided to keep a respectful distance while I gathered my thoughts. I ran various introductory scenarios through my head, "Hi, I'm Luke, remember me from the other night?" "Hi, what's your name? I'm Luke D'Angelo. Thanks for the jar." Yech. I cringed at my tongue-tied efforts and wished that she would turn around and wave at me, eliminating the need for introductions. But she kept her eyes fixed on the path in front of her wheel. After a time, I saw her brake. She climbed off and left her bicycle in the middle of the path. I stopped and watched as she moved into the orchard, toward the rock outcropping. Then I lost sight of her.

Drawing up next to her Schwinn, I came to a halt. I scanned the area in the direction of the rocks but Celeste was nowhere in sight. Where was she? Late afternoon clouds gathered on the horizon as though watching my predicament. A conversation of thunder, followed by a hot breeze, announced a brewing storm.

Another loud roll of sound made me catch my breath. "Cripes," I said to no one in particular. Maybe it would pass quickly. I walked to the rocks and saw what looked to be a cave hidden behind the boulders. There were many caves in Faith Junction and tales of hermits and strange creatures inhabiting them abounded. Only last week, Josh and Alec had told me about an unkempt, surly man dubbed "The Leatherman" because of his handmade hide clothing. He was said to have lived in dank holes in the area for most of his adult life. According to legend, he was fond of abducting children whose crushed bones were used to whitewash the stones at the entrance of his abode.

A rush of fear went through me when I saw that all the stones at the entrance to this cave were covered in chalky dust. I told myself it was merely coincidence and approached the milky rocks, trying to avoid stepping on anything white as I clambered over large boulders and peered into the dark maw of the place. Celeste could be anywhere nearby; perhaps she had not entered the cave. I scanned the outcropping above me. Why would she be in a dingy old hole in the ground that could be filled with bats and God knows what else? Thunder rumbled louder and a few thick drops pelted me.

I heard a moan and jumped back from the entrance, landing on a smooth stone and wincing in pain as my ankle twisted. I tried to keep my imagination in check, half expecting the Leatherman himself to fly out of the mouth of the cave, grab me up and drag me into the dark depths where I would be gutted and my bones added to the whitewash pot. Fighting off the fear, I stood my ground and listened hard trying to figure out what it was that had startled me. A gust of wind carried the scent of rain past me and then the moaning sound reached me again. This time I recognized it as someone crying.

The baleful, exquisite sound washed over me and caught in my chest. I gritted my teeth and tried not to let it affect me. I wanted to rush inside and wrap Celeste in my arms and comfort her, help her in some small way. I clenched my fists knowing that I was intruding on a private moment, that I should leave her alone, but there was no way I could do that.

Then the sobbing stopped. I moved under the ledge of the cave. Rain fell harder now and the sound of singing drifted up to me. I could tell she was trying to calm herself with song—I do the same thing. It pleased me to think we had something in common. I was embarrassed about my singing. When Alec and Josh had caught me crooning that day I was searching for cicadas, I had been mortified. Hearing Celeste's melodic voice rise out of the earth made me happy and more comfortable with my habit.

I recognized her hymn as one we sang in church. "Ave Maria." After awhile she moved on to tunes from *West Side Story* and I heard her snapping her fingers. Satisfied that she was no longer so desperately unhappy, I moved out into the rain. But I could not bring myself to leave her presence yet.

As "I Feel Pretty" resonated from the cave, I scaled the rocks above Celeste's hideout. I climbed over boulders and tree stumps until I reached a spot thick with brush. From there, surprisingly, her voice rang out even more clearly. And then I saw why. A small hole opened to the space below. I peered down and could see a flashlight glowing on the floor of the cave. My foot slipped and several stones tumbled into the small shaft, landing noisily below. I stepped back from the edge of the hole and held my breath. Celeste stopped singing. I knew she must be looking up to see the source of the stones. Perhaps she feared a cave-in. I bit my lip, aware I was acting like a total fool. This entire endeavor was not like me at all, and I was confused by my actions.

The rain came down in buckets now. I feared that she would exit the cave and find me. A sweet damp smell rose from the earth and for once the Spi-Sea plant stench had receded. I hurried to my bike and drove off down the muddy path, and as I reached the spot where the main road met the dirt turnoff to the orchard, the clouds rolled back in thick banks that reminded me of waves at the shore. In a matter of moments, the rain had stopped and the sun shone brightly. As I pedaled home I could feel the heat drying my drenched shirt back. My feet pumped to the rhythm of Celeste's songs and my heart raced beyond the beat.

CHAPTER THREE

M y house was two blocks from Deanna Barton's, but our lives were worlds apart. For one thing, our small house could fit inside her garage. Then there's the fact that my family operated at top volume. At Deanna's, the only thing loud was the stereo, which I heard as I stood in front of the ornately carved door of her family's white colonial.

Deanna's house was the last one on a dead-end street. From that vantage it looked out at a wide expanse of lawn, the windows and doors glaring at the lesser houses on the block. On the front porch two double swings guarded either side of the entrance.

A smiling woman dressed in a billowing white sundress greeted me. "Deanna's in the rec room with a few others. You can find your way?" asked Mrs. Barton in a manner that indicated it was not a question at all. She floated to the back of the house and I found myself thinking that she should be tethered like one of the balloons in the Macy's Thanksgiving parade.

I headed down the hall toward the loud rock music. This was the third time I had been to Deanna's. I knew there was something disturbing about the house, though I had not yet pinpointed what. Perhaps it was the white walls and furniture that gave the home a hospital-like feel and caused me to wonder who was the patient. I eventually decided that all the Bartons were.

I entered the room as a song ended. Josh stood on the opposite side of the room flipping through a stack of records.

"Put on another one, Josh," said Deanna. Her eyes turned toward me and lit up. "It's about time you appeared," she said.

She crossed the room and hugged me. She's a tall, thin, elegant girl with almost no breasts or hips. Her hair lay flat on her head and extended halfway down her back in an auburn sheet. Behind her I saw Josh make a face and a motion with his hands as though he were breaking something in two. I reddened as I knew he was alluding to my having once said that I always feared hugging girls like Deanna for they seemed so easy to break. Against me, her heart beat behind her ribcage as though it were an imprisoned bird. I pulled back and nodded at Josh who grinned madly. Alec sat in a corner thumbing a comic book and did not look up.

"More music," said Deanna. "That's what we need, Josh."

Deanna's voice lilted, but her eyes held something other than happiness. She turned them from mine quickly. A loud blast came from the stereo and The Beatles' "I Want to Hold Your Hand" filled the room. As Deanna sang along and Josh clapped his hands, I reached over and turned off one of the many lights that illuminated the small space. Then I settled onto the floor and let the sounds of my friends rush over me. There was something comforting in the companionship of this group. Since moving, I had been acutely aware of not fitting in anywhere. Sitting in the Barton rec room I was finally able to believe I belonged.

A flash of white moved and caught my eye. Curled up on a puffy chair, with skin as pale as her slacks, was a girl I didn't know. I averted my eyes and found Deanna's.

Deanna giggled. "You haven't met my cousin Susie, have you? She's visiting from California."

Susie, the girl on the chair, removed a bottle of nail polish from her pocket and uncapped it. The smell permeated the room. She ignored the rest of us and began painting her toenails bright red.

Deanna giggled again and linked her arm in mine. "Don't pay any attention to Susie. She's got a rather strange way of interacting socially. Isn't that right, Sooz?"

Susie wiggled her toes and blew at them with lips as red as her polish.

Even sitting down curled into herself on the chair, I could see she was an attractive girl, much more filled out than Deanna. As she bent to her task, I found myself sneaking peeks down her low-cut blouse.

Josh put another record on the turntable, a Chubby Checker number. As the sound flowed through the room, I broke away from Deanna and headed for the bar where I poured myself a Coke. Then I took a seat on a white vinyl barstool, facing Susie.

Deanna and Josh gyrated on the wooden floor doing the twist. I knew he liked her and this was the closest she had let him get. "He's doofy," she had said once when Alec asked her how she felt about Josh.

Finished polishing her toes, Susie cast her eyes up at me and for an instant I saw her lips turn up slightly at the corners. Her black hair hung Cleopatra style and her dark-rimmed eyes completed the look. That hair and those eyes were out of sync not only with the bleached surroundings of the Barton household, but with her own pale clothing. The confusion was enough to draw me to her. I sensed a kindred spirit.

I crossed the room and sat down at her newly polished toenails

"You want me to paint yours?" she asked and I could not tell if she were serious. I licked my lips.

"I'm joking, silly," she said, reading the puzzlement on my face.

"Thank goodness," I said and we both laughed.

She wiggled her toes and said, "These are red toes. I have no use for pink or other faded tones. If you're going to do something, do it boldly."

Her voice had an unusual cadence and her accent had a slight western twang that was new to me. She pushed back her black hair behind her ear exposing a pink nape. A smell of lemon and fresh mown grass came from her and I wanted to bury myself face down in her....

Deanna gave me a shot in the arm and brought me back to reality.

"Maybe we should go over to the quarry for a night swim," she said. "How's that sound?" She smiled a bit too long, and I figured she must have already been hitting the bottle of rum stashed beneath the Coke table. There were two givens at a Deanna gathering: Mrs. Barton never appeared and the liquor never dried up. Deanna had apprised me of these facts on my first visit. All the booze any of us wanted was available in a coat closet across the room.

I looked over at Susie. Deanna saw where my eyes were directed and read my mind. "Susie doesn't swim."

I found this hard to believe. "But she's from California. Beach Boys. Surf's up."

Deanna giggled. "She's from the desert. And she hates the water so she'll probably stay here."

"I'll keep her company then." While swimming with a group of teens sounded like fun, spending time with Susie held my interest more.

Deanna waved her cup in the air. "Hell, no. She'll be fine. Won't you, Sooz?"

Susie stood and stretched and headed out of the room without answering. Deanna shot me a quizzical glance. Deanna's definitely tipsy, I thought.

Josh put on another 45. No one made a move to leave, the liquor having induced listlessness.

I sat down on the floor and said to Deanna, "We saw Celeste Carey today."

"That girl makes me nervous."

I said, "I'm beginning to get the idea that she has that effect on a lot of people."

"There's something odd about her. It's always been that way."

"Did you grow up with her?"

Deanna nodded. "Kind of. She doesn't go to school. Never has." She reached for the bottle of rum and did not bother adding any Coke to her glass.

"But you knew her?"

"We were friends for a bit. As much as anyone could be, what with her father trying to keep her away from everyone."

"I'd like to get to know her."

Deanna extended her arm and pushed her sleeve up exposing a tanned forearm. "She did this to me."

I studied her skin and saw a jagged scar in the shape of a small lightning bolt. It appeared to have been tattooed by an expert. "She tattoos people?"

She pushed her sleeve back over the mark and shook her head. "Not at all. She does weird things. I'd be careful if I were you."

"What kind of weird things?"

Thunder rumbled in the distance again. Deanna rose and went to the window. She said, "It's threatening to rain again. It's been this way all week."

"Alec and Josh seem to think she's beyond understanding."

I looked over to Josh but he was absorbed in selecting records. "Fuckin' A!" he said, holding one aloft as he danced with himself sitting in a chair. Alec continued to read his comic book. I wondered how many drinks both of them had consumed.

Deanna stretched. "I do wish it would get it over with already and rain." She faced me abruptly as Susie entered the room and sat down again. "Stay clear of Celeste. That's the best thing anyone can do."

I wanted to ask Deanna more about Celeste but I could tell the subject was closed. Besides, with a creature like Susie drawing near, my thoughts were elsewhere. I could tell there was something between us, some undeniable chemistry. The feeling wasn't as intense as with Celeste, but it was palpable.

Susie laughed a throaty laugh, and Deanna asked, "What's so funny, Sooz?"

Susie cocked her head in my direction. "Him. He keeps staring. Is he always that way?"

Deanna rolled her eyes. "Don't mind Susie. They do things differently in California."

Susie said, "How about a game of spin the bottle? Bet we do that the same as you."

Deanna shook her head and wobbled a bit. "I don't know if that's such a good idea. What if my mother walks in?"

Susie held a hand up and silenced her cousin. "She's out at the pool with her pitcher of martinis, as usual. How drunk are you? You know she never comes in till bedtime."

This was fascinating new turf for me. Girls were creatures I had admired from afar till only recently. I had grown four inches in the last year and though not tall by any accounting, I had suddenly become the object of female attention rather than derision. I was not sure how to act or what to do, but knew how important it was to act as though I did. To my relief, Josh hopped off his chair and relieved me of being master of ceremonies.

Josh finished his Coke and placed it on the floor. "One bottle, as requested," he said.

"Way cool," said Alec. He tossed his comic book to the floor and joined us.

We gathered in a circle on the floor, and an awkward silence filled the room. Suddenly Susie grabbed the bottle.

"I'll go first," she said, and she pointed the bottle right at me.

"Hey," said Deanna. "You're supposed to spin it."

"California rules," Susie said, shooting a sideways glance at me.

"I'm not sure I like this," said Deanna.

"You can go next," said Josh.

"Now what?" asked Deanna.

Alec said, "Now Looner has to kiss Susie."

"That's right," said Susie, pursing her lips.

I stood.

"Where are you going?" asked Deanna.

I motioned to Susie to follow me. "If you don't mind, I'd like a little privacy."

Susie hesitated, then shrugged and stood. "California rules," she said, pushing her hair back behind her ears.

"Where the hell would a dumbass dirtbag like Looner have learned California rules?" asked Alec.

I opened the door to the small closet that housed the Bartons' liquor. Susie stepped inside and I followed. I drew the door closed and could hear Deanna giggling outside.

"Hurry up, you two," she shouted.

We stood in the semi-dark, light creeping under the door. My eyes adjusted and I could make out the curve of Susie's neck. Her lemon and grass scent filled the small space and I could feel myself stirring. Her face turned toward me.

I leaned down and let my lips brush gently across her neck, then moved up to her mouth, letting instinct guide me. I pulled her toward me and she kissed me hard. Her hand snaked down my stomach and as I held my breath…the door opened and flooded us with light. Josh, Alec and Deanna stood there laughing hysterically.

"It's supposed to be ONE kiss," said Deanna, "not seven minutes in heaven."

"Yeah, dirtbag, get out of there," said Alec with a grin. We moved into the room again, neither of us looking at the other. My heart was alive in my chest. I wanted to go back into that closet and explore every inch of Susie.

The lights flickered and thunder rolled through the room. Electricity charged the air and the storm broke through the heavens with a fury, rain pelting the windows and soaking the sash within seconds. Wind whipped the curtains wide. Deanna rushed to the windows and slammed them shut. Lightning crackled nearby outside.

"That was really close," Deanna said, peering out the window. "God, I hate thunderstorms."

Josh went over to her and slung an arm casually around her shoulders. He said, "Think of it as God bowling." She moved away from him.

"It's God moving furniture, dirtbag," said Alec. "And crying about it."

"The rain is angels weeping," said Susie.

Susie moved away from me. Whatever had been between us in the dark was over. The storm had done that. I tried to find her eyes but she reached down to a stack of records and read the covers.

It rained for much of the next hour, and when it let up, I left for home. The lightning and thunder had moved away, and the drizzle that remained felt cool, cleansing. As I walked, tromping through deep puddles, a female face floated in front of me. I shook my head, annoyed at myself, for the face belonged to Celeste, not Susie.

I kicked a stone and told myself how stupid I was. Celeste was a fantasy; I had barely met her. Susie was real. Susie was available, interested. Susie's were the lips that had locked on mine that night.

But it was Celeste's face that continued to haunt me.

CHAPTER FOUR

I started keeping track of Celeste Carey's comings and goings in a
notebook. I covered page after page with my pencil and pen
scratchings that bore witness to the insanity that possessed me from the
moment I had met Celeste. Flipping through the pad, I could see how I
grew more and more obsessed with Celeste. At first there were only
scattered entries in the book, but further on, the pages grew cluttered and
crammed with notes. Her life became the reason for my existence.

I learned her routine easily, for she passed by my house on the way to
town and back. I was satisfied when her bike rolled by like clockwork,
impatient if she were late. In the mornings she zipped by my front porch
at nine a.m. A towel and swimsuit rested in the pink and white straw
basket on her front handlebars. She was headed for the town pool for
private diving lessons. Once I followed her and watched. She never spoke
to anyone except the instructor.

At lunchtime Celeste returned, wet hair matted down her back. She
would not reappear until suppertime, when she would pass my house and
cross to the next block—where I had first encountered her—to wait for
the ice-cream truck or DDT truck. There were no kids, only retired
couples, on that street.

Her afternoons were the last piece of the puzzle for me. After a full week, I still didn't know where she spent them. There weren't too many places for teens in Faith Junction, and Celeste never was at any of them. She was completely outside the mainstream scene. My notebook showed that I looked for her at the movies, at the library, at Ben's and at the quarry. I even tried the cave several times, unsuccessfully. Alec and Josh told me that she spent a lot of time tending her father's apple orchards. The orchards were the finest in the area, always bearing more and better fruit even in times of drought. There was never a drought at the Careys' it seemed.

The last Monday in June, I agreed to meet Susie at the quarry. Even though I had only met her a week ago, I thought that this might be the day that Susie would let me go all the way with her and I was delirious with joy at the thought of finally experiencing sex. I looked at my watch for the fiftieth time and could not believe that two p.m. was still an hour away.

I glanced out the front window and saw Celeste on her bike riding down the block. My heart skipped a beat. Without another thought I raced outside and climbed on my Schwinn. There was plenty of time before I had to meet Susie.

I kept what I thought was a safe distance back and tailed Celeste as she pedaled out of the neighborhood toward the orchards. Soon she verified what I had suspected, as her bike bounced over the ruts in the dirt path toward what I had taken to calling the Leatherman's Cave. I should have been satisfied to discover where Celeste was spending her afternoons, but I still had time to kill, so I followed her. I did not understand what the draw of the dank underground was for either of us.

I waited until Celeste was out of sight and then walked my bike along the dusty ruts to the cave entrance. As always, I avoided glancing at the ash-like dust that coated the entrance boulders. I listened hard, but heard nothing, so I sat down. A blue jay squawked nearby. The smell of summer was thick and ripe and fortunately the Spi-Sea plant was not stinking too badly. I could actually smell the apples. I noticed how pretty the view of the orchards was from where I sat. A chill passed over me as I realized the Leatherman himself had probably sat on the same rock I had chosen and stared out over the orchards and rolling hills. I jumped up and swatted the chalky stone from the seat of my jeans.

The June sun beat down on me and sweat trickled down my brow. After a few minutes, curiosity got the better of me. I approached slowly and entered the cave trying to be quiet lest Celeste know I was there.

I glanced at my watch: 1:15 p.m. I still had at least a half an hour to kill before heading to the quarry, which was a short ride from my home in the opposite direction. I smiled thinking about how pretty Susie was even if she was a bit obsessed with keeping her toenails painted perfectly. This week they were neon pink. I loved the way her tiny toes curled into mine when we stretched out on the couch to watch television. So what if her voice had what I had by now decided was an annoying nasal twang that reminded me of the whine of my dentist's drill. The sound often caused me to forget whatever we were discussing. She was attractive and female, a real piece according to Josh, so what more could a guy like me want?

I headed farther into the cave and wished I had brought a flashlight. A loud voice made me jump.

"If you're going to follow me around, we might as well introduce ourselves."

I heard a match being struck and could make out Celeste as she bent and lit a lantern. The soft glow filled the darkness and illuminated her features. Her golden hair fanned around her bare shoulders. She had on cutoff blue-jean shorts and a striped halter top that revealed her curves. I tried not to stare, but she was so attractive I could not take my eyes off her. The light danced around her, drawing me toward her. I was sure I had never seen a girl like Celeste before. Her physical appearance was striking enough. But there was something soft, warm coming from her to me. All I wanted to do was lose myself in that pillowy texture. Something told me that if I ever got close to her we would both be doomed, but I longed for her all the same.

I must have been staring senselessly, for she waved a hand in my face and held me with a hard gaze.

"I'm Celeste. Who are you?"

I cleared my throat. "Looner. I mean Luke. I'm Luke D'Angelo."

She sat on the ground and crossed her legs Indian style. She motioned for me to join her and I did, folding my legs awkwardly; I was never flexible enough to sit that way comfortably.

"Luke. I don't know why you're following me, but I assume there's some reason."

I shrugged and tossed a stone that bounced off the metal casing of the lantern. "I'm new around here. I thought maybe we could be friends."

She laughed. "Just 'cause I gave you a jar doesn't mean I want you for a friend. Haven't they all told you the stories about me?"

She reached into her pocket and took out something that glinted in the light. A handful of jacks? She moved them from one hand to another. There was something odd about them. No matter how hard I stared, I could not get a fix on them. They seemed to change shape in the soft light. I figured it was the darkness and lantern playing tricks with my vision.

I said, "I make my own judgments about people."

She cocked her head to one side and stopped tossing the metallic objects. She closed her hand around them. "Don't lie to me, Luke. You can say anything you like, just don't lie. Especially not here." I nodded and she tossed her head in the direction of the cave's entrance. "I'm surprised you had the guts to come in here."

"I've seen scarier places on my way to school in the Bronx."

She smiled. "Everyone knows this isn't a safe spot. The Leatherman might get you."

I had been right about the origin of the cave. "Then why do you come here?"

"You ask a lot of questions."

"You're not at all like what they said you'd be like."

"You really ought to be going before you get in trouble. Most parents don't like it when their kids come to this cave." She paused. "What did they tell you I'd be like?" She turned the wick up and the glow grew a little brighter. Her hair gleamed in the soft light. I wanted to reach out and touch it. She met my gaze. "Remember the rules. No lying in this cave."

I blinked and licked my lips. "They think you're strange."

"And?"

I looked at my sneakers.

"That's not all. Keep going."

I spoke softly not wanting to say the only other thing that blared in my brain.

"Speak up!"

"I heard that you can burn people."

She sat back on her heels. "Ah. Deanna Barton." She narrowed her gaze. "You're telling the truth. That's good."

"You don't seem that odd or mean."

She laughed and I completely forgot where I was. The sound was high, tinkling, blinding. I finally realized what that sound triggered in my memory. It reminded me of the chapel bells that summoned communicants to accept the Host at church on Sunday. On hearing it, I was ready to surrender to the Leatherman if she so ordered.

She shook her head and her eyes grew dark. "Thanks for telling me that. No one talks to me much."

"That's ridiculous."

"This is a small town. You'll learn soon enough."

A low rumbling came from deep within the cave and I looked over at Celeste who appeared unfazed by the noise. I took my cue from her, relaxed and said, "You seem perfectly normal to me. You seem like one of the nicest people I've met at Faith Junction." I wanted to kick myself for uttering such inanity and was grateful for the semi-dark.

Celeste did not seem to mind my familiarity. She held her hands palms up to the ceiling. "This place is special." Her eyes twinkled. "You haven't explored it yet. There's a lot more to this cave than most people know."

"Is this where you go in the afternoon?"

She pursed her lips and ignored the question. "I'm lucky to have found it. And I guess there's a reason you've found it too."

"It's OK if you don't want to tell me. I mean, there's no reason you should have to tell me anything about yourself, is there?"

She stood and dusted off her shorts. "You want to explore it with me?"

The invitation appealed to me immensely. What better way to spend a hot afternoon than on a tour with Celeste Carey as my private guide?

My heart raced. What better way, indeed. I glanced at my watch and my stomach sank. How could it be ten past two and me due to meet Susie at the quarry ten minutes ago?

"Oh, man. I've got to leave. I can't believe I'm late." I stood and my legs wobbled beneath me, a fact that did not go unnoticed by Celeste. She smiled and made me want to stay even more.

"That effect isn't unusual here. You'll learn to gage time better if you keep coming back."

I backed away from her, and headed toward the bright light at the mouth of the cave. As I retreated, I watched her toss whatever was in her hand on the ground. The jacks again. This time I knew for sure that they were the oddest jacks I had ever seen. I stared. They seemed to have a whirlwind around their tiny prongs. At first I thought they were tiny tornadoes, moving about each other on the dirt floor. I blinked and tried to focus my eyes on them, but before I could focus clearly she scooped them up and stuffed them in her pocket.

"Have fun, Luke," she said and added. "You'll probably go bowling later. And then to Ben's. That's where all the kids go on Mondays."

"I'll see you tomorrow," I called and ran from the cave. I grabbed up my bike, threw my leg over the bar, and pushed off hard, taking off at top speed.

As I rode I heard her singing fading into the background. The notes of "The House of the Rising Sun," repeated in my brain, long after Celeste's voice had faded.

It was not till I reached the paved road that I was able to force Susie Driscoll back into my consciousness. But Susie would not stay there. She became Celeste. There was nothing but Celeste. Every blade of grass, every rock in the path, every bird overhead, was linked in my mind to Celeste.

When I arrived after a twenty-minute hard ride, the quarry lay still and welcoming, a shady oasis from the hot afternoon sun. No one else disturbed the silence. I scanned the scenery. Susie must have gone home in a huff I reasoned. Who could blame her? I was half an hour late and Susie was not the type to stand for my dalliance.

My shirt was soaked through and I figured I might as well cool down. I headed down to the diving rock that hung above the deepest part of the quarry. I took off my shorts, shirt and underwear and dove into the water, paddling out to the center of the quarry. The cold water cleared my head. And the air, oh the air. It hovered sweet and pure in a pocket tucked away from the Spi-Sea smells. I wished Celeste were there to enjoy the beauty and serenity of the scene. I sang aloud, enjoying the echo the quarry gave my voice. Then I swam back to the diving rock and looked around. Here and there an occasional shopping cart poked through the surface of the water, having been tossed in by a drunken frat member home on summer vacation.

I was about to climb out when I heard a female voice. "Do you always treat your women this way?" The voice belonged to Susie. There was no doubt that she had been observing me.

I tried to act nonchalant and wondered how long she had been watching. "I got stuck doing some chores for my mom and couldn't get away." The lie rolled easily off my tongue.

"Didn't you ever hear of a telephone, Luke?"

My teeth chattered. The water stayed icy cold in the quarry till late August. I wished I had my shorts or a towel nearby. Susie, far from caring that I was naked, stared unabashedly, a fact that unsettled me more.

I grabbed onto the slippery rock and hoisted myself up and out, scraping my thigh against the rough granite. I walked past Susie, found my shorts and held them to my crotch. Susie said nothing. She wore a sly grin.

"This really isn't fair," I said as I stepped into my cutoffs. In spite of the cold water, her presence obviously aroused me.

"It's perfectly fair," she said. "Truth in advertising."

I drew her to me and we kissed lightly at first, then with a growing passion that unleashed something wild and pent up in me.

She pulled her head back. "You're all wet and cold."

I pressed my face to her breast. "Warm me up."

We sat down on the rock. She stroked my hair and I let my lips travel down to her stomach. She lay back and we hugged full length. God, she felt wonderful.

I kissed her lightly and she shuddered. She whispered my name. I realized that it was not her voice in my ears. It was Celeste's.

I pulled Susie to me. She yielded to my touch and I could feel her hard nipples under my chest. I wanted that lemon and grass scent to be mine. I wanted to bury myself in her, all of her. Celeste faded into the background at last.

As I raised my head to look at Susie, I received the shock of my life.

There, high above us on the bank of the quarry was an unmistakable figure, her arms stretched up to the sky. I tracked where she pointed and saw dark clouds gathering overhead. Celeste Carey's head turned toward me and I knew her eyes were trained on mine. Then she ducked beneath the lip of the ledge and was gone.

Thunder rumbled. I stopped kissing Susie and bolted upright. She sat up and said, "What the hell is going on?"

I shook my head and reached for my shirt.

"You look like you've seen a ghost or something."

Fat drops of rain landed on my head and back. The wind whistled through the quarry and the clouds blotted out the afternoon sun as if evening had fallen.

"I've got to go," I said.

"You melt in the rain? There's an old shed over there we can use if you like." Susie pointed to the wooden structure near the dirt path.

I stood.

Susie put her hands on her hips. "What the hell are you, queer or something?"

I ignored Susie and found my bike. The rain fell in buckets now. She followed me and the downpour soaked us. Her thin shirt clung to her breasts as she shouted, "Don't ever call me again. Wait till I tell my cousin what you didn't do!"

But nothing could stop me from leaving. I didn't care if she put it in the school newspaper.

"You're loony for sure. No wonder they call you that!" Her nasal twang echoed in the quarry as I rode away

The rain drenched me from top to toe as I pedaled hard through puddles and rutted dirt. Lightning crashed nearby and a bolt of fear shot through my chest. I rode home as fast as I could.

As I pulled into my driveway the rain let up. The afternoon thunderstorm was over, violent, brief and memorable, like so many others that rolled over the town and my life that summer.

CHAPTER FIVE

On Tuesday morning, activity filled the house and sent the lazy summer atmosphere into hiding. My mother started cooking before I rose and the wonderful smell of bread baking filled my nostrils as I spooned my cereal and buttered my toast. Even thoughts of Susie and Celeste took a back seat. My kid sister, Joanie, was due to arrive that afternoon for one of her periodic family visits.

Although I loved my sister, and would do anything for her, a mix of dread and embarrassment seized me between bites of Cheerios. Joanie lived most of her life in a school for the mentally deficient. Most kids uncharitably called them Retard Schools. This visit was her first to Faith Junction, and I knew that she and I would be the object of much talk among my new friends.

My mother and father harbored extreme guilt over sending Joanie away to board at the Raritan School. We did call Joanie every evening at dinnertime to stay in touch. Or at least Mom and I did. Dad, the new VP of Sales for Farmer Paper Products, had a heavy travel schedule that kept him away much of the time; he was due back in Faith Junction over the weekend. We always asked Joanie about her day and what she had eaten, and told her what was happening in our lives. "The six o'clock news," is what Mom called our nightly updates.

But the guilt was still there, and when Joanie made her several-times-a-year visits home, my family tended to over attention. All of us circled round her as though she were a goddess reclining on plump pillows, or a queen awaiting her subjects' next offering.

For the most part I did not mind all the attention lavished on my younger sister. Joanie always could make me smile and I loved her very much. She and I spoke a special language. We did not rely on words. Rather, certain things were repeated constantly between us till I felt on some level that we were truly communicating. Her eyes glistened sometimes as she rapped herself in the head with a favorite wooden block that remained in her pocket. I would pick up the block and rap myself and the two of us would laugh. Other times we would repeat the motion and shout. On some level Joanie and I understood one another very well.

"Eat up," said my mother as she waved a wooden spoon at me. She stirred a pot of turkey soup, one of Joanie's favorites. "I want you to ride over to market and pick up some heavy cream."

I yawned and sat back in my chair. My mother kept talking. "I'm making sunshine cake and need to have some whipped cream to put on top." Joanie loved sunshine cake and so did I.

"I'll go by as soon as I get dressed. You'll have it before lunch." For Mom's sunshine cake I would ride five miles.

My mother nodded and continued stirring her pot. She wore a yellow apron over green capri pants. She was always a walking citrus grove of color. She once admitted that one of the ways she cheered herself and the world up was by wearing garishly colored clothes. When we went out, she always garnered visual attention, which to an awkward teen was a cause of great embarrassment, but which often led to her making interesting, if not downright odd friends. She turned to me with a serious look on her face. "Luke, I have a favor to ask of you."

I squirmed in my seat. Like her cake, her favors were legendary. I could be stuck at home for the next two weeks canning peaches or cleaning closets or worse.

"I'd like you to take her out with you once in a while. Do you think you could do that?"

I pushed back abruptly from the table. The last person in the world I wanted to be seen with in public besides my vibrantly colored mother was Joanie. Joanie always spoke her mind and embarrassed me. It was one thing to play with Joanie at home, quite another to be seen in public with her.

"How much cream do you want?" I asked my mother.

Mom shook her spoon at me. "A pint will do nicely."

I opened the back door and the scent of my mother's newly planted lilies growing next to the back porch steps wafted into the kitchen. The wind was blowing uncharacteristically from the south which meant the Spi-Sea plant was belching processing smells on those to the east of Faith Junction. I breathed deeply, relishing the sweet air.

"Don't forget, I want you to take Joanie around with you," said my mother.

I let the door slam shut behind me. I was cursed. There was no other word for it. What would all the friends I'd acquired in Faith Junction over the past few weeks think of Joanie? I could not imagine Josh and Alec doing anything except laugh at her. And Deanna would never want me at one of her parties once my sister came to light. After they met Joanie, I knew the script that would follow. Heck, they would be avoiding me for all sorts of reasons that were excuses.

I pedaled furiously, trying to lose myself in the rhythm of the wheels as the rush of morning air raised goose bumps on my arms. In a few minutes I turned into the parking lot of Hynd's Corner Superette. A bus roared by spewing exhaust. I thought, Even that smells better than Spi-Sea fumes.

Once inside, I headed to the dairy counter and dug to the back of the shelf for a cold carton of cream. As I turned around, I bumped into Celeste Carey. The collision sent the carton of cream flying. It splattered on the floor and Celeste giggled.

"I didn't mean to scare you," she said.

I reached into the case and found another carton. Celeste brushed blonde pigtails behind her ears and I could smell something sweet coming off her. I wanted to draw in more of it, but she backed away.

"I have something to show you," she said. "Can you come for a ride with me?" Her eyes sparkled.

"Sure," I said, trying to appear nonchalant which was never easy around her. Her tanned and trim legs poked out of white cutoffs this morning. She wore a pink and white checked halter top that clung to her in places I wanted to explore.

After I paid for the cream and tied the bag to my handlebars, we biked languidly out of town. She didn't say a word, but I thought I knew where she was headed. Sure enough, she chose the path between the bird sanctuary and the orchard. I followed her in silence. Soon, we reached the entrance to the cave and she turned toward me.

"You're not scared of the dark are you?" She took a red flashlight out of her basket.

I shook my head and followed her into the cool blackness. I would have followed her anywhere.

We reached the spot where she had entertained me a few days earlier. I stopped and figured whatever it was she wanted me to see had to be there.

"Come on," she whispered. "It's not all that far, but it's worth it."

She headed deeper into the cave, her flashlight trained on the ground. The walls grew narrow, until we had to walk single file. At one point I had to turn sideways to squeeze through. I prayed nothing would scurry across my feet or through my hair.

Suddenly, the narrow walls opened. Before us lay an underground lake that reflected her beam of light.

Celeste stopped. "Isn't it gorgeous here?"

We stood and gazed at the inky depths before us. She ran her light over the surface of the water. "Sometimes, I swim here."

The lake looked far too foreboding to me. Who knew what lurked beneath the surface? She must have seen the expression on my face, for she laughed.

"Are you afraid, Luke? Someday you should join me and take the plunge." I was relieved when she pointed her beam of light at a sheer wall and said, "Let's go this way."

At first I thought she was crazy. How was I going to be able to scale a rock wall in my Keds? But then I noticed there was a path cut in the stone. I placed a sneaker toe in one of the holds and up I went behind her.

We scaled the rock wall easily and came to rest on a ledge high above the floor of the cave.

"Over here," she said, pointing the way. Celeste lay flat on her stomach and pulled herself into a narrow passageway. I followed her fearing my shoulders would get stuck and leave me wedged unable to move in either direction. Instead, a few yards later the cave widened and spewed both of us out, like twin births, into the cool morning air.

I stood and dusted off my jeans, squinting in the bright sun. Celeste did the same to her shorts. I noticed she watched me intently.

As my eyes grew accustomed to the strong light again, I became aware that we were high above the floor of the valley. I shaded my eyes, peered over the ledge and suffered a bout of vertigo. I stepped back and grabbed onto a tree branch.

Celeste pointed to a large rock. "That's my ship. Come on."

Once again I followed her lead. The two of us climbed up and took at seat at what would have been the prow. I took in the view. Below us smoke belched out of the concrete stacks of what I recognized as the Spi-Sea Shrimp processing plant. The hill faced the back of the dreaded plant. We were so close it did not matter which way the wind blew. The scent overpowered everything else.

"God, I hate that smell," I said, covering my nose with the tail of my shirt. "Dead fish and tomato sauce. Sometimes I dream about it and I wake up and realize the wind has shifted in the middle of the night. What a nightmare. And it's inescapable."

Celeste eyed me curiously. "A lot of people say they don't even notice it."

"Their noses are broken."

She smiled. "It's awful, but I have to admit it doesn't bother me. I can practically tell the days of the week depending on the different processing smells."

"There are differences?"

She laughed that laugh again, sending chimes into the air. "Sometimes they just boil the shrimp and that's the strongest. Other times they make a whole lot more sauce and it's nicer, I think."

"Why do you come here?"

She shrugged.

"There are so many pretty spots you could have picked."

Her chin jutted out fiercely. "Pretty isn't everything."

She was right, of course. But like most males, I was a fool for pretty.

Celeste's rock ship faced the back of the plant where cars were parked by the dozens. To the right of the plant lay an ugly development of two-family homes populated by many of the factory workers and beyond those lay rolling hills. Atop the closest hill, to the north of the plant, perched the Crandon Dam. We sat high above all this. The stone arches of the dam sloped precipitously down toward the plant and held back water that glimmered in the strong sun. Evergreens rimmed the shore.

"I like to watch the seasons in those trees," said Celeste, following my gaze to the dam area. "Behind the pines there are oaks and maples. The colors in the fall are spectacular."

I had to admit the contrast between the factory and the verdant hills was captivating. And I could tell the hum below and serenity beyond comforted Celeste. It had that effect on me too.

She looked down at her sneakers. "I've never taken anyone here before."

The sun beat down on us furiously and the sky above shone bluer than I'd ever seen it. Instinct drove me. I leaned forward and touched her hand. She didn't pull it away. The heat coming off her was more than that generated by the summer sun. My heart came alive in my chest and I pulled her to me and brushed my lips across her forehead. My mouth found hers and the kiss was sweet. I wanted more. I wanted it all.

She pulled back and ran her fingers over her hair. "I promised I'd be back early."

My heart sank. I had misread her. She was too kind to tell me to take a hike, but then again....

I jumped off the rock and Celeste followed. The smell of dead fish hit me in a wave and I grimaced uncontrollably. Celeste laughed and that silvery tinkle made me smile in spite of myself. It was wonderful being around her.

She asked, "Do you ever buy it?"

"What?"

"Spi-Sea shrimp cocktail."

I shook my head. "I don't even want to look at the jars of it that they sent us in the Welcome Wagon when we moved in."

"It's pretty nasty stuff. I'm surprised the plant has lasted."

"Maybe someday it'll close down and we'll get to enjoy this place as it should be."

She shook her head. "I'm not sure I'd like that."

On some level I knew what she meant. There was something about the imperfection of it all that made the spot captivating.

We made our way back to our bikes in silence. As we pushed off, I asked her on impulse, "Are you doing anything this afternoon?"

She shook her head. "Once I help my dad with some irrigating I'm free."

"Why don't you come over? My mom is having a party for my sister. She's twelve."

She shook her head. "I wouldn't know anyone there. I'm not the party type."

"It's not that kind of party."

She cocked her head. "You have a sister?"

I took a deep breath. "No one's coming except me. And you, if you will. My dad is traveling. He's always traveling."

She blinked.

"My sister doesn't live with us."

"Where does she live?"

"At the Raritan facility. She comes home for her birthday and for the summer and she comes for Christmas."

Celeste pursed her lips as my words sank in. "That must be difficult for all of you, especially for her."

"Not really. We're used to it."

She smiled and said, "Kind of like the way I'm used to the Spi-Sea plant?"

"Very funny," I replied, shooting her a look that let her know I understood she was being a wise-ass.

She said, "Come on. I'll race you to the road." She stood and stretched her legs and pointed to a small dirt path. "We can go back this way."

We walked through the woods, the sun playing hide and seek in the leaves overhead. Then we clambered down boulders till we reached the spot where our bikes lay.

We set off and I watched her pull ahead of me, her flawless calves pumping hard on the pedals. I followed close behind, matching her pace. Contentment surrounded me. I felt I could remain that way forever, trapped in a mobius strip of pedaling with perfection right in front of me.

We reached the junction with the main road and she applied her brakes, stopping abruptly. I turned my wheel to avoid hitting her.

She wagged a finger at me. "If you're going to be my friend you must never let me win again."

"Who says I let you win?"

She glared at me.

When she spoke she sounded like a different person. "You better go ahead of me. A storm is coming."

I glanced up at the cloudless sky. "There's no way in hell it's going to rain."

She saw the direction of my gaze and said, "Suit yourself. You won't make it past the McGees' before you're drenched. The crops need the water, so it's a good thing."

A chill passed over me. Her voice seemed to belong to someone else. I wanted to shake her and put her back in the mood she had been in seconds earlier. That moment had ended, ripped apart and scattered into the hot dust that swirled about us.

Celeste held her hand above her head and held me with her gaze. "I didn't mean to burn Deanna. I want you to know that."

Thunder rumbled ominously.

"You should go," she said.

I watched the horizon, watched clouds racing toward the sun. She was right about the rain after all.

"What about you?" I asked.

She shook her head. "I'm not heading back to town for a bit."

She looked at me for a second. I followed her fingers and watched her wiggle them at the sky. Thunder rumbled as if on cue. I wondered what game she was playing.

She laughed. Lightning flashed in the distance. She moved her fingers again and large drops of rain pelted us. "I told you so." Her smile was back. "It's going to pour buckets."

The rain came hard, coating the pavement with a thin sheen. The lightning grew closer. Still Celeste kept her arm above her head. I had the distinct feeling that Celeste was not pretending, but was orchestrating this storm to impress me. She was succeeding in scaring the heck out of me. I pushed off and pedaled hard, not looking back, afraid of what I might see.

I suppose a prudent guy would have sworn not to see her anymore, would have gone home and never thought about Celeste Carey ever again. A prudent guy would have written her off as a flake, a kook, a dangerous girl beyond convention.

Prudence, as always, eluded me.

CHAPTER SIX

My sister, Joanie, stands five-foot-one, trapped in a pudgy body, which often jerks uncontrollably. We didn't know exactly what was wrong with Joanie, or how to deal with her, so that's why she spent most of her life at the Raritan School. There was no name for her condition. We considered her retarded, a phrase my parents rarely uttered, and then only in hushed tones, and that's what she was labeled. We loved her madly.

Though she was clearly young, her milky eyes with dark brown centers were the eyes of an old person. Some days, an inner light poured out of her. On those days Mom said Joanie's eyes reminded her of chocolate kisses that could melt anyone's heart.

Each year, July and August with Joanie took on the air of my favorite holiday, Halloween. I've always enjoyed Halloween with its controlled safe scares and dressing up, allowing you to be whomever you want for a day. Summer days with Joanie draped around us like cheap costumes which fooled no one, but which delighted us wearers nonetheless. The one who was most delighted with her part each summer was Joanie.

Joanie liked popcorn, basketball and climbing trees. She's never far from a bag of the yellow stuff or a bright orange ball, and she always sported some item of red. The day of her birthday she entered the dining room wearing her favorite red baseball cap perched on her short curly brown hair, carrying a bowl of popcorn. Her popcorn munching was infectious and I found myself indulging. As I strung crepe paper streamers from the dining room chandelier, I reached across into Joanie's bowl and scooped up a handful. Joanie chuckled approvingly.

I stuffed too much popcorn into my mouth and turned my back to her. Joanie squealed with laughter as she knew what to expect.

I faced her and raised my palms to my cheeks. And then I pressed hard, spewing popcorn across the green and gold Oriental carpet in the dining room. Joanie squealed again and clapped her hands together. "Pimple!" she shouted. "Pimple!"

I wiped the back of my hand across my mouth and went back to my crepe paper hanging. From the kitchen I heard Mom yell at the effect of my human pimple stunt.

"Luke, don't get her excited. It's almost dinner and you know how difficult it is for Joanie to sit still. And I hope you're not eating popcorn or you won't have room for dinner!"

I raised my finger to my lips and motioned to Joanie to be quiet.

"We've got at least another half hour till dinner, Ma."

"You heard me. Settle down and read or do something constructive."

Something constructive. That's what my mother always said. I sighed.

Joanie crossed the room and found her basketball. She flashed a toothy grin and tossed the ball at me. "Game?" she said.

"Game," I said. I followed her out to the driveway hoop.

I retrieved my own ball from beneath the bushes at the side of the house and took a shot. Basketball with Joanie had its own set of rules and was fun for reasons other than the enjoyment of throwing the ball into the hoop. When Joanie played basketball she lost her awkwardness. Her hands stopped flapping, her eyes stayed focused on the task and she looked normal. Joanie played ball for the pure joy of it, not unlike the way she climbed trees or ate popcorn. Everything else in her life was a struggle, but basketball, tree climbing and eating popcorn were effortless.

I watched her make her way around the driveway in preparation for her game. As usual, it was as though she sprouted wings when she arrived on the court.

Joanie never shot hoops. She could arc the ball into the net if she wanted, but she did not. Rather, she'd hit targets with her basketball. She's a basketball marksman.

I stood and took a few foul shots as Joanie raced along the perimeter of the court. Periodically, she grunted loudly. After her third circuit of the driveway she wheeled and nailed her target, which this time was a large rock where the driveway met the street. I had seen her hit a squirrel off the electrical wires. Once she took out the window on the top floor of the house, but she never did that again after my mother went screaming mad and grounded us for two days. If I took the time to place a couple of cans in the fork of a tree branch, she would knock them to the ground in no time.

Joanie waved her hand at me to get my attention.

"Shoot," she said and waited for me to comply with her order.

She liked to hear the rhythm of the ball as I prepared to take my shots. Once I became absorbed in my free throws, she would forget about me and concentrate on her marksmanship.

I watched Joanie out of the corner of my eye. As my ball arced into the hoop I suspected she was as curious about what I was doing as I was about what she was doing. What she was doing was pacing the perimeter looking for a likely target. Not really looking. You never knew where Joanie was looking. I could swear she was ready to peg the rose bush in the backyard by the way her head inclined. But instead, she sent a seeing eye throw past my head and nailed the birdbath on the side of the house. The impact sent several bathing chickadees flying. Joanie clapped her hands and let out a loud chuckle. I sent another shot into the hoop and then another. We continued our ball playing. In no time my head cleared and I thought I might be able to make some sense of what was going on in my life with Celeste. Basketball had always had that effect on me, allowing my mind to wander, then focus with clarity.

Joanie bounced her ball beside me.

"You want to take a shot?" I asked, meaning the hoop above my head. She stared at the ground.

I hit another basket. The ball thudded to the pavement and rolled to the grass.

Joanie grinned and nailed the birdbath again. Her ball landed square in the water-filled trough. Having been scared off, there were no birds in the area this time, but that did not lessen Joanie's pleasure at her accomplishment.

From the kitchen window we heard Mom. "How many times have I told you to keep your basketballs out of the birdbath? Leave the birds alone!"

Joanie and I laughed. Joanie retrieved her ball and stood with a contemplative look on her face. I knew this meant she was seeking a new target.

I faced the hoop and sank another shot.

Out of the corner of my eye I saw Joanie turn and whirl. She unleashed her basketball at top speed. Poor friggin' squirrel, I thought.

Someone screamed. I turned and saw a flash of white slump to the ground.

"My God, Joanie," I yelled and I raced to the fallen figure. Joanie's basketball lay next to the prone girl's head. I recognized the girl and caught my breath. Susie.

"Are you all right?" I kneeled next to her ashen face.

Susie sat up and gulped air.

"You'll be OK. You just had the wind knocked out of you." I motioned to Joanie behind my back to come over. "I'm sure my sister would like to apologize. We were playing a game and I know she didn't mean to hurt you."

Joanie grunted. Susie coughed and sat up. She smoothed back her hair. Her eyes moved from mine to Joanie's and then back to mine again.

I tried to explain, "My sister wasn't thinking…."

Joanie tugged on the bill of her cap. I could tell she was feeling worried at what she had done.

"Joanie's not like you or me. She's got some problems…."

Susie cut me off. "Maybe I should call the police and have her arrested."

Joanie shifted from foot to foot. She rocked side to side and her hands began to flap in a manner that indicated she was growing increasingly upset.

"It was a mistake. She didn't mean anything by it." I reached out and pulled Joanie toward me. "She thought you were a target of some sort. It's a game we play."

"She knew what she was doing," said Susie, glaring at Joanie whose arms moved furiously. "What's she trying to do, take off?"

I shook Joanie's arm, and tried to get her to stop flapping. "Tell Susie you're sorry. Stop that!" I was immediately sorry for my harsh tone.

Joanie went limp. She stared straight ahead.

"Come on, Joanifer, tell my friend you didn't mean to peg her with your ball."

Joanie opened her mouth and a small dribble oozed out the side of her mouth.

Susie smoothed her pants. "Would you look at that? She's drooling. You're talking to a raving idiot like she can understand you. What the heck is wrong with her?"

"She understands me fine. She's not an idiot," I said. My head began to pound. "All she did was hit you with a ball." I wanted to take Joanie's ball and peg Susie with it myself. I drew myself up to my full height and glared at Susie.

She backed away from us. "You're as nuts as she is, aren't you," said Susie. "Stay away from me." She turned and walked briskly down the path away from us.

When we could no longer see her, I sat down hard on the grass and lay back. "Geez, Joanie, don't do things like that," I said to the sky. I wondered how long it would be before Susie told everyone what a lunatic I had for a sister.

A little while later, we went inside and celebrated Joanie's birthday the way we always did, with macaroni and cheese, followed by huge bowls of popcorn and Mom's sunshine cake with whipped cream. I kept hoping that Celeste might appear and join us.

After the cake was eaten, my mother cleared the plates. I heard her say, "Would you look at that?"

I walked into the kitchen.

On the wall was a brilliant rainbow. We tried to figure out which window caused the light to shatter and reflect in the colorful hues, but gave up after awhile. The rainbow came from nowhere. Joanie joined us and grunted in approval when she saw the perfect arch. She clapped her hands in glee and reached under the sink for a jar.

We watched Joanie place her jar against the light on the wallpaper and then pull it back. She held the jar up to the light, looking for a rainbow within.

"It's a rainbow, Joanie, you can't…" I said, but my mother shushed me.

Then Joanie placed the jar on the wall again. After several attempts she gave up and left the jar on the floor.

"Game?" said Joanie to no one in particular. She went outside and began navigating the perimeter of the driveway again.

"Game?" she said. "Game?"

"Game," I called through the window, but I did not join her. Instead, I watched the rainbow fade from our wall and found myself thinking once again about Celeste.

CHAPTER SEVEN

Early the next day, the morning after Joanie's birthday, Alec set out to find Celeste. He rode first to the swimming hole. Anne Clare and her sister Philippa called to him from the diving rock where they sat listening to their transistor radios. But in spite of the fact that the Clare sisters were two of the finest-looking girls in the neighborhood, Alec was not to be dissuaded from his goal. From the quarry, he boldly pedaled to Celeste's house, but she was nowhere in sight. Luckily for him neither was Mr. Carey.

Alec headed downtown where he stopped at Ben's and joined me in our usual booth. Alec slumped against the seat back and stared disconsolately out at the parking lot.

"What the hell is wrong with you?" I asked. The frigid air of the diner raised goosebumps on my arms. I was grateful for the chill, as my parents were not interested in air conditioning anything in our house. "Here's air conditioning," my father would say, throwing open a window and letting in the humid air. Once or twice, I slept in the basement on an old cot, but lately even the concrete floors had lost their natural coolness. And worst of all, the Spi-Sea plant was running night shifts several times a week. Fish and tomato smells now belched at all hours.

Alec shrugged and waved at Ben who immediately threw a pile of fries into the fryer.

"You have a fight with Josh or something?" I asked, not willing to be put off so easily.

Alec shook his head and let his eyes find mine. He leaned forward in his seat and the pain coming off him was palpable. I knotted my napkin with my hands, suddenly aware that he was about to tell me something I was not sure I wanted to hear.

Alec held me with his blue eyes. "It's Celeste," he said.

I sat up straight and my heart began to race. "What about her?" Though my chest beat like a drum, I played it as cool as I could, not wanting to reveal anything about Celeste to anyone. I didn't need to worry. Alec was too preoccupied with his own thoughts of Celeste to sense anything about my feelings for her. He stared at the table and played with the wrapper from my straw and told me of his morning ride in search of her.

"What do you want to drink with that?" asked Ben from beyond the counter.

"A Coke," said Alec. He shot me a glance. "I wish I had some of Deanna's rum for it."

I tried to sound casual. "Do you think Celeste is OK?"

Alec shook his head. "How the hell would I know?"

His concern and anger confused me more than ever. Why was he so worried about her?

He ran his fingers through his hair. Then he let out a sound I had never heard him utter before, a low heartfelt moan that embarrassed me with its heavy sentimentality. "You've got to help me, Looner."

I licked my lips and now it was my turn to avert my gaze. I studied the ceiling fan and concentrated on the lopsided whirring that filled the room.

Ben plopped our sodas and fries on the table. "Who died?" he asked, wiping his hands on his white apron. Tufts of hair sprouted from his ears. There was more hair in his ears than atop his head, whose gleam in the harsh overhead light rivaled that of the chrome exterior of the diner. I shrugged my shoulders and Ben, never one to pry, headed back to the grill.

Alec continued. "I've been everywhere I can think of and I can't find her."

I sipped my Coke.

"She's mad at me. I know it."

"She'll show up sooner or later."

"What if she doesn't?"

I shook my head. "What on earth is all this about? Why should she be mad at you?"

Alec bit his lip. "I screwed up bad with Celeste. I realized it a few days ago."

I speared a French fry and moved it around in the catsup. Alec had no way of knowing of my feelings for Celeste and this was not the time to discuss them.

"I woke up in the middle of the night after having a dream about her. I was in the middle of this, this…tornado." He spread his hands wide.

I watched him and he continued.

"She was up above me peering down. Ever since then I've been waiting to run into her."

"Do you think that's such a good idea?"

"What the hell is wrong with you, Looner? This is THE girl of my dreams. I'm not going to lose her."

Alec always had a penchant for the melodramatic. I let the heavy sentiment slide and continued eating the fries. "But I thought you two had only dated once or twice and it didn't work out."

"I never called her again. I was supposed to, but after the second date I got scared. I didn't want to like her that much."

"What were you scared of?"

"I'm not really sure. Her dad for one thing. Geez, he's a creepy son of a bitch."

"Aren't most dads?"

Alec shuddered. "Not like him. He was really awful on Halloween. That was the night that Deanna got burned."

"On her arm?"

"We decided to play a prank out there and scare Celeste."

"You went to her farm?"

He nodded. "Her father came after us with a shotgun and next thing I knew there was this bolt of lightning crashing next to her house. Then another one. Then it was like some horror show with lightning everywhere."

"Where was Celeste?"

"She joined us. Deanna got so scared she grabbed Celeste's arm. She swears she got burned by touching Celeste."

"You don't believe Celeste did it?"

"Hell, no. There was so much electricity in the air I think that's what happened."

I toyed with the idea of telling Alec that I was crazy about Celeste and that I was wondering about her strangeness myself.

Before I could say anything, Alec went on, "After that, Celeste kept saying stuff that made no sense. Like she could do things to make it rain or snow."

A chill passed over me. Hadn't I been curious about just those powers? "Did you ever see her do anything like that?"

"Do you think I'm nuts? No one can do that."

I held my tongue, though I wanted to tell him that I thought perhaps she might think she could, even if she couldn't.

Alec drummed his nails on the table. "Do you have any idea where she might be? I've tried everywhere, even the library."

I chuckled. What little I knew of her included the fact that Celeste was not the library type.

He stared at the table. "How can anyone disappear in this town? It's too freakin' small for that."

"Maybe she's out in her orchards somewhere, up in a tree."

Alec shook his head. "Her bike would be there. I'd have seen it. She'd never walk all the way to the orchard."

"You ride to her house?"

Alec eyed me. "Not after the last time I went there. Old man Carey is too quick with a shotgun."

I couldn't help myself and I laughed.

"It's true, you asshole."

"So maybe she's hanging out in her room or something at home."

He shook his head. "She doesn't feel right at home. Her dad tries to get her to stay there, but she gets out whenever she can."

I leaned back in my seat. "What do we do now?"

"We need to find Celeste."

I sipped from my Coke glass. Then I held Alec's gaze. "I've got an idea where she might be."

"Oh, do you now?"

"Yeah, I have a good idea in fact."

"An idea. A Looner idea." Alec stood and threw a five on the table. "Anything is better than sitting around here."

I grabbed a few more fries and drained my Coke. We exited the diner into the humid afternoon where the wind blew from the south and the Spi-Sea plant blasted into my nose. I longed to return to the chilly crisp air of Ben's. Instead, I picked up my bike and studied the sky. Dark clouds gathered to the west, a harbinger of the late afternoon thunderstorm that was predicted.

"She wasn't born here," said Alec.

"So? Neither was I. I like her already."

"Not like you, Looner. She was adopted by the Careys as an infant."

The way he said this indicated there was something Alec was leaving unsaid.

I said, "Why on earth do you act like being adopted is so odd?"

"It's not that she was adopted. They never found where her real family came from. She just appeared out of nowhere. And my folks say old man Carey hasn't been the same since that time when he found her."

"What are you saying?" Celeste was beginning to appear even more complicated than I had originally thought.

Alec sighed. "She's different, Luke. They're different."

I arched an eyebrow as Joanie popped into my mind. "We're all of us different far as I can tell."

He continued, "Carey's orchards always bear fruit. Even in times of drought they somehow get irrigated. Sometimes you can see the clouds gathering and dumping rain over there."

I nodded, amazed that Alec was talking about making rain fall. Hadn't I thought the same thing recently? Hadn't she said she had to help her dad with irrigating the orchards?

"No one likes to talk about it, but if you ask me there's something

strange going on over there. Old man Carey is one creepy sonofabitch."
He looked over his shoulder and then climbed onto his bike.

I wanted to ask him some questions, but I could tell the discussion was closed.

Alec stared ahead. "So are you going to tell me where we're headed, Loony?"

I pointed toward the road that led to the orchards. "It's not far."

Alec let me take the lead and we rode out of the town toward the orchards. Soon we were on the dirt path leading to the cave I knew Celeste frequented.

"This is the old Leatherman's place," said Alec as we dismounted. "I haven't been here in ages. How'd you know about it?"

"I'm a quick learner." I clambered up the boulders that led to the ridge and motioned for Alec to follow.

The two of us sat quietly. To the east the Spi-Sea plant belched its noxious fumes at a furious pace. We were enveloped in a sickening fishy tomato smell that made me want to gag. I thought about holding my nose but didn't want Alec to see me do that. Instead, I cleared my throat and pointed to a gap in the rocks at our feet.

"She's probably down there."

Alec cocked his head and raised an eyebrow. "Where?"

"Sometimes she hangs out down there." I pointed to the opening and he peered inside. "It's kind of nice," I said, listening hard for signs of Celeste.

"If you're teasing me, dirtbag, I'm going to beat the crap out of you," said Alec.

I rolled my eyes. "Now I'm scared," I said.

"I mean it, Loony. This is not the kind of thing to tease about."

"Screw you."

Thunder rumbled in the distance. I glanced up and saw storm clouds rolling furiously toward us.

"Looks like we're in for a blow," said Alec.

Within seconds fat drops of rain pelted us.

"We can always take cover inside if we need to. You might as well get down there anyhow if you want to see Celeste."

I clambered down the rocks. Lightning flashed and the rain grew harder. The sun went dark as though someone was using a dimmer switch. Soon it was as if night had fallen.

We raced into the cave out of the storm. Drenched and chilled, we stood and watched the wind whip through the trees. A loud clap of thunder was followed by a crack of lightning. We held our ears and tried to see which tree had been hit.

"Geez, that was awfully close," said Alec. He took a few steps backward and peered out through the wall of water that streamed down the cave's entrance.

My heart skipped a beat as a familiar voice said, "It might get even closer. Maybe you want to come inside a little more."

I glanced at Alec and then took in Celeste whose yellow halter top and off-white cutoffs left me speechless for a few moments. I cleared my throat and forced myself to focus on the task at hand.

"Alec's been looking for you everywhere," I said, nodding my head in the general direction of Alec. Suddenly I grew aware that taking Alec to Celeste's hideaway might not have been the best idea. She had never told him about it. She had admitted to me that she had never taken anyone to her lookout except me. Maybe she felt the same about the cave. She could very well view my act as a betrayal of her trust. I bit my lip as I realized what I had done.

She turned and walked back into the darkness.

"Where are you going?" asked Alec.

The beam of Celeste's flashlight found our eyes. "Are you two going to stay out there or come in here?"

She trained the light on the ground. We followed Celeste deep into the cave and reached the spot she had taken me to on that day of our meeting. A small lantern glowed warmly.

Celeste said, "Might at well make yourselves at home. That storm will be with us for a while."

Alec sat on the floor Indian style and I joined him.

Celeste turned up the wick on the lantern. "Nice and cozy in here," she said.

I glanced at Alec. He was transfixed, watching Celeste's every move.

I couldn't get a read on what was going through Celeste's mind.

She sat down opposite us. "What brings the two of you out here?"

I licked my lips. Alec cleared his throat, but said nothing. I had never seen him so tongue-tied.

"Alec wanted to talk to you," I said.

"I see," said Celeste. "So I have you to thank for bringing him here."

I cringed. She was clearly annoyed at me. She pushed a strand of blonde hair behind her ear exposing the white skin of her neck. I knew Alec was looking at the same place as I was.

Celeste glanced at me and my heart pounded. The silence hung over us. Then she said, "The only one I want to be talking to right now is Luke."

I froze. She smiled at me and I could feel the air charge with anticipation. This was not what I expected. Alec jumped to his feet no longer tongue-tied and I rose as well.

"No wonder you knew where to find her." He stood opposite me with clenched fists. "You sonofabitch."

Without warning he lunged at me. I dodged quickly and avoided his grasp. "Alec, wait a second…" I said, holding my hands in front of me.

He faced me panting. "How long have you two been together? When the fuck were you going to tell me? Is this your idea of a joke, Looner?"

"It's not like that," I said.

He shot me a look of disgust. "Come off it. Anyone could tell you were a goner the first time you saw her." He jerked his head toward Celeste.

She had a curious look on her face. A loud crack of lightning landed somewhere nearby above us and a few rocks from the ceiling came down around our feet. Outside the storm increased in intensity.

"I thought we were friends," he said.

"Alec, I don't know why you're getting so worked up," I said.

"You make me sick, you bastard," said Alec.

I stared at the ground not knowing how to defuse the situation, anger beginning to roil in my veins.

Celeste cleared her throat and we both looked at her. "I've been meaning to ask you, Luke. What time do you want to get to the Fourth of July picnic?"

That did it. Alec lunged at me again. This time he connected and knocked me on the ground. He climbed on top of me and picked up a large rock. I grabbed his throat with my hands and pressed hard. My head was about to be turned into mush.

Celeste's voice was low and soft. "Leave him be, Alec. That's not the way to solve your differences."

The rock stayed over my head. Alec was like a caged animal and I was not sure her words had any effect, but then I felt the anger go out of him. It was as though she were Circe and he could not resist. He dropped the stone and climbed off me. Alec turned and retreated into the dark, heading out of the cave.

"Wait," I called, but he ignored me.

I sat up and blinked. Celeste reached in her pocket and withdrew her jacks. She threw them on the ground and studied them.

I wiped the dirt off my pants. Three silvery tornadoes spun at my feet, caught in the lantern's glow.

"He'll be fine," she said. "A bruised ego heals a lot easier than a bruised head."

I rubbed my elbow and watched the glinting objects move about the floor. I focused hard, but once again I could not get a fix on the tiny tornadoes.

"And let's not forget Miss Susie," she said, throwing another spinning object into the pile.

I moved next to her and reached out to touch one of the whirling toys. Before I could grab one, she scooped the jacks up and put them in her pocket.

"That's how people get burned," she said. "Storm's almost over. You should get going."

I reached over and touched her on the arm and I noticed her skin was strangely cold. The only burning I experienced was in a knot lodged in my stomach. Celeste paused for an instant. Her eyes found mine. And then she laughed that tinkling laugh, sending light up from my toes surging through me all the way into the dark recesses of the cave. I continued to grip her forearm, aware of something coursing through her and into me. No lightning came down from the sky to strike me. Rather, a sense of peace and calm took root in my chest. My confusion over what had just occurred melted away. I had a hundred questions to ask her, but I found I could not formulate them. Instead, I was entranced, content to bask in whatever it was that hung between us.

"We can't stay long," she said.

"I have to take my sister out for ice cream," I said.

And then her lips found mine. I would swear there was something eternal in that kiss. A dazzling darkness paraded across my eyelids and took my breath away.

She drew back from me and held my eyes. "I like you, Luke," she said. "You make me smile."

Inside I was grinning from ear to ear, but for Celeste I tried to appear coolly interested. I wanted to kiss her again, but that was not to be the case as she broke free of my arms. The sense of loss was cold, immediate.

She rose and dusted off the seat of her shorts. "Alec will be OK. He'll be angry for a few days so stay out of his way."

"You shouldn't have done that to him."

"He did it to himself. He's the one who left, just like he did last time. Watch this," she said. She picked up her lantern and snuffed it out. The cave went so dark I could not see my hand in front of my face.

"Total darkness is awesome, isn't it?" said Celeste.

I held my breath, not sure what to expect, hoping for another kiss, or more. She slipped a now-warm hand into mine. "There's a rainbow of dark out there if you look carefully."

I peered at the blackness, but had trouble finding any gradations.

"It takes time to know it. Darkness gathers so quickly and powerfully. Can you feel it?"

My heart raced. In spite of my arousal, her words caused me to focus on the dark. The blackness had a cold presence, or was it my imagination going into overdrive at her suggestion? The hairs on my arms stood on end. I was no longer calm or at peace. An uneasy anxiety knotted my stomach.

Then a small glow appeared. I felt calm flooding into me again, and was grateful Celeste had her light with her and had chosen to rekindle the flame. My racing heart slowed at the comforting illumination and her presence. As we stood there quietly, I became aware of how the dark receded in waves before the lantern. I could make out the dim outline of Celeste and knew I could stay there forever basking in the warm glow.

"That's more like it," Celeste said as the soft radiance filled the cave.

As the light increased I realized it did not emanate from her lantern. Nor did she carry her flashlight. What lay on the ground was a jar, similar to the one she had given me in the DDT haze that dusk. The small clear baby food jar was open. I felt a chill run down my spine. Could light be coming from a jar?

She said, "The speed of dark is one of those things that no one seems able to control. Have you ever noticed that?"

I shook my head, not at all sure what she was talking about. "What's going on, Celeste?"

"The speed of light gets so much attention. People should really focus on the dark more." She shrugged. "It's as powerful as the light, maybe even more so. One of these days we'll learn how to harness it, maybe even keep it at bay."

My mouth went dry and I did not know what to say. Something odd was happening in the Leatherman's cave, something that defied logic.

She turned and I gratefully followed her out of the cave, the light fading behind us. We climbed onto our bikes and overhead, the sky shone blue. Behind me the cave lay dark and secretive.

Before she could leave me, I said, "Tomorrow is the fourth. Are you really coming with me to the picnic?"

She smiled. "Like I asked you before, what time are we going to the darn thing?"

I stammered and hated myself for my nervousness. "I'm taking my sister over around noon."

She laughed and once again I was enchanted. I was completely willing to forget about whatever it was that had transpired in the cave if only I could hear that laugh again. She pushed off and began the trek along the dirt road home.

"I'll meet you at the picnic grounds about noon," she shouted. Then she glanced back and called, "Race you to the road?"

She did not wait for my answer, but was gone, leaving me in the wake of her tinkling laugh. I pushed off and in my hurry caught my sock on the pedal. Celeste glanced back as I tumbled to the earth. She slowed for an instant, giggling at the sight of me sprawled on the ground.

"Shit," I said. I righted my bicycle and once more attempted to ride. Celeste seized the advantage and pedaled hard.

"You're such an asshole," I muttered to myself. I pushed vigorously against the pedals and ignored the huge ruts in the dirt path that threatened to send me flying. I gripped the handlebars as firmly as I could as I made my way toward the pink bike and tan legs before me. I remembered her admonition from last time and decided to show off a bit.

Celeste rode wildly but she was no match for me. After all, I had my masculine pride to defend. As we reached the road I found the strength to pour on more speed. I flew past her and pumped a fist in the air.

What I did not see was the moving van barreling down the highway in my direction.

"Luke, watch out!" shouted Celeste.

My head jerked toward the roar of the rig's engine. In my heart I knew it was too late. As a last hope, I swerved to avoid being crushed but the driver swerved in the same direction, straight at me. There was no way the van could stop in the short distance between it and myself. The smell of the Spi-Sea plant assaulted me and I was sure it would be the last thing on earth that I would ever smell. The faces of my parents and Joanie flashed before me.

I could see the eyes of the driver in the cab of the van as he leaned on his horn blaring a too-late warning. He was horrified at what was about to happen. I held my breath and waited for impact.

Suddenly a large gust of wind rose up. Before I could blink again, I felt my bicycle lift into the air. What happened next is a blur, but I remember that I came to rest on the side of the road as the moving van screeched to a halt.

The driver tore out of his cab and raced toward me. "Son, are you OK?"

Celeste joined us. She touched my arm and a feeling of peace moved over me. I was alive. Alive! And she was at my side. All was right with the brightly colored world.

The driver said, "You were dead meat, boy. I don't know what the hell happened, but you sure are one lucky sonofabitch."

I looked over at Celeste.

The smallest smile passed over her lips and then she grew serious. "We should be more careful, Luke. That was too close."

I looked all around me. As quickly as the wind had arisen, it had disappeared. In my dazed state I suspected that Celeste had somehow caused that windstorm, and I turned to her to get to the bottom of the event, but when I saw how pale she was I did not have it in my heart to cross-examine her. Besides, the trucker would think the two of us insane.

I wrapped an arm around her shoulder and she leaned into me. I realized I was supporting her. We walked to the side of the road and we sat together in the tall grass. Two flies rose up and buzzed about my head. I swatted them away and they returned to the unmown field. Green stalks rustled gently and the driver watched as we gathered our composure.

The driver shifted from foot to foot. He eyed his wrist and checked the sun overhead.

"Why don't you get on your way?" I asked.

He glanced over his shoulder, then back at us. "Are you two kids feeling OK? I have a radio in the cab. Maybe I should call your parents or something."

Celeste said, "There's no reason to alarm them. Nothing happened."

The driver scratched his head.

She went on. "I live five minutes from here and I'm headed home. We're both OK." She nudged me, "Aren't we, Luke?"

"Perfect."

A CB radio squawked in the cab of the truck. The driver glanced at his watch again and raced to answer. "Shit," he said. "I've got to make Philly by nightfall."

We waved good-bye as he pulled his rig onto the highway but he did not return the hand gesture. He was engrossed in his conversation. As the truck disappeared over the horizon, Celeste turned to me and flashed a mischievous grin.

"I don't suppose he'd like having to drive all the way in the rain. It might slow him down to the speed limit."

I shook my head, not sure what she was saying.

Then she lifted her hand to the sky. I glanced up and saw billowing clouds of gray rolling in from the west. The light went out of the day and a breeze whipped my legs. Thoroughly chilled, my heart began to pound. Up ahead I knew the driver was in for a long ride.

She turned to me and said, "Go home, Luke."

"Celeste, I have to understand what happened here."

"Maybe someday you will."

She was on her bike pedaling furiously. Her laugh floated back to me and I knew that I might never have the answer. But at that moment it did not matter to me if I ever understood the mystery of the girl I called Celeste.

CHAPTER EIGHT

The morning of the Fourth of July dawned hot and muggy. I showered and combed my hair, nervous at the prospect of going out with Celeste. I couldn't believe she had agreed to attend the picnic with me and my brain hummed with anticipation. The only sour note was Alec, whose storming off in anger had left me uneasy about our future as friends. We had not communicated since being in the cave and while I believed that we could get through this misunderstanding, I had my doubts about how easy it would be.

I turned my thoughts to Josh and Alec's tales of picnics past. For the past few weeks I had already been looking forward to attending my first ever Faith Junction Independence Day Celebration. Attending with Celeste made it all the more a festive occasion. To my surprise, the thought of Celeste by my side gave me the strength I needed to be out in public with Joanie. I feared Joanie's behavior and wondered how Celeste would react to her, but determined to make the best of it. I bit my lip worried at all the things that might go wrong. Besides Joanie acting up, I might run into an angry Alec. Surely Josh would take his side, as they had been friends long before I arrived in Faith Junction.

The door to my bedroom creaked open. I leaned over and threw a book at Joanie as she entered. The paperback missed and landed at her feet.

"You're supposed to knock before you come in," I said, smoothing my hair back and trying to straighten it a bit. My mirror showed it defying me, springing into its usual kinks on this humid day.

Joanie rubbed her arm and shifted from foot to foot. She said nothing.

"As long as you're here you might as well sit down." I shoved clothes aside and made room for her at the foot of my bed. Joanie perched on the mattress and inserted a thumb in her mouth.

"You looking forward to the picnic, Joan girl?" I asked as I dug a shirt out of the laundry hamper and sniffed it. The scent on this yellow and white striped one was not too bad. I slipped it over my head onto my torso, took one look and tore it off.

"What's the matter, Luke?" said Joanie. "Clothes making you itchy?"

I shot her a withering gaze then felt guilty. Embarrassed, I said, "I'm trying to find the right thing to wear."

Joanie nodded. She wore a Yankees cap and her favorite red shorts topped with a white T-shirt.

From downstairs came my mother's voice. "Luke! Joanie! We're leaving in ten minutes."

I opened my drawer. One shirt lay in the bottom, a brand new white and red polo shirt that I had objected to vehemently when Mom had brought it home. Beside it sat Celeste's empty baby food jar. Since last night I had stared at that jar a hundred times, afraid to find out what might happen if I unscrewed the lid. I remembered the happenings in the Leatherman's cave the day before and wondered if this container had similar properties, but I did not want to learn about the glass jar right now. Instead, I extracted the shirt from its resting place and felt the starchy new cotton between my fingertips. Definitely clean. I removed the pins from the collar.

Joanie clapped her hands. I slipped the shirt over my head and studied my image in the mirror. Joanie covered her mouth with her hand and giggled.

"Lookin' good!" I said. I turned sideways. I didn't look like such a scarecrow in this shirt, and then there was the fact that the red and white colors were in keeping with the Fourth of July.

I realized with a start that Joanie was ferreting around in the bottom drawer, which I had failed to close. In a second she had grabbed Celeste's jar. She held it up to the light and I held my breath.

Joanie rocked back and forth.

"Give it here, Joanie," I said and extended my hand.

"Joanie's jar," she said. She clutched the glass to her chest and rocked.

I tried another tactic. "How do you like this shirt? Your favorite color, right?" I never took my eyes from the jar.

Joanie stared at my chest and her arm dropped to her side.

"The Joanie seal of approval," I said and she grinned. I bent over and retrieved a half-eaten box of Cracker Jacks from beneath my bed. I rattled the popcorn and peanuts and Joanie squealed and watched me, her fingers wrapped firmly round the glass. I held the box over her head just out of her reach.

"Yummy, who wants a treat?"

She stretched her arms up and jumped, holding the jar tight in one hand. After a couple of tries, I let her have the box. She focused on her new object of attention and let the jar fall onto the bed. As she tore into the snack, I casually placed Celeste's jar on my desktop.

I breathed a sigh of relief and extended a hand to my sister. "Mom's waiting for us," I said. "Let's get a move on." We exited my room as she happily munched stale Cracker Jacks. I made a mental note to re-hide the jar in a new spot when I returned home. Joanie would no doubt find it again were it to remain where I left it in plain view.

Downstairs, my mother and father were packing things into the car. Mom, not one for red, white and blue, was decked out in lime green pedal pushers with a matching headscarf and tangerine top. Her high-heeled lemon yellow mules flapped against her feet as she bustled from the house to the car and back again. Dad slid into the driver's seat and I sensed that things were going well between the two of them. He wore blue shorts and an old striped polo shirt that I remembered from years past.

Mom came out and gave us all the once over. She held a hand up and pointed a tangerine nail at Dad's feet. "I'm not going anywhere till you take off those socks, Joe." I stared and saw that Dad had on black socks with his brown fishermen's sandals.

Dad shook his head. "But I hate it when the bugs get my ankles."

Mom had her hands on her hips in her I-am-not-about-to-be-defied-on-this stance. I knew she would never give in. "You look like you belong in an X-rated film," said Mom.

"Like you'd know about those, Gina. They're just socks. I like them."

"Lose the socks, Dad," I said.

"No socks, no socks," said Joanie.

Dad rolled his eyes. "I guess I'm outnumbered." He reached down and undid the straps of his sandals, peeling off his socks and leaving them in the driveway.

"Much better," said Mom, sliding into the front seat beside him. She turned her head and took us in. "Would you look at this bunch? What a beautiful family!"

Joanie grinned from ear to ear, and Dad began whistling. It was as though the sun were shining inside our car. The drive over to the park took about five minutes and when we arrived at the designated field a crowd swarmed appealingly over the grounds.

"We're going to find a free picnic table," said my mother as she removed a hamper from the trunk.

My father removed two chairs and a blanket. He said, "You two can scoot for a bit and have fun."

"Look for us over there," said my mother, pointing to a hilltop that held wooden picnic tables.

"Come on, Joan girl, let's see what we can see," I said. Joanie rocked happily from side to side, then she took my arm and we strode downhill toward the main field. It was almost noon and I wondered how I would find Celeste in the crowd.

Faith Junction took the Fourth of July seriously. At home in the Bronx the holiday was an occasion to blow up things like piles of dog crap and old plastic models. The adventurous threw cherry bombs and ashcans down storm sewers where their blasts echoed mightily, or into public toilets which often ruptured from the explosion. Here in squeaky clean, if stinky, suburbia the holiday followed different patterns. There might be less to do on a daily basis in Faith Junction, but on the Fourth of July limitless options presented themselves.

"Look, look," said Joanie, pointing to a cordoned-off part of the field.

She dragged me along behind her till we could go no farther. We joined the crowd at the roping and watched as a baby bike parade made its way around the perimeter of the area. Men and women bedecked in red, white and blue outfits topped with straw hats held clipboards and nodded as children rode by on tricycles decorated with crepe paper and plastic toys. A tiny Betsy Ross passed before us, as did an Uncle Sam in diapers. Joanie squealed with glee. "Look! Babies! Look, look!" she said, her hands gripping the rope that marked off the area.

A loudspeaker, hung overhead in a tree, squawked to life. "The pie-eating contest will begin in fifteen minutes. Come on over to field three and bring your appetites. Winner is guaranteed free pie for a year at Ben's Diner!" A dozen or so people headed up the hill in the direction of field three.

The bike parade finished up and the judges circulated through the tricycles pinning ribbons on each of the children. The top three winners rolled to the center of the field where a photographer captured them with their families. As the sounds of bluegrass music from a stage area farther down the hill reached us, Joanie and I continued our walk. Within seconds Joanie squealed again. I followed her gaze and took in a Ladies Auxiliary booth draped in red, white and blue bunting.

"Oooo, hurry, hurry," Joanie said, dropping my arm and starting to run. I followed in her wake and we stopped at the counter. Before us stretched yards and yards of fabric displayed on large tables. Behind the bunting of the main table, a half dozen women in colonial costumes sat sewing pieces of material together. Joanie reached out and stroked a bolt of bright red cotton strewn with yellow flowers.

One of the women put down her sewing and smiled at us. I wanted to leave and go play basketball or baseball or eat pies. I wanted to do anything that wasn't associated with fabric, but Joanie was entranced and rooted to the spot. She patted the fabric gently. "Pretty. So pretty," said Joanie.

I said, "My sister loves the color red." I tugged on Joanie's arm, but she wasn't about to move. She pursed her lips and grunted. The smiling woman approached us and in a kindly gesture, unfolded the bolt of cloth. Joanie clapped her hands together several times.

I asked the woman, "What are you sewing?"

The woman smiled. "You must be new to the town."

Beside me Joanie gripped the fabric tightly in clumps and I knew it would be difficult to get her to let go of it. I wondered how I was going to distract her, focus her attention elsewhere.

"Yes, ma'am. We've only moved here a few weeks ago." I tried to extract the fabric from Joanie's hands but her death grip grew stronger.

The woman smiled at Joanie. "Some of us are sewing a quilt and others of us are helping out with tree-toppers."

"Tree-toppers? What are those?"

The voice that answered my question startled me, for it was that of Celeste Carey. She must have slipped out of the crowd and now stood beside me.

Celeste said, "They're colorful flags. The high school kids make them and then find the tallest tree they can to tie them to at the tippy top."

The woman at the booth said, "There are a lot worse things that kids could be out doing."

Joanie tucked the long fabric bolt under her arm.

The woman said, "We try to help the students out as much as we can with their sewing."

"Hear that, Joanie?" I searched my mind for a way to pry Joanie away from this booth. "We can make a flag and fly it from the top of a tree." I knew the tree climbing part would appeal to her. I reached in my pocket and withdrew my wallet hoping that if I paid for a bit of the red cloth, Joanie might follow me to another spot without a scene.

The woman waved her hand at me and said, "Listen, that's a remnant and it's not much anyhow. It's my gift to her." She nodded at Joanie. "I think she'll enjoy making a flag."

I let go of Joanie's arm and she grunted approvingly.

"I can pay you. It's fine," I said, but the woman planted her hands on her hips and shook her head.

"I won't hear of it."

"Thanks so much," I said.

Celeste leaned in to Joanie's ear and said, "I'd be happy to help you make a flag, Joanie. I'm Celeste."

Joanie grinned. Her eyes fixed on Celeste and then Joanie reached out and gently stroked her hair, which glistened in the sun. Celeste giggled and Joanie smiled at her.

"So shiny," said Joanie. "Luke's friend is shiny."

"Like you," said Celeste.

Celeste linked her arm in mine and the three of us set off for the picnic area. Joanie beamed and carried the fabric in front of her as though it were a box of eggs.

Celeste said, "Flag making is one of the few things I can do pretty well."

"Why would you say a thing like that? Seems to me you do everything well."

Celeste smiled at me and I could swear it was like having a flashlight beam directly into my eyes.

Suddenly a hand grabbed my shoulder and spun me around.

"What the…" I said.

Alec's narrow and bloodshot eyes held mine. Still gripping my shoulder, Alec squeezed hard. I refused to wince and instead met his gaze aware that my blood was beginning to pump wildly through my veins.

"I figured I might find you here, dirtbag," said Alec, his voice thick, the words slurred. His nails pressed through my red and white polo shirt into my flesh. I could smell alcohol on his breath. It was only noon, yet he was having trouble standing up straight. His body rocked from side to side so far that I wondered if he would topple over.

I knocked his arm away and we stood nose to nose. He tried mightily to keep his balance.

Celeste said, "Cut it out, you two. This is supposed to be a fun time."

We stood locked in a primitive hormonal battle that had been fought since the time of Adam. I knew that there was no stepping back and that one of us would act, and both of us would someday regret it.

"You couldn't stay away from her, could you?" said Alec in a voice that seethed. "Some friend."

Celeste moved toward Alec. I motioned with my hand for her to stay back; instead she tried to step between us. He shoved her away hard and the sight of him touching her roughly caused something to snap inside me. My fist connected with Alec's jaw, and he staggered backward and fell to the ground. Alec lay sprawled on the grass for a few seconds, then he half rose and rubbed his chin.

"Stay away from her and from me," I said, my fists clenched at my side. I wanted to jump on him and pound the crap out of him even if he did have me by five inches and forty pounds.

Celeste hugged my arm, preventing me from doing anything else rash. Alec lay back in the grass and stared up at the sky. He must have been too drunk to rise and hit me.

He said, "Enjoy yourselves. You deserve each other. Who the fuck cares."

Joanie had been watching the scene unfold. She caught my eye, then she began making strange noises that I knew meant she was disturbed.

"Ereeew, ereeew," went Joanie.

"Geez, Joan girl, don't go getting wound up," I said, trying unsuccessfully to find her eyes.

"Awweeee," said Joanie, blinking rapidly and staring off into space. A small crowd was already gathering and watching. Joanie squealed loudly and threw the bolt of fabric down. She stomped her feet and rocked from side to side. She was nearing a complete meltdown and rather than have to deal with that I decided to leave Alec there. We could always pick up our dispute at a later time. I grabbed Joanie's arm and propelled her forward. "If we hurry we can make the last pie-eating contest," I said. "You know how much you love pie, Joan girl."

Celeste fell in behind me, and as Joanie, Celeste and I headed to the picnic grounds, I was aware of Alec's eyes burning holes in my back. I glanced over my shoulder then back to Celeste.

"Forget him. He's a loser," said Celeste, her lip quivering slightly.

I wanted to believe Celeste was being straight with me, but that lip quiver unnerved me, made me wonder what was going on in her head with regard to Alec. Could she prefer him? My stomach sank then settled. That couldn't be. After all, Celeste strolled with me, not Alec. My insecurity banished, I decided to enjoy the day as I had never enjoyed a Fourth of July before. A tiff with a former friend would not intrude on my happiness.

I turned my attention to Joanie. "Hup, two, three, four," I said to my sister, tugging on her arm. She smiled at me and I was relieved to see that she was already a little calmer. Halfway up the hill we stopped at an old oak. The three of us sat down in the shade and Celeste stroked Joanie's hair. Joanie flapped her arms and I bit my lip, waiting to see if Joanie would erupt at the touch. Instead, Joanie stopped whimpering and sank bank against the tree.

"Joanie's tired," Joanie said. I handed her the bolt of fabric and she hugged it to her chest.

Celeste said, "Tomorrow, I'm going to come over and help you make a flag out of that fabric, Joanie. That's what you're supposed to do, and I'm going to help you."

Joanie grinned broadly.

"Thanks," I said to Celeste.

Celeste and I accompanied Joanie to the pie-eating table. We watched Joanie down a cherry pie in less than sixty seconds. She didn't break the record or win a prize but she beamed brightly and tugged on my arm, red juice dripping down her chin. She danced in circles humming and buzzing loudly and I knew she was having fun. I was grateful to Celeste for not minding Joanie's strange behavior. Most of the people at the festivities were deferential and kind to us and I was grateful for their good will.

Later, Celeste and I entered the three-legged race. We never crossed the finish line but when we tumbled to the ground I knew I had won something far greater than a ribbon. Being so close to her was an immeasurable reward. Joanie squealed with delight at the sight of our tangled limbs and joined us on the ground.

After collecting our ribbons for participating, Joanie proudly pinned them to her chest. Celeste stood between us and said, "Follow me."

She headed down the path that led to Lake Parrot, a manmade lake where two aerators worked round the clock in a vain attempt to stop green algae from forming on the surface. Except for a few slimy spots near the western edge, the degradation had not yet begun this season, and the lake sparkled in the late afternoon sun. As we walked to the banks, hoots and hollers of joy rose up and greeted us.

"What's going on down there? Swimming races?" I asked.

"You'll see. I know Joanie's going to adore this."

The path was a narrow, evergreen-lined one. Eventually it opened to a clearing, where we stopped and took in the scene. A dozen teenagers were gathered around a tall tree that stood next to the dock. The group of boys and girls joined hands ring-a-rosy-style and chanted. We drew closer and I could see there was something in the center of the ring that held their focus.

"Do you know them?" I asked Celeste. "What are they doing?"

Joanie began to grunt and squeal, but the tones were no longer those that signaled enjoyment. I could tell she was feeling tired and overstimulated and hoped she would be able to process this latest exciting moment without erupting. I knew she could take only so much activity before her brain overloaded, but I did not want to leave yet.

"They're just some townies. Not ones I know, but they probably know me. Word travels pretty fast in Faith Junction."

One of the teens in the circle caught sight of us and I saw her lean over and whisper to the girl at her right. Their chanting stopped and soon all eyes turned to us. I looked over at Joanie. Her cap was askew, her T-shirt stained with cherry juice. Her shorts hung too low on her hips and her arms flapped wildly as she hummed and buzzed.

A tall boy said, "You want something?"

I blinked. Then I saw what was at the center of the circle. A large flag.

Joanie saw it too and she clapped her hands excitedly. I didn't think we should push our luck, but she was not to be denied. She dropped my hand and headed into the center of the ring where she squatted on top of the colorful flag.

"Hey, get off, klutz," said one of the girls. "We spent a week making this flag."

I called to Joanie, "Let's go, Joan girl. We don't want to hurt the flag."

Joanie popped her thumb in her mouth and rocked back and forth on her heels, a behavior she engaged in when exhausted. Then she lay back on the flag, stuck her legs out straight and stared at the sky, her eyes glazing over. I sent a worried look Celeste's way.

Celeste followed me to the edge of the flag.

"Make her get up," said one of the girls.

I ignored the growing hostility and addressed my sister. "Joanie, we've got to let the kids have their flag. You shouldn't be laying on it like that."

Joanie rocked from side to side. She grabbed the bolt of red fabric from my hands and held it to her tightly.

Celeste said, "Listen, I'll help you make one that's a hundred times better than this one, okay?"

Joanie pressed her eyes tightly shut and hummed.

"She's got to the count of ten to get off, or we make her get off." One of the taller boys loomed beside me.

I closed my eyes and tried to stay calm, and when I opened them, from out of nowhere a flash of lightning raced across the sky.

"Where'd that come from?" asked one of the girls. "The sun is out and it's not supposed to shower."

I noticed several of the teens eye Celeste and I found myself doing the same. She avoided my gaze and stared off into the distant sky.

The wind stirred the trees. Dark clouds raced overhead in counterpoint to the light blue sky. Another bolt of lightning flashed overhead and sent the group of screaming teens scurrying to the pool house next to the dock for cover.

When the last of the group had entered the safety of the changing rooms, I turned to Joanie who, still sitting on the flag, watched the electrically charged sky with wide eyes. Her fists were clenched and her jaw set.

"This is it, Joan girl. You've got to get off that flag now. Rain's coming. We should go inside."

Celeste had her face to the heavens. Her blonde hair whipped madly about her head and shoulders. Her eyes glowed with a strange light and I was frightened to look at them.

Joanie stood and pointed at the sky. She left the flag and walked toward the spot where the bolts of lightning had flashed above us. The sky had not changed its blue color and the sun was still strong. Joanie pointed upward and I followed her gaze to the bank of black thunderheads. As quickly as they had gathered, the clouds rolled back. Joanie chuckled and danced from foot to foot.

Soon the teens came out of the changing house. A couple of the boys picked up the flag, shooting angry glances our way.

"They're going to put the flag up now," said Celeste. Her skin was pale and she leaned on me. "On the highest tree in the park which has been this one for the past thirty years." She pointed at a tall fir.

Joanie nodded and grunted. She flapped her arms and spun around like a top. I knew that we were on borrowed time, but I wanted to see what would happen next. The group carried the flag over to the tree. For a minute I thought that Joanie might try to climb the tree before the designated boy, but Celeste took Joanie by the hand. That was enough to calm Joanie and keep her still.

A tall, thin boy draped the flag over his shoulder. To good-natured cries of, "Be careful, Benji," and, "How's it hangin'," the boy began his ascent. He climbed swiftly and surely.

In a few moments, he was up in the high branches. We watched as he tied the flag to the topmost branch. A chorus of appreciation rose from the teenagers and the climber joined in their glee, shaking limbs and raining pinecones on them. The girls squealed and gathered up the cones, throwing them at the boys. A breeze stirred the trees, and the flag spread out over the crown of the fir, its glorious red, white and blue emblazoned with the names of each teen who had helped in the project.

Without warning, the boy at the top of the tree lost his footing and tumbled down a few branches. Several girls shrieked. I gasped loudly and heard Celeste moan. We all held our breath as Ben bounced along like a loose Christmas ball. But Ben was as light as the tree limbs were strong. Soon he caught hold of a sturdy branch and stopped his fall.

"Be careful, you idiot," shouted one of the teens. Nervous laughter erupted.

Beside me Celeste leaned heavily into me and seemed to grow as tired as Joanie.

"What a fantastic day this has been, eh, Joanie?" said Celeste. She nudged Joanie in the ribs. Celeste's eyes met mine and she said, "Some days should never end."

My arm encircled her waist. I had almost put the incident with Alec completely out of my mind. With Celeste by my side all things seemed possible. Ben jumped to the ground and the teens drifted away in packs.

We moved from the lake back to the picnic area where my parents took one look at arm-flapping Joanie and began packing their things.

"This is too much for her," clucked my mother, her yellow mules slapping against her heels. "Joe, sweetie, don't forget the lounge chairs."

My mother smoothed Joanie's hair and linked her arm in hers, soothing her as best she could. "Luke, you can help your father," my mother shouted over her shoulder as she towed Joanie toward the parking lot.

"If it's ok, I'm going to stay here for a while," I said to my father. He looked at me and at Celeste and nodded, a small smile on his lips. "See you at home later, son," he said, shouldering the chairs and picnic basket, now and then swatting at his ankles. "Damn mosquitoes," he muttered as he walked away.

For what remained of the afternoon, Celeste and I continued to enjoy our time together. We joined in a relay race. We ate hot dogs and hamburgers till we could hold no more. We told each other of our pasts. She was a good audience, laughing at my jokes in the right places, smiling into my eyes and sending silver into my veins each time she burst into laughter. When she slipped her hand in mine and mentioned she was looking forward to seeing me again the next day, fireworks erupted in my chest. I felt like a kid at a birthday party who has just opened the present that he desired most.

As the hours passed, though the sky above held its blue brilliance and the sun shone, the brightness of the day evaporated. I could see more color drain from Celeste's face with each passing hour. I knew, but did not want to admit, that something was wrong. In spite of the thrall that captured me, that made me want to squeeze every last drop from the final moments of the holiday, I had the feeling that the dimming around me stemmed not from the waning sun, but directly from Celeste.

That night, sitting in the ball field, as rockets exploded overhead, I was aware of the creeping darkness that gathered around us. Instinctively, I cursed the blackness. I drew Celeste close as the evening's finale burst into color overhead. She returned my kiss and light flooded me. Our time was now. Whatever was hovering out there could be damned and wait forever. I shivered as I fought off the thought that perhaps it would not wait that long.

CHAPTER NINE

The next day I rose early. The thought of Celeste's arrival had me feeling as expectant as I did on Christmas morning. While my stomach flip-flopped, I forced myself to eat breakfast and chat with my mother and Joanie. My father had hit the road before we had risen. When Celeste knocked at 10 a.m. I hurried to let her inside. I heard my mother laugh, and as I threw the door wide, I knew I was smiling. Celeste grinned back at me, refreshed and renewed by sleep. I helped her take several stuffed bags from her bike.

"How many flags are you going to make? You could outfit the flagpoles of a small country with all this stuff," I said, poking into one of the brown paper sacks.

She knocked my hand away playfully. "This is serious business. They say it takes an artist to get it right and you're in the hands of one."

I grabbed her hand and squeezed it. She felt warm, as though she had been sitting out in the sun and I wanted to bask in her heat.

Joanie appeared at the front door holding her basketball.

I called to her, "Joan girl, look who's here to help us make something special."

Joanie ignored Celeste and me. She ambled down the steps toward the basketball hoop.

"Hey, where are you going? Is that any way to treat a guest?"

To my relief, Celeste chuckled, unfazed by Joanie's anti-social behavior.

I tried to explain. "She's often tense in the morning. Basketball loosens her up a bit. She's not so much ignoring you as trying to collect herself."

Celeste said, "So are you going to help me get this stuff inside or what?"

I reluctantly let go of her hand and took the bags from Celeste. As I started to enter the house, I heard Joanie grunt. I turned and saw her standing stock-still. My heart raced. I dropped the bags I was carrying as Joanie unleashed the basketball at Celeste. I darted forward, blocked her shot and yelled. "Cut it out, Joan girl. Celeste's not here to play basketball."

Celeste said, "Would it help if I tried?"

I shook my head. "She'd just storm off into the house. She's in one of her moods."

Celeste nodded. Then she dug into one of her bags and withdrew a bright red plastic jewel. She found a thick, black ribbon and slipped the fake gem on the silk, fashioning a necklace. Celeste held the creation high and walked to Joanie.

Joanie stared at the ground not wanting to meet Celeste's gaze. Celeste approached and gently placed the ribbon with the jewel over Joanie's head. "Princess Joanie. You should have jewels, you know."

I wasn't sure how Joanie would react. She was not usually one for girly type things. She would as soon wear a baseball cap as do her hair, a fact my mother was not shy about chiding her.

Then I saw Joanie lift the gem up to the sunlight. Tears streamed down her face.

Celeste turned to me with a stricken look. "I didn't mean to make her cry. I'm so sorry."

But I was the one who was sorry. Joanie cooed softly and swung the necklace to and fro. I had rarely been able to move Joanie like that.

"She loves your gift," I said. "She's crying because she likes it so much."

Joanie reached out and grabbed Celeste's arm. Then she wrapped her in a bear hug so tight I had to go over and separate them.

Celeste chuckled as she stepped away from Joanie.

"You've got a buddy for life now," I told her.

Celeste's eyes were as damp as Joanie's. "I've always wanted a sister. I grew up alone and had an imaginary one. I wasn't much good at connecting with girls my own age."

I stepped between Joanie and Celeste and held my arms out, elbows bent. Each of them took one and we headed into the house where Joanie showed my mother her necklace. I stammered an introduction of Celeste and my mother smiled broadly, then returned to the kitchen. Soon we spread Celeste's supplies on the floor.

"This is going to take a few days," said Celeste. "It's not something you can knock off in an hour or two. At least, it's not something I can do in that time."

"A few days?"

She nodded and I beamed.

"I think we can handle having you around for that long."

Joanie smiled too.

We set to work. Or I should say, Celeste did. She unfolded Joanie's red fabric and took out a measuring tape. She removed some magazines from one of the bags and pushed them toward Joanie. Joanie pushed a bowl of popcorn back at Celeste and she grinned when Celeste popped a few pieces into her mouth.

"Popcorn's the best!" Joanie said. "Yum!"

"I want you to pick out some things that you like. Rip out the pages and we'll see what you come up with."

Joanie took the magazines and settled into the couch. She slowly scanned the pages. I knew this would occupy her for the next hour.

"You're incredible with her, you know," I said.

"I feel like I know her in some way. There aren't many people I can say that about."

"There aren't many people I feel I know that well either."

She looked away.

"You okay?"

She shook her head. "I'm sorry. Sometimes I get upset."

"I didn't mean to upset you."

"It's not that." She took a deep breath. "I lost my real parents in a plane crash. And sometimes this feeling comes over me. It's hard to explain. I never know when it's going to seize me."

"I wish it hadn't happened to you. I'd feel terrible if I lost my folks or Joanie."

She sighed and put down her scissors on the crimson fabric. "I like you, Luke. Maybe it's because you're like me, an outsider."

"You've lived here your entire life, haven't you? How much of an outsider could you be?"

"I was an infant when that plane crashed. No one is sure how or why I wound up here."

"You could find that out I'd bet."

She bit her lip. "I'm not so sure I want to."

"Nonsense. It might make all those rumors finally go away. And maybe that feeling would go away too."

"Rumors mean nothing to me." She turned her attention back to the fabric and said, "We're going to make a special flag. One third for Joanie, one third for me and one third for you. A holy trinity of a flag."

I banished her troubled comments to the back of my mind. She was still the most exquisite creature I had ever seen with that cascading blonde hair and golden eyes that invited me to tumble into them and lose myself. So what if she had a past that was not easily understood and bothered her.

As she cut she talked. "I'm sure you have a lot of questions. The other kids must have told you a lot about me."

I shrugged.

She snipped and said, "It's all right. I understand that I'm different."

"The only thing different about you is that you're better than most kids I've met around here."

She shook her head. "If only that were true."

I rolled my eyes and she sat back on her heels.

She said, "One thing I do know. People have a way of twisting things. Sometimes I think my dad is right that I should stay away."

"Is that what he says?"

"If he knew I was here he'd have a fit. I'm not allowed to go into

84

anyone's house or go to Ben's or anywhere."

"That's crazy."

"As you can see, I often ignore him and do what I like."

I smiled.

She continued, "When I was real little I was friends with Deanna for a while, but it kind of fell apart."

"You two are certainly different."

"She's not above asking me for a favor every once in awhile, but that's not exactly friendship. I know what she's up to. So now I stick to myself and everyone is happy."

"I don't see how shutting yourself off is going to help anything."

She laughed that tinkling laugh again and my mind wandered. I barely heard her as she said, "In the long run, you may be right, for all the wrong reasons. No matter what I do I can't escape what's meant to be. I suppose that's why I'm here."

Her golden eyes met mine and I thought my heart would burst through my chest. I sat back on my heels and held my breath, not sure what she was going to tell me.

She plunged forward. "My dad has told me the story of how I got here thousands of times." Her eyes caught mine with a searching glance. Satisfied that I was still a sympathetic ear, she continued. "He found me after a plane wreck up in the north orchard." She smiled. "That's the place you always follow me to, silly."

"With the Leatherman's cave."

She nodded.

"Is that why you go there so often?"

She ignored the question, clearly agitated and needing to let her words out. "My father rescued me." Her hands holding the fabric began to shake.

I reached over and put my hand over hers. It was like touching the hood of a car with your bare hand on a below-zero day. When she had hugged me hello a few minutes ago she had possessed all the warmth of someone who had been sitting outside in the sun for the past few hours. Now it was as though all that had somehow dissipated, been drawn off. I had never felt anyone grow that chilled so quickly.

"It was a terrible accident. I keep wondering why I lived."

"It just happened that way." I rubbed her hand between mine trying to raise the temperature, trying to find something to say that would comfort her.

Her eyes grew wide as saucers. "I have nightmares about that crash. Even though I was an infant, I swear I can remember it."

"We all have nightmares. It's more than understandable why you'd have them."

"Everyone who knows me loses, Luke, and everyone I care about I lose." Her bottom lip trembled. "I should do you a favor and walk out that door and never come back."

"You're being ridiculous," I said. I wanted to tell her that I felt richer than I'd ever felt in my life since I had met her. But I didn't.

She shook her head sadly. "You'll see. I'm trouble."

Her gaze met mine and I made up my mind to remove that look of sorrow from her eyes. I had no idea it was an insurmountable task.

I said, "Tomorrow, I want you to meet me at Ben's in the afternoon."

"I don't know if that's such a good idea. I don't go there very often."

"It's time you started living like everyone else around here. You've set yourself apart long enough for no good reason."

"But my dad…."

"Around one. Meet me there," I said firmly.

Suddenly Celeste leaned over and brushed her lips against mine.

The sensation that caused was heady. It was as though a whirlwind had caught me up for an instant and taken my breath away. From across the room I heard Joanie giggle and I knew she had witnessed the kiss. She smacked her lips loudly and held up a picture of a basketball.

Celeste trained her eyes on the fabric at her feet and I knew there was nothing to be said or done at this particular moment. I settled in for an afternoon of flag making, knowing that it was the future moments that held more whirlwinds that drove me on.

CHAPTER TEN

Meeting Celeste at one p.m. the next day was not an easy task. Joanie had swimming lessons at the town pool in the morning and I was responsible for staying with her. The lessons ended at 11:30. Usually we went for a soda at the pool snack bar afterwards and then Mom picked us up and took us to lunch at Joanie's favorite place, the Burger Queen in town, which wasn't too far from Ben's.

I knew that if I followed this routine, I would never get to Ben's by one. I downed my soda and waited for Mom's Pontiac to appear. I paced back and forth and cursed her slowness. Of all the days in the world to be late she could not have chosen a worse one.

When Mom's blue Grand Prix rolled into view I lunged into the street. Mom honked and waved, her hair swept up in a ponytail tied with an orange ribbon. I stepped back from the curb and motioned to Joanie who sat on a bench. My mother rolled down her window and peered over her yellow cat's-eye-shaped sunglasses. She said, "We'd better get a move on if we want to beat the lunch crowd over at the BQ."

I opened the back door and Joanie climbed in humming to herself. She liked the routine of swim and lunch and never lost control on these days. Once she had settled in I climbed into the car and sat beside my mother.

"Luke," said my mother, "where in the world are you? You look like you lost your best friend."

I stuck my hands in my pockets and said, "I'm not coming to the Burger Queen."

Mom blinked.

"I'm going to meet some of the kids. I promised them I'd be there by one."

Mom pursed her lips. I knew she did not like my going off suddenly. Joanie would like it even less.

"It's just for today, Mom. It's important."

Surprisingly, Mom was an easy touch. "You deserve to be with your young friends. I know you'll be your usual sensible self. Joanie and I will be just fine at BQ. Right, Joan girl?"

Joanie squealed with delight. "French fries, catsup. Do you want a burger?" She tossed a small ball in the air in the backseat. I knew she would continue saying this until she had finished her meal. I started to feel guilty at leaving Mom to spend the afternoon alone with Joanie. I had spent enough time with my sister to know that prolonged encounters were often exhausting. By bedtime Mom was usually tuckered out, though she never complained. One of these days I feared Joanie would aggravate the wrong person.

When we arrived at town I asked my mother to drop me at Ben's. As I walked away from the car, my mother stuck her head out the window and said, "Next time you'll take her with you, won't you? To meet some of your friends?"

My heart sank at the thought of bringing Joanie to the diner. I stuck my hands deep into my pockets and stared at the ground.

Mom rolled up her window and waved. In spite of my anger at her suggestion, a lump rose up in my throat at the sight of the two of them leaving, Mom's orange ribbon fluttered in the breeze.

I glanced at my watch: 12:45 already! Joanie and Mom faded into the recesses of my mind as quickly as they had turned the corner. Overhead the sky was bluer than ever. This was the perfect day and I was on my way to a rendezvous with the perfect girl.

My reverie was interrupted by the assault of the Spi-Sea Shrimp plant. The rank smell coated my arms and filled my lungs.

Suddenly a wind came up out of nowhere and pressed into my back. "Hey, not so hard," I said to the sky. I looked around, grateful no one was in my vicinity to hear me addressing unknown forces. The wind grew gentler. I laughed and climbed the stairs to the diner where I slipped into a booth at the rear of Ben's. A smattering of teens sat at the counter and almost every both was filled. Several of the kids, like the Clare sisters, I recognized from Deanna's parties. They nodded at me and I smiled back.

Within seconds, Celeste appeared. I heard a hush go over the diner and looked up as she came toward me. Her hair, still wet from her shower, hung flat against her head and made her golden eyes stand out more, something I didn't think was possible. She shined. I blinked a couple of times and tried to focus. Her beauty was like that. I could not possibly take it all in one glance. But then I saw the thin line of her mouth and knew there was something wrong.

I looked around and realized that I was not the only one who was having trouble taking his eyes off Celeste. The rest of the diner watched her move through their ranks.

I smiled and whispered, "Don't let the kids in here bother you. You're better than any of them."

She nodded and slid into the booth opposite me. She stared at her placemat. Behind me a girl giggled and whispered to a companion. I wanted to stand up and tell her and everyone else to mind their own business and leave her alone.

We ordered lunch. Every time I looked up I could see someone's eyes focused on us. It was worse than being in a fishbowl. I started to wonder if I was right in asking Celeste to come here.

Celeste reached across the table and took my hand in hers.

"How are you doing?" I asked.

"I never come in here for more than a cone." She licked her lips. "This is really odd to be sitting here."

"It has to get easier in the future if we come back in here. It's a small town and you're a novelty is all."

She set her jaw. "Screw them. I've never wanted to come in is why I haven't. They have nothing to say about it." She glared over my shoulder and I knew she was focusing on the giggling girl in the booth behind me.

She met my gaze. "I have to tell you something, Luke. I've been thinking about this since yesterday. It's not going to be easy and you may not understand it, but I do have to tell it to you."

Two boys in the booth to our right stared openly. I stared them both down, first one, then the other. Celeste and I went back to our Cokes.

Her pained eyes met mine and my heart thumped in my chest. I wanted to wrap her in my arms and comfort her the way I did Joanie when she had a nightmare.

"Your friends are right to tell you I'm weird."

"Like I said, they'll get used to seeing you here. It'll be easier the next time. You want another Coke?"

She raised her hand and I fell silent. "I was trying to tell you this yesterday." She closed her eyes for a few seconds and bit her lip. Then she met my gaze. "I've always been odd. But I've always assumed that there was a reason for it and that eventually I would find out why."

"I'm not buying it, Celeste."

She shook her head sadly. Then she held up her hand and pointed it out the window to the sky. "Would you like rain or hail?"

"What do you mean?"

"Pick. Rain or hail."

I looked at the cloudless sky.

"If you won't pick I will. Hail," she said.

I watched her close her eyes and concentrate. Suddenly the previously clear sky darkened. The lights in the diner flickered. The two boys in the booth beside us looked through the window up at the approaching storm. I saw one of them nudge the other with an elbow and nod toward Celeste, who sat with eyes closed and a strange look on her face. Small pellets of ice hit the glass window of the diner, slowly at first, then they increased in size and intensity.

Ben came around from behind the counter, stared at the sky and whistled.

Celeste opened her eyes and held my gaze.

"It's a summer storm. That's all," I said, not willing to go along with the idea that she had anything to do with it. "You read the weather report and got lucky."

She banged her fist on the table. Ben and just about the entire diner watched us now.

"This has nothing to do with luck, other than it was my bad luck to have been born with this...this...curse." Her eyes filled with rage.

I didn't know what to do. I couldn't believe that Celeste Carey could affect the weather. Who could?

"Okay, weather girl, make the sun shine if you can."

She shook her head. "You don't believe me, do you? I should make it stay raining for the next three days. But I'm not that good."

"Come on, maestro, sun, please, now."

She raised her head from her arms and stared at the sky. Then she pointed. The clouds parted and the sun appeared, making the ice on the ground gleam. The girl behind us gasped.

My heart skipped a beat and a chill went down my back. There was no way she could do this. Was there?

Celeste lay her head on the table. "I'm so tired."

"I don't know whether to hug you or run," I said, unable to understand what I thought I had witnessed.

"No reason to hug me, Luke."

I leaned back in my seat. Her voice was as flat and cold as Ben's pancakes.

"That's the other part of what I need to tell you. I'm not the girl for you."

"Excuse me?" Thunderbolts exploded in my brain.

She raised her head. "I thought there was something between us, but I was wrong."

I felt as though she had stabbed me in the heart. "But what about yesterday? How can you say that? We've been having a great time together."

"It's me, Luke. There's nothing there. There never is and there shouldn't be."

"How can you say that?"

"I did, and I mean it."

"What about that time in the quarry? When you were up on the ledge watching me."

She smiled slightly. "That was pretty awful of me. I should have let you have your fun."

My head swam. I didn't want to understand what she was telling me. It was over and it hadn't even begun. What had happened since yesterday when I thought we were on our way to being an ideal couple?

In the bright afternoon light it seemed as though the sun had come to rest around her and I ached as her words settled over me. I wanted to bask in the glow, but it was gone. She had become unattainable again, which if anything made her more desirable.

Suddenly the door to the diner banged open. I watched Josh scan the room and rush toward us.

"Luke, come on, buddy, get outside," he said out of breath.

I eyed him, wondering what prank he was up to. No jar or receptacle was in his hands.

He said rapidly, "Someone's up on one of the utility poles. You've got to see this." He circled his index finger around at his temple and gave first me then Celeste a knowing look. "Nutty as peanut brittle."

There was nothing I could think of to say to Celeste, so I threw a bill on the table and followed Josh outside trying not to think about what she had told me.

"Damn," he said, casting an eye back at Celeste. "Alec told me you were with her. She is such a piece. Looner, the fast worker." His machine gun laughter cut me.

Our feet crunched on the remainder of the hail, which was melting rapidly in the now-returned sunlight. I was not in the mood to discuss Celeste or Alec with him.

I asked, "Where is this crazy person?"

"Follow me," Josh said. "Things are going to get interesting." He led me across the street and pointed at a light pole.

I shaded my eyes. At the top was a figure.

My stomach lurched.

This was not what I expected at all. Joanie clung to the utility pole up at least thirty feet. She held the ball she had bounced in the car earlier. She waved it in one hand and hugged the pole with her other arm. Most of the kids had filed out of the diner now and stood in the parking lot pointing upward.

"Do me a favor and go across the street and see if my mother is still at the BQ," I said to Josh. I wanted everyone to go back inside and leave me alone with Joanie, but that was not going to happen.

"Go over there yourself, dirtbag. I want to watch this."

"That's my sister up there," I said. I leveled my gaze at him and he took a step backward.

"Whoa," he said. "Looner has a sister?" He glanced up. "On top of the utility pole?"

"I'll explain later. Please, go see if my mother is over there."

"Hey, man, sorry about the comments about your sister." Josh sank back toward the diner and I yelled to Joanie.

"Joan girl. What are you doing up there?"

"French fries, catsup, do you want a burger?" she said. She stared at the sky, one arm wrapped around the utility pole. She looked up to the top where electrical wires waved in a breeze. In an instant I knew she was contemplating a move in that direction.

"That's high enough, Joanie. Why don't you come here and we can head home?"

Joanie grinned down at me. Her red baseball cap was askew. This was not her usual type of tree to climb. This was much higher and I was afraid she might lose her balance.

"I'm not kidding, Joanifer. Mom is gonna give us heck if we don't get back soon."

She pursed her lips and turned her face to the sky.

"Where's Mom, Joanie? How'd you get away from her?"

"What the hell is she doing?" I heard one of the kids from the diner say. "What a messed-up freak."

I clenched my fists and tried to shut out the comments.

"Who the heck is she?"

"Some stupid wacko loser," came a voice I wanted to silence. The banter distracted me and left me fuming.

From out of nowhere, Celeste slipped her arm in mine. What she had unleashed in me moments ago, leaving me in emotional turmoil, faded. I could feel her warmth invade and calm me.

Sirens wailed and a fire truck rounded the corner. Some well-meaning person had called in the volunteer hook and ladder company.

"Shit," I said to no one in particular. "This is going to scare the crap out of her."

I moved away from Celeste and into the center of the street. I waved at the truck and tried to flag it down, but it continued to barrel toward me.

"Turn off the siren. Turn them off!" I shouted to no avail. The truck drew to a halt and two men in full firefighter gear alighted. The siren faded as the engine stopped. Someone told the firemen what was going on. I could not believe the size of the crowd gathered in the street.

Joanie grunted and I could see a look of fear in her eyes. "It's going to be fine, Joan girl," I shouted up to her.

I stepped between the two firemen as they approached. "You're going to scare her."

The taller of the two shot me a withering gaze. "Who the hell are you?" He brushed by me and placed his foot on the bottom rung of the pole. The other fireman shaded his eyes and looked up.

"She's my sister."

"You coming down, honey, or do we have to come up and get you?" Joanie didn't answer.

I said, "I wouldn't climb up if I were you."

The shorter fireman put his arm on his co-worker and said, "Hang on, Bobby."

The taller fellow named Bobby ignored him and hoisted himself up.

I took a deep breath. "She doesn't like being touched by strangers. She's not well, she's a little slow. Going up there could be disastrous. She's not your usual kid or cat up a tree." I glared at the taller fellow.

"What's wrong with her?" asked the tall one as he peered down at me.

"Nothing that I can't deal with," I said.

The fellow called Bobby shrugged his shoulders and slipped off the pole.

"Be my guest, big shot," he said. "You've got ten minutes and then we have to act."

Joanie clung to the pole above us, her head buried in her arm, her ball tucked into her hood behind her neck.

I wanted all this to be over and for us to be back at home watching TV or shooting hoops. Sometimes the world gets too big and this was one of those times. I took a deep breath and called to her in as calm a voice as I could. "Joanie, I want you to do me a favor and come play some basketball with me."

She shook her head and refused to take her eyes from her arm.

"Don't make me have to come up there and get you. Come on down like the big girl you are who got herself up there."

I became aware of someone behind me, and turned angrily expecting to find the fireman called Bobby smugly awaiting his chance to interfere. Instead, once again Celeste Carey slipped her hand in mine. I squeezed her fingers, grateful for the friendly touch.

A familiar smell made me smile. Celeste held a large bucket of popcorn retrieved from Ben's. She smiled and handed the bucket to me. I took the treat and held it aloft. A soft breeze rustled the trees nearby sending the scent of buttery popcorn to my nostrils.

Joanie's eyes came off her sleeve and she saw the bucket. "Popcorn, do you want a snack?" she asked.

I reached in and grabbed a handful and ate it. "It's for you, Joanie. Unless you don't want any and I get to eat it all."

Without hesitation, Joanie descended from her perch. Just like that. You never knew what, if anything, would work to distract Joanie. In a few seconds she stood on the ground. She lunged for the bucket of popcorn and I breathed a sigh of relief. Across the street a few people clapped.

Suddenly Joanie's eyes went wide. She dropped the popcorn and shrieked. My heart raced as she held her hands to her ears. The crowd fell back. Joanie shook and jolted a few times then fell to the ground. I knelt beside her. There was nothing I could do; touching her would only make it worse. She closed her eyes and lay on the ground mumbling loudly. I knew she was hiding from the crowd.

Mom's Grand Prix rounded the corner. I could see the look of worry on her brow as she drove into the diner's parking lot. Mom alighted from her car and caught sight of Joanie and me. She raced towards us, her orange and green madras pants pumping wildly, her ponytail with the orange ribbon bobbing. Her cat's-eye sunglasses fell to the pavement. Joanie stopped blubbering as soon as she heard our mother's voice.

"Thank goodness you're all right," Mom said, gripping Joanie around the middle. Mom, who wasn't much bigger than Joanie, turned to me with wide eyes. "I don't know what got into her, but as I was paying she must have trotted off. I've been driving around trying to find her. She's never done that before and she better not ever again!"

Joanie grinned and found the popcorn bucket. She stuffed a handful of kernels into her mouth.

Joanie said, "I found Luke. Do you want some popcorn?" She offered the treat to Mom who took a few pieces.

I helped Mom get Joanie up, then I turned to thank Celeste for helping resolve the incident, but she was gone, though the warmth of her touch lingered in my hand. My arm tingled where she had rested her fingers.

Right then I made up my mind not to give up on us yet. Heck. There had to be an us if I felt this way. That was clear to me. I could wait for her forever if need be. Eventually she would come round to my point of view. How could she not?

Josh clapped me on the back and said something about heading over to Deanna Barton's. I declined without caring what he thought of me, or Joanie, or my relationship with Celeste. He and all the town kids could drown in the quarry. My head throbbed and I knew I had to get away. We climbed into Mom's Pontiac and left the gathered crowd to talk among themselves about the crazy D'Angelos. I certainly knew that feeling. I sighed. It had been nice while it lasted, but now they all knew about Joanie. I reached over and hugged her to me.

She grinned into my face and handed me some popcorn. "Joanie can fly," said Joanie.

"Right," I said.

In front of me, Mom cranked up the car radio and tapped her long orange nails on the steering wheel. Her ponytail swung wildly and irritated me. "Sunshine cake for everyone," shouted Mom above the radio as we turned toward home and left the crowd gawking at the diner. There was no turning back for any of us that day.

CHAPTER ELEVEN

I didn't see Celeste for the next three days. Joanie's disappearance from the Burger Queen, and her climbing antics, left my mother jittery, which meant she kept both of us close to home, finding chores and activities for us to do. Dad was still on the road and the three of us pretended that nothing had happened, that we were one big happy family. As I cleaned the garage and weeded the garden, I kept running over and over in my head what Celeste had told me. Each day around lunchtime I called the Carey household, and each time someone picked up the telephone. My "Hello," was returned with a hard click at the other end of the line. When I dialed back a busy signal buzzed at me. The third day that I dialed and got the click I was angry and sure it was intentional.

Finally, I had had my fill of sunshine cake and popcorn and Mom's singing. Joanie could amuse herself for an afternoon. I went to the garage and mounted my bike.

My mother, in lime green capri pants, appeared in the garage as soon as she heard the door go up. In her left hand she held a spatula. Her face wore a worried expression. Without looking at her, before she could say a word, I pushed off and ignored her plaintive, "Luke, where are you going?"

As I hit the end of the street, Josh turned the corner and almost collided with me. We pulled our bikes to a stop. I waited to see what he had to say but I was not in the mood to hear about his latest self-stimulation or to have him tease me about my sister. And if he was going to stand up for Alec I was out of there in a second. He must have read the look on my face.

He stuck his hands in his pockets and said, "What's happening? I haven't seen much of you lately."

I shook my head and pushed off past him.

He turned his bike, caught up to me and said, "Guess you won't mind a little company."

We took the path that headed out of town.

"Where we going?" asked Josh.

I said nothing and pedaled hard.

"Look, if you want to be alone I understand. Heck, I spend enough time alone in my room."

We passed by the dirt road that led to the Leatherman's cave. Josh let out a sigh of relief that I didn't make the turn, but his mood soon changed as he realized where we were riding.

"You've got to be kidding," he said, panting from the hard pace I had set. "Look, there's crazy and there's absolutely raving mad," he said.

I leaned sharply over my handlebar and pedaled as hard as I could, letting the wind whip his words out of my ears. I didn't care if he accompanied me or not, but I was hellbent on my destination. After a few more minutes of all-out riding, we reached the entrance to the Carey farm. I slowed my bike to a halt and Josh caught up.

"Now what?" asked a winded Josh.

"We pay a call on Celeste at home." I wiped the sweat from my brow with the back of my hand. "It's about time someone did, don't you think?"

"Shit, no. You're freakin' loony for sure," said Josh.

"Yeah. I guess I am," I said. "It runs in the family." I rode down the dirt path to the front porch with Josh gamely following close behind. "I'm sick of all this bullshit about people being afraid of her father, and sick of her jerking me around like some puppet."

"Looks like Luke's got his Irish up," said Josh.

"And if you don't like my sister, I don't give a crap," I said.

"Who said anything about your sister?"

"Alec can kiss my ass."

Josh blinked. "You going to ring that doorbell or what?" he asked with a sly grin.

We dismounted and climbed up the bowed wooden steps. I looked around for a doorbell but there was none.

Josh chuckled. "Friendly folks out here," he said. Then he added, "We can leave now. Come on, Luke. There's no need to do this. I understand about your sister, and no one understands a thing about Celeste."

I studied the front of the old house, a turn-of-the-century, colonial farmhouse. Paint peeled from the green wooden siding, and a front window was cracked. With a loud creak, the interior door swung open. I jumped and I heard Josh take a step backward on the porch. He gasped.

In the doorway stood a mountain of a man who had enough heft for two sizable human beings. His eyes were cold blue pinpoints that looked as though they could shoot lasers. I licked my lips and clenched my fists. The man scared the bejesus out of me. And then I saw the shotgun in his hands. Alec's warning about gun-happy Mr. Carey came back at me.

"We should go," whispered Josh.

Mr. Carey glared at us from behind the screen door. "You fellows lose your way or something?" he said. His voice was gravelly, menacing. He rubbed a hand over thick gray stubble and inside I could hear a radio playing music from a different era.

"Yes," said Josh. "We're trying to figure out how to get back to town. Sorry to have bothered you. I think I remember which way to go." He laughed his rapid staccato laugh and I nudged him hard in the stomach.

I said, "I was wondering if Celeste was at home. I'd like to talk to her." I pulled myself up to my complete five-foot-four inches, which brought me up to his armpits.

Mr. Carey unlatched the screen and made his way onto the porch, which sagged further under his weight. I held my breath. He favored his left leg, which he tapped with the butt of the gun as he spoke.

"You I don't recognize, unlike your friend there," he said, pointing a hairy finger in Josh's direction. "Who are you?" He fixed his gaze on me.

Mr. Carey wore a flannel shirt and jeans. His gray hair was tied back behind his head in a long braid. In spite of my fear I wondered if Celeste helped him with his hair, if she washed his clothes, or had mended the place on the pants where they were patched. It helped me to stay calm to think of him in a domestic situation.

"Hey, you deaf or something?" Mr. Carey shouted and I jumped.

"I moved here with my family a few weeks ago. I'm a friend of your daughter's."

He narrowed his laser eyes at me and I tried not to blink. My heart pounded.

"Celeste doesn't have friends. You should get the hell off my property," he said, turning back to his door.

"We're going, Mr. Carey," said Josh but I grabbed him by the shirttail.

"You're wrong about that. She has lots of friends. And we're two of them."

Mr. Carey faced me and was about to speak when a loud noise rumbled across the pasture toward us. I heard a scream and my hair went on end. It was Celeste who had screamed, she was in distress. What had he done to her?

He shook his head. "She's over in the upper barn practicing that stuff she always practices. I don't think she's got the hang of it yet and doubt she ever will, but she sure does try."

The yell of pain erupted again from the direction of the barn.

Mr. Carey leaned on his shotgun. "She's okay. She just messes up, is all. If you go up there you better be really careful as she's worse than a kid with a chemistry set." He turned and faced us again. Then he said, "Kaboom!" so loud that Josh fell backward off the porch and landed in the dirt. Mr. Carey went back inside, slamming the door behind him.

He hollered through the screen, "Next time I'll shoot first like I usually do. I wouldn't come back if I was you." The interior door banged shut.

"Friendly fellow," said Josh. "Now what?"

"Now Celeste." I strode uphill towards the barn where I could hear Celeste singing. As I walked, I periodically heard loud popping noises, which drowned out her words.

Josh looked over his shoulder as he tagged along behind me. "I swear if that man sticks his head out that door again I'm out of here, Luke."

I reached the barn and pushed the door open hard sending it clattering against a wall. The smell of burning hay and gunpowder hit my nostrils. The barn lay dim and dark in the afternoon light. Celeste stopped singing and in a few seconds my vision adjusted. Celeste sat a few feet away from me on the dirt floor and I smiled at her.

"Get out," she said.

"I'm happy to see you too," I replied. Josh followed me into the barn.

"If my father sees you he'll shoot you both. You should leave."

"He's the one who told me where you were."

"I don't care who told you, I'm busy and want you to go."

Josh jerked his head toward the door and I could tell he wanted to leave, but I ignored his signals.

"What are you doing?" I asked Celeste.

"Nothing that's any of your business."

Josh cleared his throat. "I'll be down by the bikes, Luke." He backed out of the barn and I could hear his sneakers thudding away from the barn.

Celeste stood. Her hair flew in tangles around her head and her eyes held a fury I had not seen in the past. She pointed a finger and to my left a small lightning bolt hit the ground.

"Is that what you want to see?" she asked. She pointed again and another one caused me to jump out of the way. "Watch the freak put on a show."

"You don't frighten me," I lied. "Why are you doing this? Why won't you see me anymore?"

"You had no right to come here," she said.

"You had no right to shut me out like that. Why won't you answer my phone calls?"

"Every time I think I have control I find that I don't. I can't even control you."

"You don't have to impress me with your magic tricks," I said.

"Magic tricks? Is that what you think I'm about?"

I could see storm clouds gathering in her face and knew I had said the wrong thing.

"You'll regret saying that, Luke." Her words cut me raw. I couldn't bear her being this angry. I searched my mind for something that could soothe her, make the situation right.

"Please don't do this, Celeste," I said. "Talk to me."

She was far past reasoning. My plea fell to the ground like dust from the barn's rafters.

She said, "Keep an eye out for the next few days and see if you still think I'm practicing magic tricks." I took a step toward her and she said, "I'm telling you for the last time, get the heck out of my barn now or I won't be responsible for what happens to you."

My hair stood on end. I could feel an electrical charge in the air. I turned and walked out of the darkness of the structure into the afternoon light as Celeste's voice echoed behind me.

"Don't ever come back here. You're not welcome."

Celeste's words stung me. I had hoped to get to the bottom of her situation, to understand more about her, to get back in her graces. Instead I had managed to drive her even farther from me.

Josh and I rode back to my house. The furious ride did little to calm me.

"Now what?" asked Josh as we dismounted.

He followed me to my room where I gathered up my collection of model cars.

Josh held up a red Corvette. "Cool," he said. "You mind if I keep this one? I always wanted to do it in a Corvette."

I grabbed it from his hand.

He followed me to the kitchen where I gathered paper and matches.

Josh said, "Did I tell you my mother found my peanut butter jar?"

I rushed outside before he could give me the details. In a far corner of the garage I unearthed an old backpack and dumped the contents on the ground. My parents would have punished me severely if they had known I'd brought them with me from the Bronx. The illegal goods had been a going-away present from a couple of my "firebug" friends, which is what my mother called the undesirable teens in our old building who had befriended me to her consternation.

"Cool!" said Josh. "Firecrackers! Cherry bombs and ash cans!"

We spent the next hour blowing up my model cars, including the Corvette over Josh's protestations. We cleaned up as best we could, and by the time Joanie and Mom returned from an afternoon movie I was ready to face anything life threw at me.

"You want to stay for dinner?" I asked Josh.

He grinned. "Hell, yeah. How else am I going to get balls as big as yours? You think your mom has an empty peanut butter jar she could loan me?"

"Don't you ever think of anything but wacking off?"

"Don't you ever think of anything but Celeste?"

"Forget it," I said and we went inside to face another evening of macaroni and cheese and sunshine cake.

CHAPTER TWELVE

The next Friday night, Alec and I uncomfortably watched each other across Deanna's rec room. I knew studying him was not a good idea, given our Fourth of July run-in, but I couldn't keep from glancing across to where he stood talking to Deanna and another girl I did not recognize. Our battle over Celeste was all the more ridiculous given her current ouster of me from her life. Nevertheless, Alec and I were miles apart and not about to grow any closer. I grabbed a cup of rum-laced punch and forced myself to look around. Tonight, the unfamiliar faces far outnumbered the ones I knew. Deanna must have invited everyone she and Susie knew and then some, everyone but Celeste.

Music blared from the record player. A couple I didn't recognize locked lips on the white sofa as The Rolling Stones whined about getting satisfaction. The windows were wide open but the white curtains hung limply. I wished for a cooling breeze, for something to blow away what I could feel building in the room.

A pair of feminine hands covered my eyes from behind and a lovely scent surrounded me with a smell I could not place as a familiar one. But the nasal voice caused my heart to sink. Susie had found me.

"I assume you know who this is." She dropped her hands and giggled.

I turned to face her, not sure what to say. She changed her scent the way she changed her nail color and a part of me pined for the lemon and grass of our first meeting.

"Relax." She batted her thick lashes. "I never told anyone what happened that day at the quarry." She smoothed her black jeans and ran a finger over my lips. Today her raven hair had an orange streak that fell across one black-rimmed eye. "It's our secret, okay?"

I knocked her hand away. "I don't care who you tell what to. Plus, I don't like the way you treated my sister."

She laughed and moved toward the window, pushing aside the damp curtains. She tossed back at me, "It's your call, Looner."

Anger rose in my chest. Josh, a silent witness to our encounter, moved alongside me as Susie faded into the crowd. "Looner sure has a way with the ladies."

I sent him a scorching look and he laughed his machine gun laugh.

"What was that about? God, you're lucky to have girls like her after you."

I eyed him and shouted above the music, "You like her?"

"Are you serious?"

"You're better off with your jars, Josh."

He shook his head in disbelief.

"I wish she'd leave me alone. Truth is, I don't know how to get rid of her. She must have better things to do with her time than bother me."

Josh whistled a low note, and said, "Women are like cats."

I shook my head and groaned.

Josh continued. "It's true. My brother in college told me. You ever been in a room with a cat and a bunch of people? Guaranteed that the cat will start rubbing the leg of the guy who hates cats."

I took a sip of my Coke. "I don't hate cats."

"You don't like Susie and she knows it. She's not the type of girl who's used to being turned down. I mean, look at her." He let out a low sigh.

"I'm not doing that, Josh."

"Fine. Look, you can count on me, buddy. I'll take her off your hands."

"Keep an eye on the nutjob Alec while you're at it." I nodded my head in the direction of Alec, who still stood across the room. Alec caught the gesture and glared at me. "Let me know when Mt. St. Alec is set to erupt again so this time I'm ready."

"You two haven't made up yet?"

I shook my head and Josh tapped his finger on his cheek. "You have a lot in common at this point."

I rolled my eyes, and Josh said, "Think about it. Celeste has dumped you both."

"She hasn't dumped me."

Now it was Josh who rolled his eyes. "Yeah, right. She invited you to a pajama party last time we saw her."

"It's a little misunderstanding is all."

"You know what? You sound a lot like Alec when he talks about Celeste." He let out his machine gun laugh.

I could feel something hot building in my chest. Josh's words irritated me. I wadded up my napkin, aimed it at the trashcan and missed. Celeste was not out of reach and he was not about to convince me that she was. Josh shot me a sideways glance, then cleared his throat and rapidly said, "I'd say this is a cause for a celebration."

Josh grabbed my arm. Before I could say a word he propelled me through the gyrating dancers straight at Alec. Alec had his hands in his pockets and watched our approach. Alec's eyes locked on mine and I wanted to crawl under the couch. Josh held his fist aloft in a victory salute as he deposited me in front of my former buddy.

This was not the place for us to air our disputes. The music was as dissonant as the thoughts racing through my head. A room full of strangers and who did I encounter? First Susie and now Alec. Why should I have expected anything different?

Josh said, "This has gone on far too long. I don't want to be caught between the two of you. Can't you kiss and make up?"

His words hit Alec and I knew they were like prodding a bear with a hot stick. What poured from Alec's eyes had nothing to do with reconciliation. I braced myself for a punch or a drink thrown in my face. I drew myself up and glared, ready to defend myself.

Alec scowled and leaned back. But instead of cocking his arm to hit me, Alec's glower turned to a grin. He wrapped his arm around my shoulder. "I really shouldn't have acted that way." The words came out slurred. Alec shook his head. "My feelings about Shuleste got the better of me."

"Sounds like about a quart of rum punch talking," said Josh, pointing to the empty cups at Alec's feet.

I couldn't believe what Alec had said. Josh was right. It had to be the punch laced with rum speaking. I was relieved that Alec was a happy drunk, not an angry one. But a part of me worried that he was drinking far more than he should have and had done so the last two times I'd seen him. I wasn't about to give him or anyone advice on alcohol consumption. They already thought I was a loony loser.

I said, "I never would muscle in on Celeste if she was your girl. I had no idea how you felt about her."

He held his hand up to silence me. "Come on, Looner. Let's just forget the whole thing."

I blinked. As he held my arm I sensed a shiver pass through him. "You OK?"

He shook it off. "Must be the air conditioning in this room."

The three of us laughed as the only air conditioning was the open window where no breeze stirred. Then Alec shivered again. Josh looked at me then back to Alec and we both studied Alec.

At first I thought it was the booze making him act strangely. But growing cold after drinking was odd. Perhaps he was coming down with a fever, a nasty summer flu. Then I felt a sinking rush of understanding. Alec's eyebrows had gone hoary and were coated in white crystals.

"Maybe you should go to the bathroom and wash your face," I suggested. "You don't look too good."

Josh leaned into Alec and stared up at his nose. "Holy shit," he said. "What the hell is in that punch?"

"What the hell are you staring at?" asked Alec. He pushed Josh hard on his chest and sent him reeling backward. Little shards of ice rained onto the floor at my feet.

Josh called out, "Hey, everybody, look at Alec. He's so cold his eyebrows and snot have frozen." He let out that machine gun laugh of his.

The majority of teens in the room ignored us, and the few who looked over gave us a look that read "loser." They quickly directed their attention elsewhere lest they be drawn into our pathetic circle. Someone cranked the record player up even more until I could barely hear Josh's shouts of

"The iceman, the iceman, what'll happen if he cometh!" Alec leaned against the wall, holding his head in his hands, dripping small clumps of ice. Again I had a sinking feeling and thought I understood what was happening. I remembered Celeste's words of warning and had no doubt that she was at the bottom of this. I wanted to run from the room, find her, and make her stop whatever she was doing.

Susie and Deanna must have heard Josh's shouts for they approached and stared at Alec. Susie gasped and pointed as Deanna giggled. "Why it's true, you DO have something that looks icy in your eyebrows." She reached out to touch his brow, then decided against it.

Susie sidled up to me. I rolled my eyes to the ceiling and heard Josh say, "Meeeeow!"

Susie took that moment to slip her hand into my front pocket and dig around.

"What the...!" I yelled, surprised, but more shocked as her fingers were icy cold.

"Alec's not the only one who needs some warming up," she said. "I'm soooo cold."

I jerked myself out of her grip and stood in front of Alec, with Susie so close behind I thought she was going to pass through me. She stuck her hand into my back pocket and I could feel the cold creeping through my underwear. Alec's eyes rolled a bit toward the top of his head, then settled into their usual spot. He opened his mouth to speak and out flew a cold spray that hit Susie's face full on.

"Oh, gross!" yelled Susie. She withdrew her hand from my pocket and wiped furiously at her face. In a disgusted tone, Susie said to Alec, "Would you watch where you're spraying? Say it, don't spray it."

"I want the news not the weather," continued Josh. He laughed hard and pointed at Alec, who was clearly in distress.

I didn't know what, if anything, I could do for him. I regretted pushing Celeste into feeling a need to show me her abilities. Alec tried to speak, but now he could not. Instead, small pellets of ice began to trickle from his mouth.

"Would you guys grow up?" said Deanna. "Stuffing ice cubes in your mouth is so middle school lame."

"Time for Twister in the garden," said Susie. "That's where the normal kids will be. Till we find willing partners." She sneered at me. "And it's warmer outside anyhow. I could use the nice summer night air."

Josh grabbed her arm and said, "Hey, want to see my third leg?"

Both girls stared at him. He tapped on his fly and I winced, knowing what would follow. Josh had an enormous hard-on, visibly bulging through his white pants. Josh twitched his penis and got the desired reaction. Deanna shrieked. Then she grabbed her cousin's arm and they headed toward the back porch where most of the crowd of teens had gathered. Josh let out his machine gun laugh.

"Damn. Like cats I tell you. That should do it," said Josh. "You'll excuse me," he added with a mock bow. "I'm off to do a friendly deed for Looner." He followed the girls to the back of the house.

Alec grabbed my arm with icy fingers. He wore a look of fear, and I dreaded what might happen next.

Alec spoke with difficulty. I caught bits and pieces of his words as he slurred them out. "What's haffening? I don unnerstan...." The effort was too much for him to continue. His eyes grew wide and he groaned.

Alec pointed to his mouth. "Sumthin's gwrong." His eyes darted back and forth like the eyes of Joanie's favorite kewpie doll when she shook it. Alec grabbed my arm and held tight. "Wha's in there?" he asked, pointing to his mouth. He leaned toward me and I moved back from the blast of cold air that whooshed into my face.

"Man," I said with a shiver and put a little more distance between the two of us.

His pitiful look entreated me and I steeled myself, moving closer. Anticipating a blast of air, I held my breath, peeked inside and tried to make sense of the sight. Tendrils of mist clung at the back of his throat and curled out into the room. I waved my hand in front of his mouth, clearing the air a bit.

Unable to control myself at what I saw, I groaned, which resulted in Alec squeezing my arm tighter. His eyes begged me to tell him what was happening in his throat.

"It's a blizzard in there," I said, not knowing what else to say.

"Wha the hell d'you mean?" Snow spewed out over his tongue. The hail grew larger and poured past his teeth.

I didn't want to watch. I pushed him toward the punch bowl and soft drink table.

"It's OK. I'm sure it's nothing to worry about," I said, but I knew my tone did not convince him. "You must've drunk an awful lot of this stuff," I said. Alec was a walking ice cave.

"I'm nat gfeeling too glood," Alec said. He gripped the table with both arms and bent his head down low. Snow erupted from his ears now too. It would have been a comical sight if he were not in such distress. I nudged the punch bowl toward him to catch the icy discharge.

"I thin' I'm goin' tabe sick," he said.

With that statement, Alec shuddered and bent over the punch bowl. The three remaining occupants of the room fled to the garden. Alec heaved mightily and I wondered what would happen next. I cursed Celeste and vowed to tell her off.

An icy blue chunk of ice flew out of Alec's mouth and landed on the cherry punch. Then another larger chunk passed from his lips. Alec slid to the floor and lay his head on the table. His eyelashes were coated in frost, his lips were blue.

The tiny icebergs floated in the midst of the punch.

I sat on the floor next to Alec. "Relax," I said. "They needed to replenish the ice in that damn punch bowl anyway. Besides, the punch sucked."

The color rapidly returned to Alec's face and I could tell the siege was over.

"What the hell happened?" asked Alec. He put his hand to his face and found the last of the hoary frost in his eyebrows. He rubbed it between his fingers.

"You want me to get you a Coke or something?"

He shook his head. "Man, I knew I never should have had that last beer after that punch. I feel awful." He rose and stood on wobbly legs. Then he glanced at me. "You don't look so hot yourself, Looner. You better lay off the stuff too."

I nodded and reached under the table for the bottle of rum I knew I would find. "Hair of the dog?" I said and offered it to Alec.

He took a swig and passed it back to me. Then he looked around. "Where'd they all go?"

I chuckled. "Seems we're not fit for human company. Not when you go around doing things like that to the punch bowl."

He shook his head. "What exactly did I do?" He leaned over and stared at the blue ice floating in the red sea. "Whoa, what the hell is that?"

I passed him the flask again and he took another swig. I didn't have to answer the question as Alec fell to his knees and slid to the floor. He spent the next hour sleeping off whatever it was that Celeste had induced in him. I sat beside him and finished off what remained of the fifth of rum. Alec snored loudly beside me and after a while I noticed I needed to find a bathroom.

When I stood up I realized that I was quite drunk. "At least I'm not cold. What's the matter, Celeste, you too chicken to make me a fuckin' iceberg?" From outside in the garden I could hear the squeals of the girls and boys who were still engrossed in playing Twister. If I could have stood up straight, I would have tried to join them. Instead, I made my way to the wall and held onto it for support. "You're a coward, Celeste. You do this stuff and you hide. Goddam coward." I made my way to the bathroom and unzipped my fly. Relieving myself was intensely gratifying and took quite some time. As I finished up, I realized that I was not alone in the john.

I slowly turned and found Susie. Her tousled hair and smudged lipstick made me wonder what had happened to her latest victim. She pulled her black T-shirt down in a nervous gesture, which in another girl would have showed off her attributes. In Susie's case all I could think of was fried eggs. I finished zipping my pants.

"What are you doing that for?" asked Susie. Her hot pink nails snaked to the back of my neck. She trailed them down my back and I felt myself stir.

I kicked the bathroom door closed and locked it. Susie giggled and I swept her into my arms. Within seconds we were in our underwear on the cold tile floor. I blinked as I caught sight of the woolly thatch of red pubic hair peeking out of her pink panties. There was something unusual about the color. I caught my breath as she slipped the pink silk undergarment down and off. I had not expected to see what rested there. I had seen enough of Josh's magazines to know what to expect. Susie's pubic hair lay in three bright vertical stripes of color.

"You like it? It was in honor of the Fourth of July."

I blinked and nodded.

She said, "Red, white and blue. It's a bitch to color but I like to celebrate the holidays."

"Very patriotic," I said. A picture of Susie sitting on the toilet with bottles of hair dye entered my mind. I snapped back to the present as Susie lay back on the floor. With one quick movement she stripped off her bra. Her small breasts definitely reminded me of two fried eggs, two sexy fried eggs.

She said, "Remember what I said? I like to do things boldly? Orange and black for Halloween is next. I'll shave it all off before then though, for a change." With that she kicked her underwear across the room.

She cupped what there was of her small breasts and leaned her face toward them. "Did anyone ever tell you about lipstick theory?"

I shook my head.

She pursed her lips. "The color of your nipples is the color family you should stay with for your lipstick." She smiled and pinched a tiny bud between her bubblegum-colored fingers, holding me with her eyes. "See, this is the same as the lipstick I'm wearing, pink blush."

If I had not been sitting down I would have lost my balance. I didn't care what color lipstick she wore, what color her lips were. I barely heard the words that tumbled out of her mouth. Every cell in my body wanted to touch those nipples and feel her beneath my chest.

"Of course, if you go to the store people look at you strangely if you whip one out and try to match yourself to the colors of the sample tubes. But I don't care. So what do you think, did I do a good job?" she asked, pointing a nipple at me.

I fell on top of her and pressed my mouth against hers. She spread her legs, and as I entered Susie I could swear I heard something, something like a sighing of trees when a fall breeze stirs them briskly. The sound grew loud enough that it became annoying and I glanced around my surroundings as Susie gyrated wildly beneath me. But the bathroom was windowless and no sound could penetrate the thick walls. I chalked the noise up to water rushing through the pipes. Then Susie absorbed all my attention, leaving the trees to rustle and whoosh among themselves. There were much worse ways to lose your virginity than wrapped in the arms of a girl like Susie.

CHAPTER THIRTEEN

Too much rum took its toll. My room spun wildly as I staggered into it later that night. I kicked off my sneakers and fell face down on my bed, but that made things worse, so I rolled back over and watched the ceiling circle above me.

The hall clock chimed midnight and I groaned, knowing dawn was a long way off. Lying down increased my dizziness so I propped my head up on two pillows and stared at the ceiling light trying to make it stay still. The walls lurched around me, reminding me of the funhouse at Playland Amusement Park.

My door creaked open and revealed my sister, backlit by the hall nightlight. I moaned at the sight of her. Joanie entered my room and threw herself on the foot of the bed.

"Game?" she asked, bouncing up and down. The movement of the mattress made me seasick. I moaned again and turned my face to the wall.

"Cut it out!" I whispered. The words hammered in my temples. I had to be quiet or I might cause my mother to find me like this. What a nightmare that would be!

"Luke, OK?" She bounced again.

I shook my head. Talking was too painful in my condition.

"Game," she repeated.

"Joanie, it's too late to play basketball," I said through clenched teeth.

She moved up the bed and sat next to my face. I turned and took her in. She wore her red cap and favorite matching shorts which was odd at this time of night. The brightness of the color made me wince, made me think of Susie's thatch of pubic hair and wince again.

"Game," she said in a demanding tone. Joanie was not to be dissuaded, but neither was I. My head throbbed and nausea threatened.

"No game," I said. "Not tonight. It's too late."

She pulled at her shorts and stuffed a fist in her mouth. I could tell she was agitated but I was in no shape to deal with her.

"Luke's no fun," she said.

Out of the corner of my eye, I watched as she looked around my room, then stood and fixed her gaze. I saw what had captured her attention a second before she grabbed for it. With a chuckle she seized Celeste's baby food jar. I had forgotten to hide the jar.

"No, Joanie! Don't touch that!"

She ignored me, smiled at the jar and held it up to the ceiling light. "Pretty colors," she said.

I reached out and yanked the jar from her hand. The glass felt warm and comforting.

Joanie burst into tears. I lay back on my pillows, head spinning.

"It was a gift from Celeste. Like your flag. Leave me alone."

Joanie bawled loudly, thick tears running down her cheeks. "It's for Joanie," she said, gulping air.

"It's mine, not yours."

She glared at me. "Mine. Pretty colors."

"There's no freakin' rainbow in there, Joanie. Besides, everyone knows you can't capture rainbows." I felt miserable the minute I uttered those words. I might as well tell a group of five-year-olds there was no Santa Claus. She stuck her lower lip out at me and it quivered.

"Can so."

The light above our heads flickered and died. I thought that perhaps the bulb had burned out, but then I realized that the clock radio on my desk no longer glowed either. I propped myself up on one elbow and looked out the window into the yard. The streetlights should have been lit, but they were not. There wasn't a light anywhere as far as I could see.

Joanie began to cry again. I thrust the jar at Joanie to shut her up and allow myself to think straight.

"Don't open it. You can hold it, but don't you dare open it, Joanie, or I'll tear apart that red cap of yours."

Her eyes grew wide at the thought of this. She took the jar and held it gently.

I stuck my head out the window and still couldn't find light anywhere. "Shit. We're having a blackout. I wonder what the hell is going on."

"Game," said Joanie.

I snapped. "No game. Ever."

Joanie flung the jar at me and I caught it before it hit the ground. She followed up with a paperback from my desk. I ducked and her throw missed.

"You stupid idiot," I said. "You retarded moron." Immediately I hated myself for my words.

She reached for a lamp and held it overhead. I cringed. She let it drop and it shattered into pieces. Joanie raced from the room. Her shoes slapped on the stairway and then I heard the back door slam.

Good. She was going to play her stupid game by herself and would leave me be. My head throbbed. I needed to rest and to think over what had happened that evening. I groaned aloud as Susie's face floated in front of me. I remembered enough about what had happened earlier in the evening to know that I already regretted what I had done with her, but a part of me was smug, satisfied. Hadn't I done what I had wanted to do for so long? Wasn't I finally a man under Josh's definition? I could hear his machine gun laugh followed by "Way to go, Lukie! You nailed her!"

I tried to recollect what happened. There was the thatch of red, white and blue hair, and then things got hazy. Snippets of conversation and a whooshing noise came back.

"Yep. I'm going to shave it all off next week," she had said after we had finished. "By Halloween it will have grown back in time to be orange and black. You're going to love it."

Whoa. Her. Me. Halloween. Where had this come from? "Aren't you going back to California before then?" I wasn't sorry I'd miss the Halloween display.

She'd laughed and poked me in the ribs. "I might not have to go back. My folks are talking about me studying here for a bit as they think the kids around here are a better influence. Then we could see each other every day," she purred and curled into me. After that things were even blurrier.

Her words rang in my ears. "Then we could see each other every day." Damn. Susie practically had us married, and I barely remembered having screwed her. I thought about the unused condom in my wallet, the one that had been there for over two years. It was so old it was probably dried up and wouldn't have worked even if I had figured out how to use it with Susie. Guilt poured over me. I lay back down on my bed and wondered what I might have said to encourage her. The late hour and booze took their toll and I dozed off.

The next thing I heard was Joanie screaming at the top of her lungs. I bolted upright in my bed as she continued to shriek loudly. I couldn't place where she was.

"Now what," I said to the ceiling, my head still pounding. I knelt on my bed and looked out the window over my headboard. The backyard was dark, bathed in night. She was out there. I could hear Joanie shouting something but couldn't understand what she said, and was still not sure where exactly she was. I rose with difficulty, and went to the largest window in my room and threw it open. I had a clear view of the driveway, but she was not by the hoop or in sight. Out of the corner of my eye I saw a shadow move and I looked up into the tall pine that abutted the house beside my window.

As my eyes grew accustomed to the dark, my heart raced. Joanie was on top of the tall pine, so high up that she was above the roofline, shouting down at me. My God. How the heck could she see to get up there? Although she normally scaled like a mountaineer, it was a moonless night, an enormous tree, and without streetlights it had to be a difficult climb.

"Joanie, get the hell down from that tree," I called.

Joanie continued to shout indecipherable words and her babbling increased in volume. I shouted back at her. The commotion woke my mother who raced into my bedroom, her eyes bleary. She pulled the belt on her yellow and green terry robe tight about her waist.

117

"Luke, what's going on? I thought I was dreaming before, thought I heard a crash." She eyed the broken lamp on the floor. "Where's Joanie?"

I wasn't feeling as dizzy as before, but I wasn't exactly hitting on all cylinders. My head ached and my mouth was cottony. "There's a blackout. Joanie's in the pine tree." I pointed to the open window.

My mother stuck her head out the window and gasped when she saw how high above us Joanie had climbed. She said calmly, "What are you doing up there, Joanie? You know you're not supposed to climb that high." She turned to me and said in a high-pitched voice, "When will she stop this climbing? In a blackout no less. I can't believe she's up there! We have to do something!"

I stood and slipped on my sneakers. "I'll see if I can get her down."

Mom peered into the darkness and shouted. "You wait for Luke. He's going to bring a flashlight. I want you down and in bed!" Then she tucked her head back inside. Her face was ghostlike, her eyes rimmed red. "Be careful, Luke. I don't have a good feeling about this."

I tied my laces and tucked Celeste's jar into my pocket. I grabbed the spare flashlight from the kitchen and headed to the backyard. In the distance, a fire siren wailed. The pine tree Joanie had chosen to climb was the largest one, not only in our yard but also on the block. Mom, Dad and I had joked about calling up Rockefeller Center and offering the evergreen to them for their Christmas tree. I approached the base and tried to figure out how Joanie had gone up into its interior. Above me I heard Joanie grunt.

"Don't you be getting sleepy up there, Joanie. You need to come down and get some rest in your bed, not in that tree."

I shined my light up and found her. I moved the beam back and forth. There was something strange about her shape. Then I realized what it was. Joanie wore the flag that Celeste, she and I had almost finished constructing. She wore it draped around her shoulders like a cape. Superman came to mind and my heart skipped a beat. Surely she meant to hang the flag, not to fly with it. I tried to remember if Joanie even knew about Superman. She had to. Her school had television and comic books.

I ducked as Joanie hurled a tree branch down. She yelled loudly, "Go away. Luke, go away!" She threw several pinecones, one of which stung me on the arm. Clearly she was still angry with me. She turned her back to me and I watched her spread her arms out. The red cape billowed slightly in a late night breeze. The words she had spoken after the diner incident came back at me. "Joanie can fly." Oh God, she could not be intending to try this, not here, not now.

"Joan girl, I'm coming up. You wait for me up there," I said, trying to keep my voice calm, trying to gain a footing. Above me I heard Joanie make a series of clicking noises in her throat. Please, don't let her get hurt, I prayed. I didn't mean to set her off. I promise to be good to her and take back all those awful things I said.

I grabbed for the lowest branch on the tree and hauled myself up into the boughs. The smell of warm pine engulfed me and I hugged the center trunk, which was sticky with sap. Above me Joanie kept her arms spread wide as she looked up at the stars. I kept talking, trying to calm myself, trying to control the situation as best I could.

"We're going to hang your flag when it's done. What the heck are you doing up there trying to hang it now?"

Joanie ignored me. Her eyes remained fixed on the sky. I wondered what she was thinking, what she might do. I didn't have to wonder for long. Without warning, Joanie leaned forward and toppled from her perch. It was a graceful swan dive. She joined with the air for one pure moment and flew noiselessly through the night. Joanie flew. Then her legs caught on one of the branches; she hung for a second and plummeted past me to earth. The thud that rang in my ears was sickening and final.

The odd thing was that right then, right after the thud, I became aware of the sweetness of the night air. Though Joanie lay sprawled and broken on the ground below, I couldn't help but draw in a deep and wondrous breath. The blackout had caused the night shift at the Spi-Sea plant to halt production. The air was fresh and clear the way I had never smelled it before in Faith Junction. Not only the air, but other things became clear to me that night.

My mother's screams brought me back to reality. She kneeled next to Joanie stricken with grief. I climbed down and dropped out of the tree, fighting off the nausea that threatened to engulf me. I raced inside where

I dialed the local ambulance corps. I could hear my mother crying. "My baby," she wailed. "My baby! What have they done to my baby!" I waited inside, praying for the arrival of the ambulance corps. Within a few minutes they arrived and placed Joanie's broken body on a stretcher. My mother screamed and screamed.

As they strapped Joanie into the ambulance, I heard a technician say, "She's breathing. Let them know we need immediate attention when we get to the ER." My mother heard the comment and she leaned hard on me. I feared she might collapse. Joanie wasn't conscious but her chest did move up and down.

"She can make it, Mom. She's going to make it," I said. I wouldn't let her die. I couldn't let her die.

Mom and I climbed into the back of the ambulance. Mom grabbed Joanie's hand and held it tightly. "We're here, baby, we're with you," she said over and over.

We raced to the hospital, siren blaring, the lights of the ambulance piercing the side windows and running colored bands across Joanie's face. Wake up, Joanie, I wanted to say. Look at the rainbows just for you. But I said nothing.

The hospital lay blanketed in darkness when the ambulance arrived. The blackout extended throughout Faith Junction. The driver shone a beam and they extracted Joanie's stretcher. The three men made their way into the emergency entrance.

"The generator should have kicked in by now," said the driver.

"How the heck are they going to function here without power?" a technician said.

The driver groused, "Who's going to keep the patients from panicking? Some of them must be terrified."

My mother had regained some of her color. Though she was afraid, she rose to the challenge. "They have to have power here. How on earth can anyone get treated? I want you to take my daughter to another hospital if this one isn't capable of treating her."

The driver turned kind eyes on my mother. "Ma'am, the next hospital is over an hour away. The lights are probably out there too. Plus, I don't think you'd want your little girl to wait that long. Not with all the head injuries and internal bleeding she probably sustained in that fall."

My mother bit her lip. "Then this hospital had better be able to treat her or there will be hell to pay."

The driver and technician exchanged glances. Joanie moaned on her stretcher and my mother went to her side. Inside the emergency room, people sat in the dark. The stretcher rolled past the huddled figures toward a door that said "Emergency, No Admittance."

"This can't be happening," said my mother. She turned to me. "Luke, I want you to keep calling home and see if your father has arrived. He's due back from Ohio tonight and will wonder where we are."

I headed to the bank of phones that lined the entryway as they wheeled Joanie into the emergency ward. I dialed home but there was no answer. My head ached. How could this have happened?

Then a thought came to me. I dialed Celeste's number. After one ring someone picked up.

I whispered her name, unable to find my full voice.

"Where are you, Luke? What's wrong?"

"It's Joanie. I'm at the hospital. She's hurt."

"I'll be there as fast as I can," she said.

I hung up the phone and found my mother sitting on a plastic chair with her head in her hands. She smiled wanly as I approached. "I don't see how they can help her without any electricity. This is horrible."

The lights flickered and glowed and power returned to the hospital. Somewhere clapping erupted.

"Thank God," said my mother. She wiped her hand across her brow.

But as quickly as light filtered into the ward, the overhead bulbs flickered and died. We plunged into dark again.

"Now what?" my mother asked. She stood and paced back and forth in the hall. "How can they run this hospital? How can they treat their emergencies?"

I licked my lips. The same thought had crossed my mind and I didn't want to consider the answer. A woman in white scurried by and my mother addressed her.

"Nurse, what are you going to do? My daughter needs help. They have to X-ray her and find out what's wrong."

The woman slowed her pace but did not stop. "We're doing the best we can with what we have."

"That's not good enough!" shouted my mother to the nurse's retreating back. "God, Luke, she may have a concussion. Internal bleeding. This is a nightmare."

I went over and wrapped an arm around my mother's shoulder. I was now an inch taller than she was. At first I had been thrilled to pass her in height, but as the days passed there were times when I regretted growing larger. This was one of those times.

She cast baleful eyes at me. "We never should have moved here. If we were in our old neighborhood we'd be able to get treatment. This wouldn't have happened. There aren't any huge pine trees back there."

I tried to calm her fears. "They'll get the lights on soon. It can't last forever."

A doctor dressed in green scrubs came down the hall and called out, "D'Angelo? Mrs. D'Angelo?"

"Over here," said my mother, gripping my arm.

He shined his flashlight and addressed her. "Mrs. D'Angelo, we're doing everything we can to stabilize your daughter. As soon as we get some power I'll be able to determine the exact cause of her injury. Till then…" his voice trailed away and I could feel my mother going limp beside me. I let her down into her seat.

Something caught at my consciousness, and I was aware of a calming presence. At that moment Celeste Carey entered the emergency waiting room. I turned and took her in. She smiled and took a seat beside me while the doctor continued to speak to my mother. His flashlight cast an eerie glow in the waiting room.

Celeste reached in her pocket and withdrew her jacks. She began toying with them, tossing them from hand to hand. Her lips were set in a thin line. "How's Joanie?" she asked.

"She's in a coma."

"Oh, no. I'm so sorry. What happened?"

"Joanie fell." I gulped. "She fell from the top of the pine tree in our backyard." I recounted the events of the evening as best I could. "They can't tell what damage she did. It has to be pretty bad though. This blackout is making things really difficult. Why did she have to fall from that tree?"

"What was she doing way up there at night?"

I hung my head. "We argued. She took off in a huff. I found her up there with the flag we were making."

"Her birthday flag?"

I nodded.

Celeste bit her lip. "We should have finished and hung it. Then this wouldn't have happened."

"She was wearing it like a cape. She wanted to fly."

Celeste shook her head and bent to the floor. She tossed one of the jacks and it spun wildly. I found I could not take my eyes off the tiny spinning tornado. Celeste added another jack and then another. Three of them circled on the concrete floor. Shards of darkness shot from them.

"I don't know if I can do this, Luke. I should be able to, but I've been having trouble lately."

I nodded fascinated by the little display at my feet. I could watch the jacks spin all night. I shook off the mesmerizing feeling and focused on the activity in the room. I said, "You seemed able to work things pretty well with Alec tonight."

She raised her eyes to me and her lips turned up slightly at the corners. "What on earth are you talking about?"

"Iceman Alec. He was spewing more snow than an avalanche."

She pursed her lips. "What makes you think that was me?"

Suddenly, thunder rumbled ominously. I looked through the window and saw fat drops of rain pelting the ground.

"That's you, isn't it?" I said.

Celeste took a deep breath and closed her eyes.

My mother shouted at the doctor. "Do something, quickly. I don't care what you do, but you have to help her."

Once again the lights flickered as the emergency generator tried to kick in. Up and down the halls people called for light. A nurse with a flashlight rushed by. The hair on my head stood on end. I felt warmth, and the feeling traveled down my arms and torso. Every hair on my body was at attention. I looked over to my mother. She and the doctor had grown quiet and must have been experiencing the same feelings. They stared straight ahead. I looked to Celeste. She gave no hint that she was the cause of the energy that was palpable in the room, yet something told me she was the instigator.

"Everyone hit the floor. Now!" said the doctor. "Quick!"

We did as he asked and around us there were screams and shouts as the people waiting in the emergency room followed suit. Outside the night sky blazed silver and I watched in fascination. A few feet from the window, a large arc of electricity descended slowly from the sky. Simultaneously one rose from the earth. My heart beat like a drum as the two streams of light merged with a crack. Then the slow-motion lightning snaked toward the building, toward the emergency room. The hospital had grown eerily quiet. The energy curled and found a gutter at ground level outside the waiting room window. I rose up and watched as the charge ran up the copper gutter and traveled toward to the roof.

"Stay down, Luke!" called my mother. But I was on my feet, drawn to what was happening. I went to the window and peered out. The electrical charge jumped from window to gutter, coursing along the hospital, lining its perimeter like a string of Christmas lights.

The hairs on my arms were still erect. Suddenly another bolt of lightning hit the ground hard and I could see it glow silver then blue in the night. It, too, traveled toward the hospital. A loud hum sounded. I looked over to Celeste and saw her holding her hands over her ears.

My heart raced wildly. Then the lights in the hospital flickered. The overhead lamps glowed weakly and then strongly. Beeping filled the night air as machines started up. Shouts of joy erupted at the nursing station down the hall. Light flooded the room and everyone started clapping.

The doctor stood and brushed off his knees. "That was close."

"I thought that we were going to take a massive lightning strike," said my mother.

The doctor shook his head. "I guess it didn't happen. The generator must be working again." He helped my mother rise and then said, "If you'll excuse me, I've got to get to my patients."

I glanced over at Celeste. With shaky hands, she scooped up her jacks and placed them in her pocket. She turned and shot me a knowing smile.

When my mother and the doctor had left I said to her, "It was you, wasn't it? The reason we have power is because of something you did."

"Luke, that may be. But it's not really important, is it?" The color had left her cheeks and she appeared almost ancient for a second.

"Of course it is. You're some kind of national treasure if you can do this. The government would love to get their hands on you."

She pursed her lips. "That would never do. What use could I be to them that would do good? Who would take care of my father?"

"Speaking of him. Does he know where you are?"

Celeste scuffed a sneaker against the floor.

I reached out to her. "How do you do it?"

She turned wide eyes to me. "I've learned to let it happen. I've struggled with this for years. And I know there has to be more to it, more that I can do."

I ran my fingers through my hair. Celeste looked as tired as I felt. I wanted to hug her to me, but I could tell she would not let me near her. I said, "I can never thank you enough."

Two nurses walked by and one said to the other, "It's a miracle that we have power. There isn't a tad of electricity from here to Delaware."

"Thank heavens for those emergency generators," said the second.

Celeste smiled slightly.

"It's ok, Celeste. Your secret is safe."

For a short time it was.

CHAPTER FOURTEEN

I visited Celeste at the cave the next day. I had a feeling I would find her underground in the heat of the afternoon. When I arrived, she sat dangling her feet in the onyx lake. The water shimmered in the glow of her lantern.

She leaned back and took a deep breath. "How's Joanie doing?"

"They had to remove her spleen. She's still in a coma." I sat down next to her.

"I'm so sorry." She trailed a hand in the water.

"The injury to her head was worse than anyone realized." I knew my hands were shaking.

"How's your mom doing?"

"She's taken up a vigil at Joanie's side. She stays practically round the clock, singing her lullabies, and reading to her from books she read to her when she was a baby."

Celeste pursed her lip and sent ripples out into the lake with her feet.

I dipped a hand in the cool water and shook my head. "She's trying so hard to bring her around. But there's nothing any of us can do except pray and wait."

She said, "I'll leave the praying to you." Then she sighed, "There's a lot I need to do at this lake."

The wick of her lantern flickered in the dark and I leaned over and turned up the flame. We sat in silence for several minutes.

"How often do you come here?"

She stretched and groaned. "Not often enough. This cave, the lake and I need each other, especially now."

I wasn't sure what she was telling me.

"This is where I can push myself to see what I can really do. Do you understand what I'm saying?"

"I think so."

She held her hands out to the flickering light. "My powers," she laughed derisively, "if you can call them powers, are nothing compared to what's here, in the dark."

I looked around, growing increasingly uncomfortable. I dried my hands on my shorts but couldn't shake off a feeling of cold wetness.

Celeste's voice was serious. "There's a balance, Luke." She looked around warily. "I'm starting to understand it, little by little." She shook a finger at me. "Don't you breathe a word about this or about what happened at the hospital."

"If I did they'd never believe me anyway," I said and we both laughed.

She held up a small jar similar to the one that she had given me that day in the DDT haze.

"I bet one of these days you'll find a use for another one of these," she said.

"Joanie was fascinated by it, said it has pretty colors."

Celeste grinned. "Joanie's quite right. And there's more in there. The absence of colors."

"I don't see anything," I said. She handed it to me and I stashed it in my pocket.

She smiled. "That's because the speed of dark, like the speed of light, isn't easy to see or control."

I rolled my eyes.

"It's very fast. The best any of us can do is hold it in our hands for a little while and warm ourselves before it goes trickling through our fingers."

I reached out to the darkness outside the halo of the lamp's glow.

"It's the nature of things," she said. "And I'm close, so close…."

Something inside me ached. I longed to curl up beside her in the cave and feel the warmth of her breath on my cheek. That would be enough for me to carry on. Her talk of dark and light opened a black hole in my chest that frightened me. I needed some affirmation of life and I wanted to find it in her. The speed of dark made me think of Joanie sailing into the night, of her flying off into oblivion. None of Celeste's talk about the dark and light, about what was visible and not, made sense, yet I was willing to forego logic if that was what it took to remain in her sphere.

"In a moment, in the twinkling of an eye….I suppose it's foolish of me. But I can't help myself." She laughed and I was happy to hear that sound again. I could see the color fill her face. She looked healthy and fit again.

I cleared my throat. "What exactly can you do? Besides make Alec into a sputtering iceberg. That wasn't very nice of you."

She withdrew her feet from the water. "I shouldn't have done that, but you got me so angry."

"No lasting effects from that, I hope."

"They're just harmless tricks."

I studied her and waited.

She said, "I seem to be able to control the weather at will. Nothing more than that. Kind of a lame superpower, eh?"

"Make it snow in here. Right now."

"I can't."

"Why the hell not?"

"The cave isn't for that." She held her hands out and turned them over, palms downward. "My weather powers shouldn't be used here."

"But isn't this where you come to recharge them?"

"Not exactly. If I try to use them here, or in any place of extreme dark, it's very painful." She looked around the space. "The dark here is overwhelming at times. It's too powerful for me, unlike the weather. And I know my limits. Or at least I'm learning them."

I looked at her skeptically.

"That's what I've found over the time. There has to be more than just making it rain."

I listened, trying to make sense of her words.

"Changing the weather takes a lot of effort. My body won't always cooperate."

"How?"

"Let's say I want to make it rain on my dad's orchards. I no sooner get the skies to open than I grow weak, tired. I have trouble breathing."

"And then you come here and do what?"

"It's like I hit some wall, and I can't get beyond it. I found that coming here, sitting in the dark, dangling my feet in the water, my thoughts become clearer. I do love the way I feel down here." She leaned back contentedly and stretched like a cat.

"But it can't be only this cave that can do that for you. Wouldn't a dark closet make you feel better too?"

She smiled. "It's not the same. I imagine there might be other caves in other places that would work as well, but I've never found one.

I thought about her jars and what she had said. "After you helped Joanie you looked so pale."

She nodded. "Seeing her lying in that coma made me realize how precious life is. I think I've finally sorted out a few things in my mind." She turned troubled eyes to me and I could feel an ache building within my chest. "I'm sorry for how I acted to you. I've been awful."

"Forget it," I said.

She went on, "I've never been one for sentimental things. And I never intended to let my heart get in the way of what I want to do. But it seems that it has."

I licked my lips. Could she be about to declare her affection for me at last? Oh God, what a thought that was. I could barely keep my mind in order as I tried to concentrate on her words. I wanted to wrap her in my arms and tumble to the ground right there.

"I can't believe I'm telling you this." She smiled and I smiled back. "I should have told Alec first."

I felt as though the wind had been knocked out of me. "Alec?"

She nodded. "Ever since I can remember I've been attracted to him." She ran her hand through her hair. "I've tried to put him out of my mind. I was sure I was over him. But seeing Joanie lying there like that, the only thing I could think about was him and how much I would have missed if it were him on that gurney." She let out a deep sigh. "I don't get it, but there is absolutely nothing I can do about it."

"I don't believe it."

She had grown pale again, as if the declaration of her feelings had somehow drained her. "I'm going to let him know. I'm going to shout it from the top of that darn Spi-Sea plant. I love Alec DuBarry." She giggled and something burned hot in my temples.

A low rumbling came to us from the inner depths of the earth. I jumped up as the sound grew louder and then faded. "Jesus, what was that?"

Celeste was unfazed. "There's an abandoned copper mine that abuts this cave. It reaches all the way to the Spi-Sea factory."

"If it's abandoned, what's the noise?"

"The old wooden slats that shore it up are rotting away and collapsing. It's nothing to be worried about. Worst that could happen is Spi-Sea will have a mess on their hands to clean up one day." She smiled wickedly, clearly pleased at the thought.

"You're not scared that this place could cave-in?"

"Not at all." She rose and wiped her hands on her shorts. "Time to move out, Luke."

"We can stay longer if you want."

"That wouldn't be good for you. Being here with me will sap you. It's time you went outside."

I stood and found my legs wobbling beneath me. "Whoa..." I said. "What the heck is going on?"

"Like I said, it's the nature of things. You'll be fine in five minutes outside."

I followed her to the entrance of the cave and stepped from the depths.

"Thanks for keeping me company," she said.

"Anytime," I said. "What does your father think of all this?"

Her face went dark. "I'm worried about him. If it were up to him I'd never leave the farm. We don't talk much, and lately even less."

"I'm sure he wants what's best for you."

"There's not a chance in the world that he could ever make a difference," she said. Before I could ask her what she meant, she quickly added, "You better get back to your family." She shoved her hands into her pockets. "Give Joanie a hug for me next time you see her."

I leaned into her, longing to kiss her once again, hoping that what she had told me about Alec was not true and that she cared for me, but she turned her head to the sky. I mounted my bike and turned toward home. The sun stabbed my eyes as relentlessly as her words which ran through my head over and over, keeping time to the pedaling of my bicycle, leaving me wishing for darkness and ignorance.

CHAPTER FIFTEEN

Good Samaritan Hospital, where Joanie lay deep in a coma, clung to a hill on the outskirts of Faith Junction. From this vantage it beckoned to customers from all neighboring areas. It could be seen from miles away, and at night the bright white cross that perched atop the main building guided the injured to its doors.

The building that housed the medical operations was a plain brick one standing unimposingly opposite a sprawling factory outlet mall, the other occupant of the hillside. The one highway that passed near the town and exited at the outlet and hospital could be seen from the upper floors of Good Sam, which was a good and bad thing; good because it gave the bored patients something to watch besides the soap operas, bad because some patients said that at night, the arc of lights they viewed on the interstate were not street lights, but were beams sent from above, guiding them from Good Sam to the portals of heaven. Those patients who claimed to have seen such lights were invariably the ones who were heavily sedated. Nevertheless, over the years the tale took on the stature of an urban legend, much like the tale of the Leatherman, so much so that long-time residents of the area requested rooms facing away from the highway, lest they be called to heaven before their time.

As I entered Joanie's room, I realized with a start that her bed faced the highway. Not wanting to tempt fate, I crossed over to the window and snapped the metal blinds shut so that in the event she awakened one night, she did not see the roadway and its heavenly beams.

Clapped to Joanie's ears were a pair of my old headphones. My mother's nursery rhymes and Mother Goose played in Joanie's head incessantly in the hopes that one of the singsong rhymes would register with Joanie and rouse her from her coma. My mother had read about such a miracle happening in *Women's Day* magazine. But so far the comforting sounds of my mother's voice intoning the rhymes had not brought Joanie back to us.

"How you doing, Joan girl?" I asked.

Joanie stared straight ahead, her eyes wide open. I reached over and took her hand in mine. In spite of the overheated room, her fingers felt like she had been outside in February without her favorite red mittens. I rubbed her hand between mine and tried to raise some warmth. Then I leaned over and took the headphones from her ears.

"Hickory, dickory dock, the mouse ran up the clock," my mother's voice sang tinnily into the room. I shut the machine off and Joanie and I sat there together in the waning July afternoon sharing the sounds of the hospital. Outside, at the nurse's station, someone was ordering supplies on the phone. Across the hall an old woman coughed several times, then moaned. After a time I cleared my throat.

"There's something I wanted you to have," I said and dug deep in my pocket. I extracted Celeste's jar, the jar that had started all this trouble. The glass gleamed in the overhead fluorescent light.

I waved the jar in front of Joanie's face. "Pretty colors, Joanie. They're all here for you." I placed the container on her tray table. "You can see it whenever you like over here, Joanie. It's yours."

Joanie stared straight ahead. I was aware of my blood starting to pulse wildly through my temples. I wanted to kick something or scream or do anything. I couldn't bear seeing her this way. I couldn't bear having caused her fall. Yet I had. For if I hadn't been out drinking, if I hadn't called her names, if I hadn't taken the jar from her….I clenched my fists.

A nurse entered and said, "Visiting hours are up in five minutes." The nurse turned without looking at me and I heard her rubber soles squeak down the corridor. My blood settled down and I approached my sister.

I leaned into her and whispered in her ear, "Joanie, get better. There's no way you can leave us. You hear me?"

The smell of disinfectant did nothing to cover what I now know, after many more hospital visits, was the scent of death. I kissed Joanie on the cheek.

"Celeste says we'll fly that flag of yours as soon as you're back on your feet. Okay?" I stuffed my hands in my pockets. "You get to pick the tree and we'll all make sure it flies forever. Flags fly, Joanie, not you."

Bells signaled the end of the visiting period.

"I have to go now. Everyone is waiting for you to get better and come home. We'll play basketball first thing."

I picked up the headphones and turned on the machine. I heard my mother in a chipper voice saying, "There was an old lady who lived in a shoe." Her lilt was in sharp contrast to the surroundings. I clapped the headphones on Joanie's ears. Suddenly, I found I was having trouble breathing.

"I'll see you tomorrow," I said, choking on the words.

Joanie's cold staring eyes followed me out the door. I walked down the hall past the central nursing station where I stopped to pour a drink of water and gulp deep drafts of air. As I sipped from a paper cup I heard a nurse say, "Minnie, you'd better check on the Barton girl. She should be eating something."

Another nurse said, "Stomach pumps never eat. Especially the thin ones like her."

"Regardless, I want someone to try to get her to take something. Minnie, she's yours so don't forget."

Barton. I glanced up at the patient board over the station and saw the name with the number 622. The room was on this floor but lay at the opposite end of the hall from Joanie. In spite of the fact that it was time to leave, I made my way to the room and peeked inside.

Deanna Barton lay still and pale in a hospital gown. She looked more fragile than ever, her auburn hair painted flat against a pillow as white as her pasty skin. I bit my lip, unsure whether I should disturb her. I coughed and Deanna turned her head toward me.

"Luke!" Her initial happiness at seeing me immediately passed. She cast her eyes down and her cheeks colored slightly.

I entered and stood at the foot of her bed. "I'm visiting my sister," I said.

Deanna nodded. "I heard that she was in a bad way. I'm sorry."

"Deanna, do you mind if I ask what you're doing here?"

She pressed her eyes shut and leaned back into her pillows.

"If you don't want to talk about it, I understand."

She licked her lips and blinked. Tears welled in her eyes. Deanna took a deep breath and said with a quavering voice, "I guess I had too much to drink. And too many pills on top of that."

I remembered the nights in the Barton rec room with dozens of bottles of easily accessible booze in the hall closet, but I didn't remember any pills. Deanna had never seemed to be someone who was foolish in that regard. She was no more foolish than the rest of the crowd who for the most part knew and respected the dangers of drinking and drugs. At her weight it would not take much alcohol or pills to put her in distress.

"Are you feeling OK now?"

Tears ran down her cheeks and her lip trembled. I went to her and held her hand, a hand so small it could belong to a toddler.

"Whatever it is, it can't be that bad that you should be winding up in the hospital over it."

She gulped great drafts of air and found her voice. "I'm sorry you have to see me like this. You have enough problems to deal with."

"Deanna, don't be ridiculous." I squeezed her hand, being careful not to exert too much pressure.

Her chest heaved twice and she took a deep breath. "I'm so lonely so much of the time."

I handed her a tissue from the box on her bedside table and sat on the edge of her bed. She blew her nose and continued, "Do you ever feel lonely? I suppose not. You've got your mom and dad and sister."

"And you've got your mom and lots of friends."

Her tears started again, this time more rapidly. I reached over and handed her the box of tissues. She took several and honked loudly. Then she pounded her mattress with her fist. "My mother is a drunk. She doesn't get up till two in the afternoon and even then she's so hung over that she won't talk to me till after five p.m., after her evening cocktail."

I didn't know what to say.

She continued, "She disappears for days at a time, Luke. I get so worried."

"What about your dad?"

"They divorced when I was two. I don't know a thing about him." She sniffed loudly.

"I overheard the nurses saying they had to pump your stomach."

She nodded and looked away.

"Why did you take all those pills?"

She stared at the wall. "I don't want to continue anymore is all. After everyone left last night and the lights went out, I realized I'm fed up and tired and a burden to her. I'm better off dead. No one will miss me."

"You're talking nonsense."

"I used to think that, but I was kidding myself." She let out a big sigh and collected herself. "Thanks for listening to me. Sometimes I think I've already gone stir crazy sitting alone in my room all the time."

"But what about those famed Barton parties? You're the life of the teenagers around here."

"If I didn't have those parties no one would ever talk to me. I only give them to pretend that I have some friends and to stop myself from being alone in that house."

"That's not true."

"Who'd want to be friends with me? My mother is a whore and an alcoholic. And she's got a medicine chest full of stuff that could knock out ten elephants."

"Deanna, you're upset."

"It's true, Luke. She brings home a different guy practically every night, that is if she comes home. I hear them. And I find the empty bottles in the morning."

I rubbed my eyes and tried to integrate what she was saying. Again, I found myself wondering about my own parents and how their relationship might be going. My father and his traveling weren't a good recipe for a relationship. Who knew what he did on his business trips? But

I'd never seen anything like Deanna described.

"Deanna, I want you to promise me something. The next time you get the urge to take pills or drink too much, give me a call. Okay?"

She rolled her eyes to the ceiling.

"I'm not the best at this stuff, but I'd like to try to be there for you. I know it's not the coolest thing to say we should cut back, but I've been doing some thinking and we're making a real mess of our lives with all this stuff. Call me if you get the urge to drink or take anything, okay?"

She let out a low sound. "I'll try, Luke." Then she turned her eyes to me. "Last night, when they lost power, Celeste was here, wasn't she?"

I chuckled. "What makes you think that?"

"I've known her longer than you and I'd recognize her handiwork anywhere." She stroked the lightning scar on her arm. "I wish we were still friends. She was the only one who ever understood me, ever seemed to care, you know?"

I nodded. "Yeah. I know."

"I wish I wasn't such an idiot."

"Why don't you tell Celeste that?"

"She'd laugh at me, or worse. And I'd deserve it."

"Maybe, but it might be that she'd love to have you back as her friend. Don't you think she gets lonely too?" I gave her a quick peck on the cheek. "I promised my mom I'd be home for dinner."

"At my house supper means a fifth of vodka."

"I'll drop by when you get out of here. I can come by your home anytime. And even here, after I visit my sister. She's right across the hall from you."

"I'd like that," said Deanna.

"Anything I can do to make your time here go faster?"

"I'll be out of here by tomorrow. At least that's what they say."

"You take care of Joanie for me, OK? I'm counting on you to keep an eye on her here till then."

She smiled at me and I could tell her mood had lifted.

"You're not your mother, Deanna. You can't help what she is, but you can be the best you can be yourself. The hell with people who can't see you for you."

She bit her lip. "I think I'll give Celeste a call as soon as I get out of here."

I left the hospital and pedaled home. That night when the DDT truck made its rounds of my neighborhood, I didn't budge from my seat at the kitchen table.

My mother hugged me and planted a loud kiss on my cheek. "You want to tell me what's bothering you?"

I shook my head.

"Luke, I know this is a hard time for you. It's a hard time for all of us, but it's going to be all right. Things have a way of working out."

I wanted to believe her.

"So you want any ice-cream money? If you hurry you could catch the truck on the next block."

I shook my head. Helping Deanna had only made me feel worse about what I had done to Joanie. The fog held no thrill and everything tasted flat.

CRSO

The next day was Sunday and my mother and I both rose early. I didn't want to admit that I had not slept, and I assumed that my mother's red eyes meant that she too had been up most of the night.

"Guess it's eight o'clock Mass for us," said my mother as she put away the remains of the morning meal. "Maybe by the time we get back, your dad will have arrived." Her voice was tight and I knew she was angry that Dad had not come home the night of Joanie's accident. He had never arrived that night, for he had flown out of Ohio to Hong Kong for a factory emergency. When his secretary called the next morning to update us on his whereabouts, I was with Mom. She had moaned loudly and let the receiver fall from her hand. "Hong Kong. How can he be in Hong Kong?" she had said, staring off into the distance.

"Mom, he's going to get here. He got the first flight out he could and his secretary said his limo should drop him here soon as possible. Don't worry about it, okay?"

"You better get dressed lickety split," she said, wiping her hands on a dishtowel. "I don't want to be late for church."

At St. Sebastian's, Mom and I sat in a pew toward the rear of the church. Mom didn't look left or right as we took our places, and then she kept her eyes focused straight ahead. I could tell she was trying not to cry. Since Joanie had been hospitalized, her tears erupted without warning. She tugged on her orange gloves and laid her hands in the lap of her green skirt.

I bit my lip and looked around the mostly empty church. Eight a.m. Mass was not heavily attended. To my surprise I saw Celeste and her father sitting a few rows up from us on the right. I shifted in my seat and tried to catch her attention, but she looked straight ahead and was unaware of my presence.

I turned my gaze to Mr. Carey who wore brown pants and work boots. A neatly pressed plaid shirt stretched tautly across his muscular back. His braid hung down between his shoulder blades and a few escaped hairs curled around the collar. His profile was strong, like his hands. Soon, Father McInerney entered and the Mass began. Throughout the service, I watched Mr. Carey, remembering Josh and Alec's comments and wondering if he would do something odd.

Mr. Carey hung one leg out into the aisle and stretched it out. I stared unabashedly, first at him then at Celeste. I hoped that the intensity of my gaze might somehow let Celeste know I was there behind her. Look at me, I repeated over and over. But my staring and mantra didn't have any effect at all on her.

When it came time for his row to approach for Communion, I watched Mr. Carey head for the railing, while Celeste remained in her seat and did not take part in the sacrament. Mr. Carey walked with a limp, favoring his left side. I wondered what had caused him to need an artificial limb. When he returned to the pew, he sat and began fiddling with his shoe. Celeste leaned over and whispered something to him but he wore a grim look on his face and shook her off with a brisk nod.

My mother and I received our Communion wafers and made our way back to our seats. As we slid into our places, I noticed my mother's cheeks were damp. With a sniffle, she took a handkerchief from her purse and held it over her eyes. I reached over and put my hand in hers, then I turned my attention back to Mr. Carey who had shifted sideways in his seat. Something was on the seat next to him near the aisle. After a few seconds I recognized what it was. While we were at Communion, Mr. Carey had removed not only his shoe, but also his entire foot! Shoe and foot lay on the wooden pew beside him. He wore a prosthesis, a prosthesis that must have been bothering him immensely.

Celeste poked her father, then looked around with a mortified gaze. As she turned her head toward the back of the church, her eyes caught mine and she immediately turned forward. She whispered to her father once again, but he shook his head and began rubbing the stump of his leg.

Beside me my mother, oblivious to Mr. Carey's plight, gulped air and shuddered. I squeezed her hand and she took the handkerchief from her eyes.

By the time Father McInerney gave us the final blessing, I had made up my mind to find out more about Mr. Carey and his missing limb. My last encounter with him at his farm had not been all that harrowing. Hadn't he just gone to Communion? How bad could he be? And why hadn't Celeste gone up to the rail?

My mother and I joined the parishioners as they headed out of the church. I looked back trying to get Celeste's attention but she and her father must have exited out another door for they were nowhere in sight.

As we reached the rear doors, Alec's familiar voice hailed me. "Luke, I heard about your sister." His face wore a look of concern. "Let me know if there's anything I can do."

I met his gaze and asked, "Has Celeste spoken to you?"

He looked down. "Why should she? She hates me, remember?"

I shook my head. It was not my place to tell him about Celeste and her feelings for him. I couldn't bear to be the messenger of his good news. She would have to tell him herself when she was ready.

"Some party the other night," I said.

He scratched his head. "I don't remember much of it. Josh said I had quite a good time. Was I acting strange or doing something weird? I had a lot to drink...."

"No stranger than usual," I said.

"Josh also said you and Susie were…" He nudged me in the ribs. "Way to go, Looner. I knew you had it in you."

I knew I was blushing. I wished I could forget what I had done. That whole night had been a disaster. I said, "Tell me about Mr. Carey."

"Guess you caught the show in there, huh?"

"How'd he lose his foot?"

Alec shifted from leg to leg. "No one really knows. Some people say a bear bit it off."

"There aren't any bears around here."

"Sure there are. Well, there used to be. Other people say he lost it in a farming accident."

"That's believable at least."

Alec looked at his sneakers. "I don't believe most of the stories they tell about him. But you do have to wonder because he keeps to himself so much."

"Wonder what?"

Alec sighed. "Another theory is that Celeste chopped it off."

"What?"

"Hey, I don't buy it either, but people say she's a curse on the Carey family."

My mother called to me that it was time to head for home.

"Meet me at Deanna's tonight," said Alec. "She's coming home from the hospital and we thought it would be nice to visit her."

"Take it easy on her with the booze tonight, Alec. She's messed up. I think we all might benefit from cutting back."

He held his hands up. "Scout's honor. No booze at Deanna's. Josh already told me that's the rule."

I joined my mother in the parking lot, not sure what to make of Alec's last preposterous allegation about the Careys. The more I learned about Celeste the more there was to uncover. Was there no one who knew the real story about this family?

"Such a nice boy. You've made some wonderful friends here already," said Mom as she turned the car out of the church lot.

A few minutes later, when Mom pushed open our back door, my father was waiting in the kitchen. He wore a rumpled gray suit and several days' growth of beard, but he had never looked better to me. Mom fell into his arms and began to cry. As I moved past them, my father reached out and included me in the embrace. It was the first time I had ever seen him with tears in his eyes. The three of us stood there, hugging for a few seconds, my embarrassment growing. I left them in the kitchen holding hands like a pair of teenagers.

Mom followed Dad around that day like a lost puppy. At times, he wore a bewildered look, but his presence instilled a sense of calm in both of us. They visited Joanie, who remained deep in a coma. That night, to my relief, I could hear them talking into the small hours of the morning. Gentle sounds filled the house and made me aware of how close they were in spite of his constant traveling and demanding job. My fears receded and I understood on some level that their relationship was grounded in something that would not be destroyed by distance. The irony that my father's physical presence meant all was not right in our world hit me. I longed to hear a limo pick him up in the wee hours of the morning for that would mean things were back to normal.

CHAPTER SIXTEEN

We were gathered at Deanna's playing records when Celeste walked into the rec room. Her hair was held back with a white ribbon and her gauzy peasant blouse was tucked into tight jeans. I had to hand it to her. She had no trouble commanding the room and within seconds the group was staring at her. To my surprise, Deanna rushed over to Celeste and embraced her.

"It's so good to see you," said Deanna.

"I've been thinking about you too," said Celeste.

I caught Celeste's eye as Deanna hugged her to her chest. Celeste looked pained, as though the mere act of being touched imparted discomfort. This had to be difficult for both of them. I was glad Celeste had shown up to hang out and have some fun with people her age. A smile spread across Deanna's face.

Alec materialized from the garden and Deanna waved at him. "Can you believe Celeste showed up? It's been so long since we had her at a party."

Alec gave Celeste a tired, beaten look. He turned away and headed in the direction he had come.

"Wait up," called Celeste.

Deanna chimed in, "Come on, Alec, where are you going?"

Alec kept walking and I held my breath.

Celeste raised her voice, "Alec, I need to talk to you."

He stopped and slowly turned toward her. "Since when?"

Celeste closed the distance between them and grabbed his hand. "This is important. Let me come outside with you where we can have a little privacy."

Alec shook his head. "Anything you have to tell me you might as well say it right here. There's nothing between us that's got to be discussed in private."

Celeste winced and pursed her lips. "I suppose that's fair. You deserve a lot, Alec, a lot more than I could ever give you."

I coughed and Alec glanced toward me then back to Celeste. Deanna wore a dreamy look on her face and had her hands clasped to her chest. I held my breath as Celeste leaned into Alec and whispered something in his ear.

Alec's head shot toward her. "What did you say?"

She leaned in and whispered in his ear again.

At first I was afraid that Alec might begin spewing snow or ice again, but then a smile lit his face and it became agony for me to watch the two of them. He entwined his hands in hers and she again spoke gently into his ear. I wanted to be the one she whispered to, but all I could do was stand there and witness the scene. Celeste looked pale and seemed to be having trouble standing. Suddenly Alec swept her off her feet and twirled her about the room. The two of them fell laughing to the couch. In spite of her joy, Celeste seemed as though she had had the wind knocked out of her.

"You OK?" asked Alec, planting a big kiss on her cheek.

"I'm fine. Just a little dizzy from the excitement."

"God, I love this place. There is no better place in the world than Faith Junction," said Alec.

He folded her into his arms and I left for the garden, sadness at my own loneliness eclipsing any happiness I felt at their reunion. They might be right for each other, but that didn't mean I could celebrate with them.

I joined Josh where he stood pouring rum into a glass of Coke.

"So much for the 'no booze at Deanna's' oath," I said.

"No booze inside the house, not outside," he said, letting loose his machine gun laugh. "Shhh," he said putting a finger to his lips, "I won't tell." A smile spread over his face as he handed me a cup and prepared another for himself. In spite of my promise that I wouldn't touch alcohol, I downed the contents in a few gulps.

Josh scratched his crotch and turned his eyes toward me. Then he grinned madly. "Hell, you know what it means every time you scratch your balls."

I rolled my eyes skyward.

"It means someone is thinking about you." He scratched again and let out a guffaw. "And in your case I think I know who it is."

With a start I turned to find Susie standing behind me. Josh poured her a tall drink and attempted to refill my cup, but I waved him off. This time I wouldn't lose control. This time I would take control. A few minutes later Susie's hand snaked under my shirt. I pulled her to me and ran my hand under her T-shirt. She broke away and grabbed the bottle of rum from Josh.

"This way to the private club," she said, pulling me toward the pool house at the far end of the yard. When the door closed behind us, the small space was welcoming and dark. Susie and I fell onto a lounge chair and soon I lost myself in her arms and lips. They were not the ones I dreamed of, but once again they would suffice for the evening.

CHAPTER SEVENTEEN

My mother, dressed in neon yellow, sat at the foot of Joanie's hospital bed in a metal chair dispensing Joanie's daily dose of Mother Goose. "There was an old woman who lived in a shoe," she sang.

I entered the room with a cup of cafeteria coffee, light and sweet the way Mom liked. I had one for myself as well, hoping it might alleviate my headache. The night before was a bad memory, and my temples throbbed every time I ran it over again in my mind. I clenched my jaw at the thought of Alec and Celeste being together. And then there was Susie. I was embarrassed at what I had done.

When I entered Joanie's room, Mom looked up and smiled at me, without missing a beat in her reciting. She turned the page and continued with her singsong rhymes. "Humpty Dumpty sat on a wall."

I placed the paper container on the ledge by the window within her reach and glanced down at the stream of cars on the highway.

"Humpty Dumpty had a great fall."

I wondered how many times Mom had said these rhymes to Joanie, not only since her accident, but also as a child.

Suddenly Joanie chimed in. "All the king's horses and all the king's men. She had so many children, she didn't know what to do."

My mother shrieked and stood up. The cup of coffee splattered to the floor, forming a caramel pool.

Mom stood there shaking at the foot of Joanie's bed. "Luke, did you hear that? Did you hear her? Oh God, let it be true."

Joanie grinned at me and then at Mom.

I grabbed the metal handrail at the side of Joanie's bed and pressed it hard. "Joan girl, what'd you say?"

"Oh God, she's awake, she's awake," my mother said. Her hands shook as she reached over and hugged Joanie. "My baby's awake."

A dark cloud passed over Joanie's face. She looked around and took in her surroundings.

My mother saw her distress and in a soothing voice said, "It's OK, Joanie. Don't be upset." Then Mom turned to me and calmly said, "Go find a nurse." She kept her voice controlled though I knew she must feel the same way I did. My heart was pounding wildly, the way it did right before the first big drop on a roller coaster. I met Joanie's gaze and saw joy then fear. She thrust her fist in her mouth. Joanie moaned loudly and tugged at the IV in her arm.

My mother soothingly said, "Don't do that, Joanie. You'll hurt yourself."

I raced from the room down the hallway to the nursing station. Within seconds several nurses and a doctor circled Joanie's bed. A wide-eyed Joanie moaned loudly at the strangers peering down at her.

"Please, she doesn't understand what's been going on. Don't frighten her," my mother whispered to the head nurse. I liked that nurse, for she had always shown a soft spot for Joanie and my mother. I moved to my sister's side and tried to calm her.

"The doctors just need to talk to you for a bit. Don't worry about a thing, Joanie. We'll be getting out of here soon."

Joanie rotated her fist in her mouth. Her eyes moved around the room and she grunted loudly, then whined. Her gaze seized on Celeste's jar. She moaned again and extended a hand toward the container, but her IV prevented her from reaching it. I leaned over and handed the jar to her.

"It's yours, Joanie. Like I told you before. Keep it."

She pressed the prize to her chest. "Joanie fly," she said.

"It's a miracle," said my mother. Tears streamed down her cheeks. She hugged Joanie and planted kisses on her forehead and cheeks. Joanie made a face and pushed her away. Then she giggled.

"Game?" she said to me.

"Game," I answered.

A doctor picked up Joanie's chart and wrote furiously. Two nurses whispered to one another. I reached into the closet by her bed and withdrew one of Joanie's favorite balls. Everyone watched as I tossed the ball to Joanie and she caught it. With a chuckle she threw the ball back at me.

Nothing ever felt so good as that game of catch.

Later that afternoon, they took Joanie for diagnostic tests. She carried the ball into her CAT scan. Her brain function had not deteriorated. The doctor said it must have been an act of will on her part. She had woken up. It was as simple as that.

CRWO

A few days later Joanie came back home. Mom insisted she stay quietly in her room and we took turns entertaining her. Mom made sunshine cake and macaroni and cheese and Joanie beamed as she ate. Dad hit the road and things were once again comfortable in the house. I stayed close to home. My mother and I chatted till late in the evenings and for the first time in my life I was aware of her as not just my mother, but as an interesting person. One morning the doorbell rang and I was surprised to see Celeste.

"I thought I'd drop by and see how Joanie was doing," she said.

I stepped aside so she could enter. "She's upstairs, in her room. She'll be happy to see you. She doesn't get many visitors. In fact, you're the first."

Celeste appeared pale and drawn. I wondered what was bothering her to give her such a ghostly appearance.

"How's Alec?"

"He's great. I'm so lucky to have found someone like him. There's nothing better than love, Luke, don't let anyone tell you otherwise."

"I'll keep it in mind," I said. I knew my voice was tight.

We headed up the stairs and found Joanie sleeping on top of her covers, thumb in mouth, red ball cap askew.

"Don't wake her," said Celeste. "It's not important that she see me."

"She'll be disappointed if I tell her you came to see her and she slept through it."

Celeste gripped the doorframe. I could see all the color drain from her face. She gasped for air.

I didn't know what was happening, but could tell it was something to worry about.

"I need to get outside," she said, her eyes pleading with me to act quickly.

When I realized she couldn't walk, I scooped her up in my arms. She could not have weighed eighty pounds. I carried her downstairs and placed her on the grass in the backyard where she gasped for breath.

"Tell me what's happening," I said.

She shook her head. "I'm a bit overtired is all. Seeing Joanie was more difficult than I expected."

Celeste leaned back in the grass and her hair fanned out in a halo around her head. Overhead thunder rumbled ominously. Her eyes shot open and she watched the sky intently.

"Cut it out," I said with a smile.

Her voice came back at a fraction of the volume I was used to, "It's not me, Luke."

I looked up at the thunderheads gathering in the distance. "Whoever the hell it is had better be prepared to take me on," I said.

"Meet me at the cave tomorrow," said Celeste.

"The Leatherman's place?"

She nodded.

"I've been meaning to ask, what do you know about the Leatherman?"

"Same as everyone else I'd venture. He was tall, dark, with long black hair. Everyone thought he was evil. They were afraid he would hurt them if he caught them."

"Add their bones to his soup pot and whitewash the boulders with them," I added, chiming in with what I had heard.

She smiled with effort. "He had several caves, not just the one I use, though the others have never been found. He slept in them at night. I found some of his old tin cans that he used for cooking so he definitely did live there. He never talked to anyone."

"What happened to him?"

"They found him dead one day, lying face down on the floor of a barn near the Spi-Sea plant."

"What was he doing there?"

"My father says he fell in love in France with the daughter of a leather worker. The leather worker said that if he did well in his business he could marry his daughter. But the Leatherman failed miserably. So he came to America. Alone."

"To start a new life."

"He wore leather clothing that he made out of boot tops and whatever he found. People left scraps of it for him. He roamed around aimlessly, scaring the little children."

She raised up on her elbow. A little color had entered her face again. Overhead, the clouds moved toward the hills and the sun poked through.

"I don't think he meant anyone harm. But the way he looked put people off. And his habits, living in the caves that way is not normal."

"He sounds interesting."

She smiled. "Some people were kind to him, others wanted to have him arrested and committed." She stood on wobbly legs.

"I bet if he were still alive today things would be different and he'd be famous."

She smiled wryly. "I don't think he'd have liked fame."

"Even if it could get him real leather suits?"

She laughed out loud. I realized it had been quite some time since I had heard that tinkling sound. Once again the feeling of hot silver ran through my veins.

"Even if it could have put him on the cover of *Newsweek*. All he wanted was his love, in France."

I met her gaze and my heart melted.

She said, "And all he found was his face in the dirt on the floor of the Spi-Sea barn." She turned and walked toward her bike. "Meet me at the cave, tomorrow, Luke. I have to get there again."

"I will," I said. I would have crawled over broken glass if she had asked. She moved away from me and fear rose in my chest. Her actions and words troubled me. She and Alec had it all, yet she seemed to grow paler each day.

My mother called from inside the house and I went back to entertaining my sister. I read to her until supper. As night settled over Faith Junction I feared that like the Leatherman I was roaming aimlessly, searching for what might have been.

CHAPTER EIGHTEEN

The next day, the Leatherman's cave lay dark and dank and I shivered as I entered. A couple of weeks ago I had welcomed its coolness as an escape from the summer heat, but with the recent change in weather I wished I had brought a jacket. As I walked deeper into the interior, I felt myself numbing at the core and remembered Celeste's warning about the affect of the cave physically on me. Already spooked by the tale of the Leatherman, the rumbling of the copper mine in the distance set my nerves on further edge. This was not a place I wanted to linger.

I reached the spot where Celeste and I had met in the past and sat down on a boulder. Weak sunlight filtered in from above and gradually my eyes became accustomed to the dark. I looked over my shoulder and wished that Celeste were there. I wondered how Celeste found this place comforting. All I wanted to do was leave. I needed warmth, light, sunshine, not the overwhelming dark of the cave.

Soon I rose and brushed off my slacks and decided to wait for Celeste outside. I would see her coming and the two of us could come back together. As I exited the mouth of the cave, shielding my eyes from the brightness, I heard a loud rumble.

"Jesus," I said aloud. I looked back and dust belched out of the cave, billowing into a choking cloud around me. I ran to the dirt path where I had parked my bike, and hid behind a boulder, sure that the entire cave was about to collapse. My heart pounded and I vowed to never again set foot in the Leatherman's place. He could have the damn spot to himself. He and Celeste would be right at home, two outsiders who deserved each other and liked to be in a black hole underground.

The rumbling stopped and the dust cloud lessened. Celeste still was nowhere in sight. This was not like her and I began to worry. I climbed on my bike and took the path that I knew led to her house. Maybe she had forgotten, or maybe her father had given her more work to do than she could finish. A half dozen other excuses paraded through my mind as I pedaled hard to her home.

When I arrived at the Careys' place, the lights were off and there was no sign anyone was at home. I knocked on the door and listened for sounds within. Mr. Carey's tractor was in the driveway, not in the barn, which seemed odd to me. His truck was gone too. Perhaps he had left in a hurry. Perhaps he was out tending his trees or running an errand in town. But where could Celeste be?

I entered the barn and shouted her name. "Celeste, are you here?" I called. My shout startled a barn swallow that flew out the open window overhead. The sun's warmth filled the room with the scent of hay. I went outside and scanned the horizon but nothing moved in any direction. "Fine," I said. "Have it your way. I hope you're enjoying yourself with Alec." Where else could she be but with Alec? Angered at her irresponsibility, I tried to block out the image of the two of them together. I headed to Ben's to forget about being stood up.

When I entered the diner, I was surprised to find that Alec and Josh sat opposite each other in a booth at the rear. I slid into the banquette beside Alec, who turned to me with a worried look on his face. I saw that Josh also wore a troubled look. My stomach wrenched.

Josh said, "We've tried calling you for an hour. Where the hell have you been?"

"Out at the Leatherman's cave."

Alec shot Josh a look that I knew meant he thought I was acting loony again.

"Some places aren't as bad as they seem at first." I elbowed Alec gently in the ribs and said, "Anyone know where Celeste is?"

Josh's face dropped further. Alec played with his straw.

There was an uncomfortable edge to the silence. "What'd I say?"

Josh cleared his throat. "You really haven't heard?"

"Heard what?

Alec said, "Celeste's sick. Something happened late last night. We were together and she collapsed."

Fear gripped me. "I saw her yesterday and she seemed a little under the weather. She was getting around ok."

Josh threw some change on the table and said, "We were just getting ready to head over to Good Sam now." He pointed a finger at Alec. "The lady killer here brought her over last night."

"To the hospital?" My head began to spin.

Alec said, "The doctors don't know what to make of it, but she's not doing too well. I'm worried about her, Looner."

"They'll figure it out, she'll get better in no time," I said without much conviction. I had tried to ignore the fact that she had looked increasingly ill each time I saw her. I couldn't do that any longer. Outside the diner, the smell of fish and tomato sauce made my stomach churn as much as Josh's words had.

"Celeste and Alec went to the movies, and then to the quarry." Josh made a smooching sound with his lips.

"Knock it off," said Alec.

Josh raised his eyebrows and shrugged. "Looner has a right to know what happened. No one blames you."

Alec ran his fingers through his hair. "It's my fault, Looner. We went for a swim, and then we were kissing and the next thing I know she was limp in my arms."

Josh stared at his feet.

Alec continued, "Kissing her was incredible. My God, it was like fireworks going off on the backs of my eyelids. And her voice, her laugh, it was as though it got inside me somehow, like some flame floating inside of me shining through my skin. Even when she wasn't conscious I could feel it, see it."

I knew exactly what he was talking about. The dazzling brightness

Celeste gave off was unforgettable. The feel of her lips on mine still left me weak.

"It's not your fault, Alec," said Josh. "People get sick. It's not like you could have done anything about it."

Alec hung his head. "God, I wish that was true. But I have this awful feeling that she's this way because of me."

I clapped him on the shoulder. "Screw it. Let's go see if we can make some sense out of this."

CRSO

Not much later we arrived at Good Samaritan and my head spun. Joanie, Deanna and now Celeste had been laid low in the past few weeks. Joanie was home and so was Deanna. I'd been to see her several times. Maybe in a few days everything would work out for Celeste too. My stomach wrapped itself around something empty.

Alec and I left Josh downstairs to his chagrin as only two of us could be in her room at a time. We exited the elevator and found Celeste's room. Her door was open.

As we entered, I saw Celeste staring out the window. Hers was one of the rooms that faced the highway. Outside, a line of cars crusaded across the highway in search of the Holy Grail of shopping, the factory outlet across from the hospital.

I motioned to Alec to keep quiet. I wanted to see what held Celeste's attention. I followed her line of vision up over the stream of cars. Her eyes were locked on a hill far from the shopping center. I stared at the green expanse and tried to place what I was looking at. I still didn't have a good feel for the town. After a few seconds I realized it was the concrete maw of the Spi-Sea Shrimp plant belching its noxious gases that rested far off from Good Sam. Celeste gazed in rapture at the operation. I wondered if perhaps she missed her special spot looking down on the plant. She couldn't be nostalgic for the stench.

Celeste must have heard us enter, for though she didn't turn her head or acknowledge our presence she spoke in a voice that was barely above a whisper. "That plant never stops. They seem to be running it more than ever lately. It's never going to end." Tubes ran in and out of her in a maze of white underpasses and overpasses.

We crossed the room and Alec sat in a chair at the foot of her bed.

I said, "There must be an increased demand for shrimp cocktail. Maybe it cures baldness or something."

She smiled. "It goes all night, some nights." She inclined her head toward me. "Like the lights on the highway." My heart wrenched at the thought of her watching those arcs alone.

I sat on the bed beside her. There was a paleness about her that was unearthly. Even her eyes had grown washed out. "I went to meet you at the Leatherman's cave."

She nodded. "I'm not much good at this."

"The next thing I know you're here."

She looked down the bed to where Alec sat at the foot, cradling his head in his hands.

Celeste looked bad. There was no getting around it. Her cheeks were ashen. Her golden hair hung limply and dully around her face. There was no trace of luster or shine anywhere in her features.

She smiled wanly. "The doctors don't know what's wrong. No one wants to tell me, but I'm not stupid."

"They'll figure it out." The words caught in my throat.

"You're such an optimist." She smiled. "I'm glad you came." She pressed her eyes closed and then opened them.

Alec licked his lips. I knew he wanted to say something to comfort her, but what could either of us say?

The silence grew heavy. To fill the conversational void, Alec said, "Josh is downstairs. He wants to see you too."

Celeste nodded. She leaned back against her pillows and let out a deep sigh.

I grabbed her hand and had to stop myself from recoiling at the cold, clammy touch. This was not the Celeste I knew. Suddenly I was frightened by what I saw pass over her face. "Celeste? You OK?"

I knew she was not. "I'll get the nurse," I said to Alec, who paced at the foot of her bed.

Her eyes were pressed together tightly and her voice came at me, a whisper that rattled in my stomach. "Stay with me."

"Celeste...."

"Hold my hands and stay with me, Luke, Alec. I don't want to be alone."

I approached her. "What do you want me to do? Is it your heart?"

"I have a big, strong heart," she said.

"We should find a nurse," said Alec, who stood beside me.

"No! No nurse. I'm sick of seeing those ghosts." She looked at me. "Would you sing me a song?"

"Celeste, not now," I said.

"Please, sing something happy."

I couldn't do it. She shook her head at my silence then turned to Alec. "We had fun, didn't we, Alec?" She pressed his hand to her chest and he nodded unable to speak, emotion choking him.

Finally he said, "This will pass, Celeste. It has to."

My mouth felt like a desert but I forced out, "Stay with us Celeste, OK?"

Her face wore the color of a New York winter sky and I was afraid that we were losing her. I leaned into her and whispered, "I'm here, Celeste. We're here." I repeated the words over and over, not sure if she could hear me. Her breathing grew irregular and a loud rasping noise periodically emerged from her chest, sending shivers down my spine. I hung onto her hand not knowing what to do.

Alec pushed a strand of golden hair back from her forehead. He traced his fingers down past her eyes and brushed his lips against her cheek, drawing in her scent. Her face was soft, the lines of the pain evident earlier erased. Celeste smiled weakly at Alec. Her eyes registered fear, changed to sorrow then concern. She shook her head and whispered, "Don't be upset."

It was so much like her to worry about others, even now. Both Alec and I had tears coursing down our cheeks. I tried hard to be courageous and summoned anger. Every ounce of me railed at her helplessness, wanting to pull her back. Being unable to do so was unbearable and I controlled letting loose the tears that were ready to stream.

Celeste sat up with a groggy look on her face.

"Celeste? What's going on?" asked Alec.

She struggled with her words. "It's passed. It's not time."

"What's that supposed to mean?" I saw color in her cheeks, more color than I had seen in days.

"Not yet."

I sank back against the bed. "Don't do that. Don't you ever do that again."

She spoke softly. "It's no use, Luke. They're not going to figure out what's wrong with me. I'm a rather complicated medical specimen and I can guarantee there's no hope for a cure." She flashed me a wan smile.

I said, "Nonsense. You'll be better in no time."

Alec chimed in, "You're already looking like your old self. It won't be long till you're going to Ben's with us again."

She nodded but I could tell that she was humoring us.

Alec said, "Is there something we can get you? I'd be happy to bring you an ice cream or whatever."

She shook her head.

"Come on, Celeste," I said. "A pizza maybe? Or some Chinese food?"

She closed her eyes. "I'm so tired."

I could see Alec's eyes fill with tears once again.

Suddenly Celeste began to shake. It was as though an electric current passed through her. Her body jerked wildly as she thrashed beneath the covers moaning. As suddenly as it came on her, the charge receded and she lay still against her pillows.

A nurse entered, all efficiency, oblivious to the distress hanging in the room. "You boys are going to have to leave for a bit." She glanced at her watch. "Miss Carey is scheduled for some tests."

Celeste waved at us, signaling we should go. I rose to leave and Celeste squeezed my hand. Whatever had happened had passed through her.

Celeste said, "I'm sorry I didn't meet you. That really would have done me some good."

The nurse nodded her head toward the door and Alec shifted from foot to foot, both of us unwilling to leave.

"The Leatherman says hi," I said, dropping one of the stones from the cave I had in my pocket into her palm.

Her face came alive. "I don't believe you did that, Luke." She clenched her fist around the stone. "If only I had the strength to finish what I started."

As the nurse watched with folded arms, Alec leaned over and kissed Celeste on the forehead. She grew pale and I could see her fight off a wave of pain.

The nurse said, "Outside. Now, boys." She snapped the curtain around Celeste's bed and Alec and I made our way to the elevator.

As we descended to the lobby, Alec groaned. "I can't stand seeing her like that. It's my fault. I just know it."

"I don't get it. A couple of days ago she was fine. Now she's barely breathing."

Alec clenched his jaw. "I think it's time we paid a visit to the Carey household. You up for that?"

I swallowed hard. The last visit to the Carey household still stung. "I'm not sure that's such a good idea," I said. "Mr. Carey is one mean bastard."

Alec raised his voice, "There's a reason she's like this. Why the hell isn't he here at her bedside? What kind of a father is he?"

"The doctors will find out what's wrong. All those tests...."

Alec wheeled on me and grabbed me by the shoulders. "Screw the doctors. They won't help her. You know it and I know it. There's something else going on. We've got to get to the bottom of this or she's not going to make it."

"She's different than the rest of us, Alec."

"I know that, Luke. She's got weird powers. I didn't believe her at first, but then she did that thing to me. Made me into a human iceberg."

"You knew it was her?"

"Who else could it be? I've seen her do a lot of strange things. I never wanted to admit that she was the one making the wind blow, or the rain come down on my block, but I guess I just learned to accept it."

His hands fell from my shoulders as the elevator came to a stop at the main floor. He stormed into the lobby. I knew that he was desperate, upset and incapable of listening to anything but the fury in his brain. And I knew that he was right.

Josh stood as we approached him. "We're going to the Careys', baboon balls," said Alec, not bothering to stop.

"But I haven't seen Celeste," said Josh.

"She says hello," I said. "I'll fill you in as we ride."

Josh picked up his jacket and caught up to us as we exited the waiting room and walked down the hallway. His words rushed at us. "Last time Luke and I went there was more than enough for my lifetime. You're joking about visiting Mr. Carey, aren't you?"

The question hung in the air and answered itself as Alec shoved the exit door wide and stepped into the last rays of daylight. Josh followed behind us, a look on his face that I knew meant he was reluctant to participate in our venture.

"So are we all in this together or what?" asked Alec.

I nodded. "One for all and all that shit."

We both stared at Josh. He turned his head to the side and for an instant I saw a gleam in his eye that signaled he was going to bolt. My own confidence wavered.

But he said, "God. The things I do for you guys."

The three of us mounted our bicycles.

"I should call my folks," I said, raising my kickstand.

Josh shot me a look of disdain. "Looner, if you do that you know you'll never make it to the Careys'."

He was right. My resolve was not strong enough to last through a phone call. I could hear it now. My mom would insist I come home for dinner. A pang of guilt shot through me. My sister would be waiting at the front door for me to pedal home and have a game of hoops. I gritted my teeth and put my head down, forcing the thoughts of home out of my mind.

As we rode, the wind was at our backs. Normally the stench from the plant would be overwhelming with this type of breeze, but I found myself drawing in deep draughts of air. Spi-Sea fish scent hung heavily in the air, but I wasn't about to care about it. I smiled and pedaled harder. Maybe I was finally starting to fit into Faith Junction after all.

CHAPTER NINETEEN

I pounded hard on the door of the Careys' farmhouse. Mr. Carey's red pickup sat parked alongside the barn, and I figured in all likelihood he was inside. If I were mistaken, I would venture out into his orchards and find him. I wouldn't give up until I confronted him. I looked up to the second floor and saw a curtain move.

"Good, he's home," I said, pointing at the window.

"Oh yeah, that's great," said Josh, looking over his shoulder as though he were seeking a place to hide. The three of us waited at the door, panting, still out of breath from the furious ride. Alec wore a determined look and that fueled my resolve.

I yelled up at the window, "Mr. Carey. It's me. Luke D'Angelo. I need to talk to you about Celeste."

As we waited, an eerie calm hung over not only the Carey home, but all of Faith Junction. There had been no rain for days and dust billowed at the foot of the stairs in the occasional unwelcome gust of wind. The stench of the plant had grown greater at the Careys', so much so that I could no longer ignore its presence.

"Geez," I said, covering my nose with my hand. "How much worse can that damn plant stink!"

Alec chuckled. "They're doubling production. Probably to make up

161

for the runs lost during the blackout," he said, shoving his hands in his pockets. "It's starting to be annoying for sure, eh, Josh?"

"Annoying!" I shouted. "It's goddamn revolting. The hotter it gets, the worse it gets."

Josh said, "According to the newspaper, everyone's on overtime and the plant's going to stay that way for the next month."

"Damn," I said. "The smell is awful, worse than ever at all times of day and night."

My two friends grinned. I tried to forget the smell and called again. "We want to help Celeste. Would you please come and talk to us?" I pounded on the door in frustration. "We're not going, Mr. Carey. Do you hear me?" My fists ached.

The door swung open and revealed Celeste's father. In spite of my determination, I felt my heart pound in fear as he loomed before us. He was even larger than I remembered, but at least he didn't have a shotgun today.

"You can quit your banging on my door. I don't have anything to tell you." He glowered at me and I licked my lips.

I had to hand it to Alec. He didn't shrink from the large, dour man who towered over us. Alec spoke up, "That's not true. I think there's a lot that needs to be said about her and you're the only one who can help."

"She's in the hands of her doctors." He eyed us warily.

"Celeste has powers, Mr. Carey. She's told us about them. We believe in her." I nodded at Alec and Mr. Carey took him in with a gaze that would have sent the cowering-behind-me Josh running. Alec glared back at Mr. Carey.

Celeste's father spoke. "Oh, you believe in her, do you? And what would she have said that these powers of hers are? She's never been able to do much as far as I can tell."

I said, "That's not true and you know it. She's the one who keeps your orchards watered, isn't she?"

He crossed his arms against his chest.

I continued, "There has to be something we can do to help her. I'm afraid for her, afraid that without the right care she could slip away from us."

Mr. Carey's shoulders sagged. He looked as though someone had knocked the wind out of him. With a sad shake of his head, he threw the door wide. "Come on in, but it's not going to make any difference at all what I tell you, or what she does at this point. You're right that it may be too late for her." I could see his eyes glisten with wetness.

We followed him as he leaned on his cane and limped his way to the kitchen where his prosthesis lay on a table in the corner. Mr. Carey pulled a chair away from the table and sat down. He motioned for us to do the same. He rubbed his bare leg where the foot was missing.

Aware we were staring at him, he said, "The darn thing aches like the devil."

"Farming accident?" I asked. Alec shifted uncomfortably beside me and Josh groaned. Mr. Carey narrowed his eyes and I regretted asking the question.

"You're a nosy bugger, aren't you?" he said. "Why the hell didn't you leave Celeste alone? All of you!"

"It's too late for that," said Alec.

Mr. Carey ran his fingers through his hair. "What is it that you want?"

"We want to know about her. About you. Maybe there's something we can do to help if you'll tell us about her."

"The doctors say she can't survive more than a few days." He wiped his damp eyes with his sleeve. "Not that they understand what the hell is going on with her. They keep saying there's some kind of storm in her heart and electrical charges in her brain too. I warned her not to get involved with the townspeople."

"I don't think they know what they're talking about at the hospital. Besides, don't you believe in miracles?"

"Miracles? There would have to be a loving God for there to be miracles, now wouldn't there?" Mr. Carey held his hand up and signaled that I should not answer. His tone left me chilled. Could this be the same man who attended church on Sundays?

"Could you tell us what you know about her?"

He let out a sign of despair, then spoke in a low voice. "I suppose I should start at the beginning, when she came into our lives."

I nodded and Alec and Josh leaned forward in their chairs. Celeste's father took a deep breath and shut his eyes.

"It's been a long time, but I relive it often."

Alec and I exchanged glances as Mr. Carey spoke.

"The night she arrived there were a lot of stars out. They reminded me of the tufts of the chenille spread that lay across my and Emma's four-poster." He reached in his breast pocket and removed a small pipe. "Emma, God bless her soul. She was my wife." Mr. Carey tapped the pipe on the table. He no longer frightened me. Instead he seemed like one of Dad's shirts when all the starch had gone out of it after washing.

"I remember thinking about how it was getting to be bedtime and soon Emma and I would be lying together wrapped up nice and cozy. God, that woman always did something to me. A day didn't go by that I didn't want to be next to her." His eyes glistened with tears as he lit his pipe. "There's nothing like being with the woman you love."

I could see Alec shift uncomfortably in his seat. I was grateful he resisted the urge to tell Mr. Carey of his feelings for his daughter. Josh cracked his knuckles and let out a machine gun laugh. Mr. Carey eyed him and Josh said, "Sorry." He stuffed his hands under his thighs.

I said, "You must have loved her very much."

Alec rolled his eyes, but Mr. Carey didn't see that, instead he nodded and said, "She's been gone fourteen years and I still can feel her sometimes." He cast his eyes about the kitchen as though she was present. "But that's not what you want to hear about."

I smiled. "I don't mind."

Alec chimed in, "Me neither."

Mr. Carey cleared his throat. "This isn't an easy story to tell." He clenched his fists. "It's not going to do any good."

"Please, keep talking. It can't hurt," I said.

He licked his lips and went on. "I remember that I leaned back into the oak tree in the front yard and glanced over at Emma. She was sitting next to me on the ground. I could smell her hair, like apple blossoms. You ever notice the way people have a scent of their own?"

A fleeting thought of Susie's lemon and grass scent went through my mind and I nodded.

"Well," said Mr. Carey, "that was Emma's scent. Apple blossoms."

Mr. Carey clearly was going to take his time with this story. We would do anything to find some shred of evidence that might give us a clue to helping Celeste so we hung on his words.

"Late evenings were our time to unwind together. That was a quiet time when we drew close and felt a part of not only each other, but of something greater that neither of us understood. That's what I used to think."

I saw his jaw clench.

"I took a hunting knife from my pocket and an apple from my shirt and carved it into slices." He demonstrated with his hand, reliving the experience. "Emma pointed her chin toward the sky. The sight of her neck arching upward, offering herself to the sky..." His voice trailed away. "She often left me dizzy and that night she elbowed me in the side the way she often did to bring me back to reality."

Alec chuckled. "My mom does that to my dad, says he's lost in space."

Mr. Carey glared at the intrusion and puffed on his pipe. "She asked, 'That one over there. It's Orion, isn't it?' I trained my gaze in the direction of her finger and passed her a sliver of apple. She popped the fruit into her mouth. She was six months pregnant." His throat caught.

The three of us exchanged glances. This was the first we had heard of a Carey sibling.

Mr. Carey said, "I told Emma, 'That's it all right.' No sooner were the words past my lips than something bright streaked across the sky. I caught my breath and tracked the flash. 'What on earth is that?' asked Emma.

"My nerves screamed mayday as Emma brought herself to her feet. She had a hard time getting up with being pregnant. 'Take it easy, Em,' I said. I studied the path of the glow and watched as it moved toward earth. I was afraid it was headed toward us, so I got up, pocketed my knife and dusted off my jeans. I tried to appear calm for Emma's sake, but she wasn't about to be fooled. 'Oh, Lord,' said Emma. 'It's a plane, isn't it! And it's going to crash!'"

He shook his head. "I wrapped my arm around her shoulders and told her we'd better go inside." He sighed. "Emma wasn't about to listen. She pushed me away and stared up as that flame above us grew brighter. The plane was on a downward path. I didn't want to believe it was about to hit the ground and I tried to distract her. I said, 'Em, come on. I want to go in.'"

Mr. Carey puffed on his pipe. "I told her that maybe they could make it to the orchard. There's open space up there and they could have a chance. But Emma moved away from me and lumbered toward the barn."

Mr. Carey pointed out the window toward the barn where his pickup truck sat. "She yelled, 'We can't just stand here!'"

He took a deep breath. "Sometimes I think that maybe that's exactly what we should have done. Just stood there."

I asked, "You went to the orchard?"

Mr. Carey nodded. "You could see the entire sky overhead glow orange as that plane passed over us, heading toward the orchard. I looked at Emma. She was horror-stricken. As that ball of fire passed, it painted her skin golden orange."

Josh let out a low whistle.

"It was a small plane and we were both relieved it missed the house. It was unusual for any plane ever to fly over our place. The nearest airport is seventy-five miles away in Sullivan County. I remember thinking that something must have happened to cause the pilot to detour this far. The plane hung low on the horizon and I held my breath. Maybe, just maybe, the pilot could arc the nose up and away at the last second." He held his hand up to the ceiling and pressed his eyes shut and we waited for him to continue.

He sighed and said, "No such luck."

Josh groaned.

Mr. Carey said, "The plane hit, and on impact the explosion rocked us so hard we fell to the ground. I shielded Emma with my body. 'Oh God, oh God,' she kept moaning. In the distance, sparks shot into the air. Horrible sounds of metal screeching made my hair stand on end. Emma pushed me off and rose to her feet a wild look in her eye. 'Hurry, Matt!' she said. I was so scared I could barely move. I told her that maybe we should call the sheriff and the fire department."

"She said, 'We can do that later. We have to get to them!' That's when I said to her that it seemed to me there wouldn't be anyone left to get to as it was one helluva crash."

He glanced at the three of us and saw we were paying rapt attention. "She glared at me and after seventeen years of marriage I knew what the look meant. We climbed into the cab of the pickup truck and headed for the apple orchard."

Mr. Carey re-lit his pipe which had gone out. The scent of cherry tobacco filled the kitchen again. "Before we arrived the smell of death greeted us. I'll never forget that smell. Burning flesh mixed with the scent of warm apples wafted into the open window of the truck. I felt sick to my stomach so I pulled to a stop and studied the orchard. Then I looked up." He shook his head. "It was amazing. The cab of the plane had lodged in the tops of two apple trees. The rear section lay in flames on the ground nearby."

Josh gasped. I clenched my fingers around my chair.

"The plane was a small one, a four-seater Cessna. Emma opened the door to the truck but I grabbed her arm and held her back. I told her I didn't think we should go any farther. Everything was burning everywhere."

Alec asked, "The plane was up in the tree?"

Mr. Carey nodded. "Part of it was, yes, sir. Emma thought someone might be up there. She pointed to the smoking cab in the treetops and said, 'That's a miracle. We have to try to help!'" He slammed his fist on the table. "A miracle."

Alec and I exchanged glances.

Mr. Carey said, "I told her she had the baby to worry about. But she said she would never be able to live with herself if she didn't do something. I knew her well enough to know I would never dissuade her, so I opened the cab and climbed down. I told her to wait and that I would go and investigate."

I let out my breath which I had not been aware I was holding. Josh muttered something and bit his lip.

Mr. Carey said, "Emma got out of the truck slowly. 'I'm coming too,' she said. I wanted to lock her inside but she was already moving toward the accident. She allowed me to link my arm in hers and we approached the tree. The fumes were awful and Emma started choking so I gave her my handkerchief and she put it over her nose. Flames shot from the rear section of plane on the ground and my heart started pounding. I realized that the fuel tank could explode at any time and I wanted to get the hell out of there as fast as I could. Only the rear section lay bent and curled around an apple tree on the ground. The front of the small Cessna, the part that lay cradled above us between two boughs, had smoke curling up out of it like a barbecue. Crispy critters for real, I thought. And then I jumped, scared out of my wits by an eerie sound."

"What was it?" asked Alec.

"I didn't know at first. So I listened hard and when the sound reached me again I placed it. A moan, and then a cry. Emma heard the same thing because she held my gaze and said, 'That's someone in pain. Up there.' She pointed to the treetops. I said, 'I'm not so sure there's anyone alive.'

"She came back at me, 'You need a hearing aid. You always have. What the hell is making that racket if it's not a person?'

"I studied the tree and told her she should go for help. I've never been much of a tree climber.

"She planted her hands on her hips and insisted, 'We have to do something!'"

Mr. Carey ran his hands over his face. "I knew she was right. I took a deep breath and reached out to the large oak before me. At least it was a good tree for climbing. I grabbed a thick limb above my head and hoisted myself up. Emma watched and called that I should be careful. As I climbed my eyes went up to where the plane's front cab miraculously lay in the arms of the tree above me. I climbed slowly and listened hard. I heard the metal creak as the plane shifted and settled into a fork at the top of the straining boughs. A wail rang out from above. Someone was definitely up there."

Alec, Josh and I hung on every word.

"'It's a child crying. Oh, Lord,' said Emma. She paced back and forth beneath the tree. 'Do something. Quick!'"

"What, what did you do?" asked Alec.

"I lifted myself up branch by branch. I could feel the heat coming from the burning interior even from low down. Another few feet and I was level with what was left of the front of the plane. I steeled myself, looked inside and saw a man and a woman. But I got dizzy then and had to close my eyes and calm myself down. Maybe they're unconscious, I said to myself. When I opened my eyes, I saw the angle of their necks and their poor twisted bodies and knew they were both dead. But then another cry rose from somewhere up there in the wreckage and sent shivers down my spine. I leaned into the cab of the plane fighting the heat and fumes. The plane shifted and tilted precariously."

My head spun as I focused on Mr. Carey's words. The scene was horrid and alive in the room.

He went on, "Emma called out, 'Be careful! Oh God, be careful! I can see it moving!' I didn't understand how the plane could not fall. I was about to back off and climb down when something brushed against my arm and then took firm hold. A chill went down my spine. I let out a yell and nearly lost my footing. Emma screamed and I regained my balance. A small dirty hand clung to my forearm. My heart raced. It was a child's hand. I calmed myself and tried to think as the heat swirled round me. Flames leapt up in the cockpit and terrified me. I pushed a seat away and beneath it found the owner of the hand. A tiny face peered up at me. There was so much blood that I couldn't tell if it was a boy or a girl. The child's eyes fluttered open and held mine."

I saw Mr. Carey's lips tremble and his eyes well.

He said, "That poor sweet child said, 'Help me. Please, help me.' The words cut into me deeply. The cloying smell of blood made me gag, but I reached inside and summoned strength I didn't know I had. I yanked hard and pulled the seat cushion completely away. And then I saw all of her. Her long blonde braids were matted red, her eyes were pools of pain. Emma was shouting, 'Hurry up, Matt! You're taking too long! It's not safe!' I told her I was trying to free the little girl. What I saw next caused a fresh wave of nausea to pass over me. I leaned back and took gulps of air." Mr. Carey's hands shook. He said, "A metal strut poked out of her stomach."

Mr. Carey wiped a tear from his eye. "The blood that covered her stemmed from her stomach and I couldn't imagine how she could still be alive. I leaned back and tried to stop the dizziness from overcoming me. The sickening sweet smell of blood clogged my throat. I wanted to run from the grizzly scene. The flames in the cockpit were so strong. The cabin creaked ominously and I got so angry at the senselessness of it all. Rock a bye baby in the treetop started to sing in my brain. The child moaned again. I called down. 'She's hurt, Emma. You better go back and call an ambulance.'"

I watched Mr. Carey pull a tissue from his pocket. He set his jaw and went on.

"Emma paced at the foot of the tree. She said, 'I won't go. I'm afraid to leave you here! What if something happens?' I told her, nothing was going to happen, that there were two dead people in the cab and this poor child who was surely a goner unless someone got to her soon."

"You couldn't get her out?" asked Josh, his eyes wide.

Mr. Carey shook his head. "She was hurt pretty bad and stuck in the cab. I asked Emma to go call. She kept circling the tree in a frenzy. Finally she left telling me she'd be back in ten minutes. I watched as she lumbered to the truck. Then the child cried out in pain and I was with her again."

I said, "That must have been so difficult for Emma to leave and for you to watch that injured child."

Mr. Carey's eyes dropped. "That child, she told me, 'I don't want to die.' She was no more than eight. I can still hear her say that to me, over and over. I told her I would get her out and to a hospital. I lied, God forgive me, I lied."

I could hear Alec breathing beside me. My stomach ached and my head throbbed.

Mr. Carey continued in a voice that cracked with sorrow, "The wind kicked up and whistled through the grove of trees. In the distance thunder rumbled. That little child closed her eyes. 'I'm so cold,' she said." Reliving the moment, he cradled his hands. "I lifted her head and placed it on a seat cushion. I rubbed her hands. Her face was the color of concrete. Why do things like this have to happen? That's all I could think about. Why? I leaned back in the tree, sickened by the smell, the death, the carnage in the cab. I reached inside and patted the girl's head. I stroked her face, and cursed God. I knew she would never see the light of day again. If she were one of my farm animals I'd have shot her already." He wound the tissue between his fingers.

"Then, something caught my eye. I pushed the seat cushion farther back into the cab of the plane and gasped. An infant lay sucking its thumb. A little girl with golden ringlets and bright eyes that locked on mine." His face brightened.

"Another child!" said Alec. I groaned. Josh stared numbly.

Mr. Carey nodded. "When she saw me, she let out a yell. I was amazed that the baby wasn't hurt. Then the plane shifted and creaked again. Another large piece of the tail ripped and fell. I was afraid the entire cab was about to tumble to the earth. My heart raced as I reached inside and scooped that baby out of her protected corner. As I held her tight to my chest, the rear of the plane cracked. What a horrible deafening sound. The front cab sheared off and plummeted down to the ground taking that poor impaled child with it. The impact ignited whatever fuel was left and flames shot up around me."

Mr. Carey hung his head in his hands.

"And down will come baby, cradle and all," said Alec.

Mr. Carey looked up with tear-filled eyes. "I hunched over trying to shield the infant. I felt a wave of nausea as I realized the child in the wreckage below was silent, burning in a funeral pyre. I couldn't save her. I didn't save her. Then there was a loud crack and the back half of the plane next to me shifted and slid down pinning the baby and me in the fork. It was terrible, terrible, so much pain. I started screaming. The cab continued to settle crushing me into the fork of the tree. Branches blinded me and jutted into my mouth, scraped my neck raw. I wished for the wail of fire engines or the siren of the local ambulance corps, but heard nothing. The flames were intense. That baby and I would be charred to death if I waited for the fire trucks. I was breathing more smoke than air and getting more and more dizzy. I wriggled the top half of my body free of the wreck and tree limbs, gasping for air, pushing pieces over the side. But the source of my pain, my left foot, was stuck, crushed in a gap between a piece of the plane and the tree."

"Oh no," said Josh.

"I tried to move the metal shell of plane with my shoulder to no avail. I had lost all feeling in my foot. I tried to move my toes but could not. The baby cried. Flames licked up the tree from below and cascaded down from the remains of the plane above. It was a living hell."

"What did you do? What?" asked Josh.

"I ripped off my shirt and fashioned a sling and tied the baby to my chest. When I was sure the child was secure, I gritted my teeth. I reached in my back pocket and took out my hunting knife. I closed my eyes and then, oh God, then I sawed through my sock. I took a deep breath and hacked at my ankle where it hung limply on the other side of the metal that held me in a death grip."

"Oh God," said Alec, clutching his stomach. I suddenly felt dizzy and gripped the table to steady myself.

"I was surprised at how easy it was to sever my foot; no different from cutting through a piece of firm fish flesh, or the joint in a chicken leg. Skin, then tendons, then bone. I watched the detached limb fall away into the burning pyre below. Then I blacked out, but it must have only been for a few seconds. I opened my eyes to a lusty wail of the baby. The pain was awful, and I fought the feeling of losing consciousness. I tugged my leg again but that hurt even more. With a mighty pull, the bloody stump came up and out. I screamed, clutched the baby to my chest as tightly as I could, and dove out of the burning tree to earth, tumbling as far as I could from the wreckage."

The thought of Mr. Carey hacking at his foot made my head spin. I forced myself to breathe evenly. It was horrible, absolutely horrible.

"Funny thing was, as I fell it felt as though I were being carried on a cloud of air to earth. I rolled onto my back gasping for breath, but the fumes from the burning plane were thick and harsh, clogging my lungs. The rest of the plane crashed to earth not far from where I lay, sending more flames into the already congested air. I couldn't move. Pain coursed through my leg from the bloody stump. My right arm seemed not to be connected to my body. I was aware of the baby on my chest stirring. She was alive. Alive! I blinked and took in her tiny form."

He stretched his good leg out in front of him. "Everything was going black. I saw her tiny hand reach up, palm facing the sky."

With a jolt I remembered how I had seen Celeste make that gesture on the ridge over the quarry. A chill went over me.

"She must have invoked the heavens with those tiny fingers. I looked up. It had to be a dream or a hallucination, that the stars in the sky overhead grew brighter, that thick clouds gathered. And then the most amazing thing happened. A steady rain began to fall, drenching us. I closed my eyes and let the darkness take me."

"She survived, and so did you," said Alec.

He nodded. "I thought for sure we'd be consumed, just like that poor child and her parents. But the downpour doused the nearby flames that threatened to engulf us. A few minutes later, Emma and the ambulance arrived. The fire department too. They rushed us to the hospital."

Mr. Carey stretched. Then he rubbed his foot, or where his foot should be. He cleared his throat. "I'll never forgive myself for what happened to that poor child, never. We named the baby Celeste. I figured it was a good name for such a heavenly creature."

"But where did she come from?" asked Josh.

He narrowed his gaze and Josh shrank in his seat. The room was deathly quiet. He said, "In all likelihood, hell."

I stood up and knocked over my chair. "What's that supposed to mean?"

Mr. Carey puffed on his pipe. "She's my daughter. I love her." He hung his head. "She's a devil child."

"You're crazy. You raised her telling her she came from hell?"

"No, son, she's the one who told me, by her actions. She causes as much harm as she does good. More harm than good if you ask me."

Alec stood in anger. "This can't be."

Mr. Carey shook his head. "Think what you want. But I know that girl. She does a lot of bad things with those storms and lightning bolts. She's burned a lot of people, burned down my barn once too."

Alec groaned. "She isn't bad."

Mr. Carey tamped on his pipe. "The worst is," he made the sign of the cross, "she's the one responsible for killing her family."

"For the air crash?" I asked.

Josh gasped several times and I thought he was going to have an asthma attack.

Mr. Carey said, "She didn't mean to do any of it. But she did. She knows it. Bad things happen around her."

Alec said, "How could a baby have done such a thing? You're lying."

"She struggles with controlling that bad side of her. I don't think you need to worry about her doing you in. Besides, in her current state she won't be hurting anyone but herself." He looked away sadly.

I licked my lips.

Mr. Carey said, "She was just a tiny baby. She really had no idea of the devastation she could cause."

Alec said, "But how can this be?"

"Have you seen what happens to her when she does something nice?" He shook his head. "It's just not her nature, makes her sick to her stomach. When she was growing up I'd watch her play with butterflies. She'd collect them and rip the wings off one by one. Once I caught her in the act and made her let them all go. She fell on the ground and writhed in pain."

I thought about all the times that I had seen her grow pale and weak after doing a good deed. With mounting fear I told myself over and over that what he said could not be true, that there had to be another explanation.

"She's a dark angel, my little girl is." He wiped a tear from his eye. "She's constantly battling what she wants to be, but it's so much larger than her. She's a fighter, I'll give her that." Mr. Carey stood and raised his hands over his head pointing to the ceiling. "And He knows it. I bring her to church trying to get Him to intercede but it does no good. Falls on deaf ears."

"But how about her feelings for me?" asked Alec. "We love each other."

Mr. Carey crossed his arms across his chest. "Oh, do you now?"

Alec looked at the floor sheepishly.

"She can't love. Love is man's paradise. Love is seeing the face of God. That'd be bound to do her in completely. It's the ultimate act of goodness to love, now isn't it?"

Quiet settled over the room as we tried to understand what Mr. Carey had told us. After a minute Alec spoke.

"I'm the one who's killing her," he said. "If what you say is true, her caring for me is making her sick. Take me out of the equation and she can go back to being herself!"

"You give yourself too much credit. I'm telling you she can't love."

"But what if she did? Then it might kill her!"

"It's too late to help her," said Mr. Carey. "Can't you understand that?"

"You can't be serious."

"Don't blame yourself, son. She always knows what she's getting into. Even if she thought she could love you and conquer the dark she's always babbling about controlling, she'd have been taking a huge risk." He stood and reached for an empty baby food jar that sat on the kitchen shelf. "She really is at home in that blasted dark." His hand trembled. "She tries to keep it away, but the dark always catches up to her. I've seen it. It's too damn fast." He sighed. "I suppose I have to be grateful I've had her here with me for this long. I can't imagine life without her." He wiped at his eyes. "My little dark angel." Then, in an exhausted voice, he said, "I think you should go now."

"There's more to tell, isn't there," said Alec, clearly hoping for a solution. "What about all the times she's changed the weather? Isn't that something she did for the good of people for the most part? For you, for your orchards?"

I said, "She wants to do that, Alec. She's trying to control the weather, trying to find some way to keep herself from doing bad. Is that it, Mr. Carey?" I thought I understood the puzzle that was Celeste.

He shook his head. "That's all I'm going to say."

"What about your wife and baby? What happened to them?" asked Alec.

All the color drained from Mr. Carey's face. He bent at the waist and held his hand to his head. "That wasn't Celeste's fault. I refuse to accept that it was. Emma died in childbirth along with the baby. I never should have agreed to allow Emma to have that baby. She was too weak and getting up there in age."

"And Celeste's parents? Didn't she have any relatives?"

Mr. Carey shook his head. "No one ever was able to find any. The plane wasn't registered anywhere. It's like they were escaping from somewhere." He looked out the window. "The worst part was I never even asked that little girl her name before she died." Tears streaked down his face. "We had to bury all of them, what was left of them, without knowing who they really were."

Alec asked him, "Can we do anything? There must be something."

"Celeste's a strong girl. But she's waging a terrible war that no one in medicine can help her with. I'm afraid all we can do is stand by and watch."

"That can't be!" said Alec. "There's got to be some way to let her be healthy again."

Mr. Carey puffed on his pipe. A tear rolled down his cheek. "Son," he said, "sometimes no matter how much you want something you just can't make it happen." He covered his eyes with his hands.

Not much later, we rode our bikes away from the Carey house speechlessly. As we pedaled, I ran what Mr. Carey had told us over and over in my mind. Could the angelic Celeste be what her father had said? Could she be a dark angel? She had seemed to suffer every time she did something good. But I hadn't seen her do anything bad. There had to be another explanation.

After a few minutes of hard riding, Alec called over to me, "This is such bullshit. Why is Celeste here? And what battle can she possibly be fighting?"

"I don't know much about angels, Alec," I said. "And I know even less about dark ones."

Josh looked over his shoulder, then up at the sky. "I'm going home, guys. I don't like any of what old man Carey told us. It can't be true."

"But if it is," said Alec, "what if it is?"

"She's trying to do good. I'm sure of it. We've got to try to help her," I said. "No matter what. I could never live with myself if I didn't."

"Me either."

"Oh Christ," said Josh. "Here we go again."

Alec pulled to a stop alongside the road. "Luke, you're the one we have to rely on. If her father is right and I go to see her it might make her worse." He shook his head. "I don't want to hurt her. She has to get better."

"But what can I do? If she's so sick because of what's happened, then there's nothing I can possibly help her with."

"There must be a way. You go to the hospital and talk to her. Maybe she'll have an idea or two."

"The cave. There might be something there that can help her. She told me it's where she goes to feel better."

Alec nodded. "She told me that too." He put his kickstand up. "I'm going to the cave and see what I can find."

We both looked at Josh who threw his hands up and said, "Fine! I'll catch up with you at the cave later. Whatever you come up with, I'm with you."

Alec clapped him on the back. None of us were willing to voice any further concerns. If Celeste was what her father said she was, we were involved in something far greater than any of us had ever imagined. And if she wasn't what he said, well, then whatever she was was far too disturbing to contemplate. The only thing we knew was that there was no turning back and the road up ahead was frightening and hazy.

CHAPTER TWENTY

Not much later, I stood over Celeste's hospital bed. Her heart monitor beeped and an IV dripped into her arm as she tossed and turned in a restless sleep. I wanted to reach out and stroke her forehead, touch that golden hair and make it all better, but I feared doing so. After what her father had said, I thought touching her might worsen her condition, plus I was afraid. She thrashed and moaned and I wondered what tortured dreams held her.

At the foot of her bed I found her chart and I picked it up to see what the latest reports were. Several doctors had made notes that were indecipherable, but at the bottom of the last page I found large red circles around the words "heart rate" and "brainwaves" and the words "Retake tests as soon as possible. Results not possible."

Celeste moaned loudly and a chill went down my spine. I had never heard a sound like that moan before this. Fear beat in my chest. I threw my caution aside, reached over and placed her hand between mine. Her cold fingers seared my skin, but I held onto her hand.

"I'm here, Celeste," I whispered. "It's going to be all right."

She kicked her legs and moaned louder. I thought about calling a nurse. Perhaps Celeste needed more medication, something to dull the pain. Celeste grew still, drew a deep breath and opened her eyes.

"Luke!" She said my name with joy and my heart raced at the thought that she was happy to see me. I nodded furiously, unable to speak.

"I'm so sorry you have to see me like this," she said, looking around the room. Her lips were parched and cracked. I tried to disguise my feelings, but she read my face. "It's not as bad as it looks." She smiled wanly.

I patted her hand and fought back tears. I couldn't stand seeing her this way. I wanted to be out riding bikes in the orchard together, and even smelling the Spi-Sea plant together would be better than the smell of the hospital room that closed in around me.

She turned her face toward me and I could see how drawn she was. Her cheeks were gaunt hollows. She said, "Do you know what they did? I'm going to be famous." She managed a weak smile. "They've mailed my results to doctors around the world trying to find out if anyone had ever seen anything like it." She shook her head. "That's not going to work. The fact is, I'm not sure how much more of this I can take."

"You're doing fine," I said, pouring her a glass of water.

I supported her head and pressed the glass to her lips. She closed her eyes and drank deeply. She leaned back into her pillows, exhausted from the effort.

"I wish that we could be at Ben's together again," she said. She bit her lip. "I'm sorry about the last time we were there. It was good of you to try to make me fit in."

I shrugged. "There'll be lots of times at Ben's for us. We'll hold a party there for you when you get out."

She held my gaze. "I don't have much time."

"Nonsense. You've got all the time in the world."

"Then the world must be about to end too."

I reached for the pitcher to pour myself a glass of water. My hand shook and I knocked the telephone to the floor. I bent to retrieve the handset.

"They can't cure me, Luke."

"They'll figure something out. You have to try to stay strong, try to help."

She looked around and said, "Where are your trusty sidekicks?"

179

"Josh had something to do this afternoon."

"Alec too?"

I could not meet her gaze. "I'm not sure what he's doing."

"I can't believe anyone would want to visit me. They probably figure I'll send them off in a tornado or something."

"They'll be here tomorrow, I'll bet."

She shook her head. "I'd rather that they didn't see me this way."

I held her hand tightly. "Tell me what I can do."

She smiled a crooked smile. "I miss the cave, Luke, the lake, the dark. There's nothing to be done about me now."

I pressed my fingers to her lips. "It's not just the cave or the dark, Celeste."

She held my gaze.

"I spoke to your father."

"You didn't."

I nodded.

"My dad has strange ideas...." Her voice trailed off.

"He's very worried about you. He told me an odd story though, about how he found you as a baby."

She turned her head to the wall. I could see tears streaming down her cheeks. I remembered how she linked her arm in mine at the picnic, and once again I thought my heart would burst. I wanted to rip the tubes from her arms and carry her away from all this. But that was senseless. I stood and paced at the foot of her bed.

"I have an idea, Celeste. I think there's something that I can do to get you better but I need your help."

She sighed. "There's nothing. It's my fault. I thought I was strong enough. Good enough."

"You're good enough for anyone."

She smiled. "If I were good enough things wouldn't have turned out this way. I was wrong."

"You have to promise to hang on for as long as you can. Can you tell me if there's anything at all that I can do to help you get better?"

She said nothing.

"Look at me, Celeste."

Her eyes turned toward me and I felt a stab in my stomach.

"It's going to be all right. I know it."

She licked her lips and nodded without conviction.

"My mother always says attitude is half the battle. Keep your spirits up. Hear me?"

She had a faraway look in her eye. "I'm so tired, Luke. I want to sleep. Everyone will be better off without me. There are things I did that I cannot possibly do. Things I did that are unforgivable. Things I've set in motion...."

I pulled the covers up around her neck and tucked her in. Then I brushed her forehead with my lips. "Rest. When I come back, things will be better. You'll see."

"My father...he's wrong about me, Luke. I'm not what he says. You have to believe me."

She lay so still I wondered if she were still breathing. I was tempted to run my fingers beneath her nostrils to feel her comforting breath raise the hairs on my knuckles. Instead, I gave her blanket one last tuck, turned and exited her room.

CREO

When I arrived at the Leatherman's cave I found Alec sitting near the entrance, head down staring at the ground. I kicked a stone toward him and he raised his eyes. I heard a loud piece of construction equipment and focused on the ridge above the cave where a bulldozer lurched across the pasture nearby.

"It's the Spi-Sea folks," said Alec. "They're expanding. Josh got scared waiting here and left, the lousy chicken."

"But they can't do that!" I said.

"My folks said the plant bought the property. No one's paid the taxes for years. The town was glad to have someone come in and take it over."

It was then that I saw the jumble of rocks in front of the cave. "Are they trying to seal it off?"

Alec shook his head. "They're going to level the entire area. Put up another stinking fish factory."

"Shit," I said. "Just what we need."

Alec ran his fingers through his hair. His face was drawn. He said, "I don't want her to die, Luke."

I clenched my fists hard and fought back the wave of emotions that his words caused to rise in me. "I have an idea," I said. "Not much of one, but we don't have many options."

Alec met my eyes with his damp ones. "Did you find anything out from her? Is there anything we can we possibly do?"

I shook my head. "She didn't tell me anything."

"Damn."

"Look," I said, planting my hands on my thighs, "it seems to me that she can't survive without this spot."

Alec picked up a rock and threw it forcefully. "I'm not sure she can survive with it."

"That may be," I said measuring my words, "but this is the only chance she has. This cave can keep her alive. She could recharge here, heal. I've seen her do it before."

"Maybe we can find another cave that works the same way for her." He eyed the bulldozer, which was now headed in our direction. "Maybe we can kidnap her from the hospital and keep her in a dark place for a long time." We both knew we were grasping for a hold in an impossible situation.

I said, "We don't have time to find out if there is any other cave, and the dark isn't going to do it for her. She's beyond that."

He picked up another stone and tossed it from hand to hand. "For all we know this cave won't matter at all." He shook his head sadly. "Who am I kidding? It's me, Luke. If she loves me she can't cope no matter what we do. You heard her father. I'm sapping her of any strength she has, so the hell with the cave."

"Maybe it's time we brought the mountain to Mohammed," I said. "That way we'd know for sure."

"There is no mountain, and no Mohammed." His eyes were cold.

"I don't believe that." I sat down beside him on the boulder and we watched the bulldozer clear a swath of land above where we sat. "And I don't believe her father either. There's something else going on with

Celeste. I feel it." Several tall birches fell with a crack. The driver inside the cab waved at us to move away but we ignored him. He shifted the bulldozer and headed back to the other side of the field toward the Spi-Sea plant.

I said, "Are we going to mope and let them destroy the one chance we have of saving her? I've seen what this place does for her. I'm not saying I understand it, but it's our only chance. There's something down there that we might be able to harness for her."

Alec looked at me and a small smile crossed his face. I laughed and he said, "Are you thinking what I'm thinking?"

I nodded. "You always were a damn good fighter."

Off in the distance we could see that the bulldozer driver had reached a trailer where several men sat surrounded by large plans. They were wasting no time building the new plant. We scrambled over the boulders that covered the entrance to the cave and found we could squeeze inside the small opening. Alec and I hurried into the depths of the cave and when we reached the room where Celeste usually sang and tossed her strange jacks, I let out a low moan. The floor of the space was in shambles, with boulders and rocks littering the dirt. A large rift in the ground prevented us from going any deeper into the cave.

"Now what?" asked Alec.

"We have to get to the lake that's below here." I looked around. "Let's see if we can fill in enough to bridge the gap," I said. We tossed rocks and small boulders into the opening in the floor. Periodically the cave trembled and shook. The earth above and below was unstable and we both knew it could give way at any moment. I heard the bulldozer moving overhead.

"We can't stay," I said to Alec. "It's too dangerous." The task now seemed impossible. "What could I have been thinking?"

Alec ignored me and continued throwing things into the maw below him. "Oh yes, we can. Why don't you go meet our new bulldozer buddies? It'll give me some time to get acquainted with our new hangout here."

"There isn't much time," I said.

"So what are you waiting for? A written invitation? Get going!"

I raced to the entrance and scrambled up the cliff where I confronted the operator of the rig, a red-haired, burly fellow in a bright orange T-shirt.

"What the hell…are you boys crazy?" he called down from his cab. "I thought I saw two people over here. This is a construction site. Get the hell out of here," he said, waving his tan cap at me.

"My friend is down there," I said, pointing to the cave.

"Your friend and you are both going to be arrested if you don't disappear in five minutes. The sheriff will be on his way in a jiffy if I call," said the driver. He sat back and lit a cigarette as the bulldozer belched diesel into the air. "My foreman is waiting for me to tell him to do that."

"You can't clear this area. That cave down there has been here forever. It's not right," I said.

"Kid, I'm just doing my job. I've got my orders, understand?"

I knew that if I continued to argue, in a few minutes we would see the flashing lights of a county police car approaching. Alec was not within sight or earshot as he was still trying to fill in that gaping hole. My heart sank at the memory of the size of the hole in Celeste's retreat. There was no way Alec could ever throw enough stuff into the maw to make it passable. Maybe the best thing would be to let the bulldozer level the place and to hell with the consequences. My idea was a long shot and what right did I have to draw Alec into it, to be so arrogant that it would solve Celeste's problems?

"Kid? Did you hear me? You've got five minutes."

I turned and headed back into the cave as the rig operator bellowed, "I'm not kidding. Get your asses out of that cave now!" His words echoed against the stone walls.

When I reached Alec, I found that he had constructed a small bridge across the large hole using a couple of logs. He grinned at me.

"Not bad for a drop-out Boy Scout," he said. "Don't look down and we'll be fine."

"You first," I said.

"Piece of cake," said Alec. I saw him tentatively climb onto the log. Then he yelled, "Geronimo!" and raced across. "What are you waiting for, Looner?"

I took a deep breath and muttered, "You can do this. It's just a hole."

I fixed my eyes on the other side and stepped onto the log. I looked down at my feet and extended my arms to the side. I held my breath and swiftly walked across the log.

Once on the other side, Alec clapped me on the back, "Hurry," he said. Soon we reached the lake where Celeste had taken me. The two of us stood side by side next to the inky water. I shined my flashlight and noticed that something was different about the surface. I could hear water rushing somewhere below us, not something I had heard in the past.

"What's going on?" asked Alec. "It didn't look like this when Celeste took me here."

I felt a pang at the knowledge that she had shared this spot with him. But what could I expect? I said, "The lake's emptying."

"Damn. They must have ruptured something with their bulldozing."

"Celeste told me that the waters from this lake restore her energy. I'm figuring that maybe if we bring her some of this water it might revive her enough to get her here. When I gave her some stones from this cave, she felt better. The water may be a cure."

"But if it's draining away, what good will it do? We'll run out of water." He turned panicky eyes to me. "And even if this does help, how will we get her out of the hospital? They don't let sick people leave just because they want to."

I held up my hand to silence him. "First, we have to figure out a way to stop the leak from draining it away," I said. "I have a feeling Celeste will go where she wants regardless of the hospital."

We studied the dark surface and surrounding rocks. Alec jumped onto a boulder and then waded into the water. "Look, over there," he said, pointing at a bubbling spot. "It's like a huge bathtub. There's a hole down over there. See?"

I followed his hand with my flashlight and could see a small whirlpool. Alec waded toward it. "Maybe we can throw something down there."

I looked around the cave. There wasn't much handy to try to toss into the lake.

Above us sirens wailed then drew to a stop. "Damn," I said. "We don't have much time. The foreman on the job caught me up there and called the cops."

"Now what?"

"I'll occupy them for a bit," I said. "You try to figure out some way to stop this thing from drying up. And then get the heck away. I'll call you after dinner and we'll make plans to get Celeste here. And bring some jars for the water."

A few moments later I greeted a policeman and the red-haired driver at the entrance to the cave. The officer spoke. "Son, this is private property. I'm going to have to ask you to leave."

"Sure thing," I said.

The rig operator said, "He's not alone. There's someone else down there. Where the heck is that other kid?"

"No one's down there. I don't know what you're talking about."

The driver narrowed his gaze. "That's not what he said before, officer."

"Son, you're going to have to tell me if anyone else is down in that cave." He put his hands on his hips.

The sound of the bulldozer starting up caught their attention. The rig driver peered over to his vehicle which was belching diesel. "What the hell is going on…" he called out. "Someone's in the cab!"

With glee I saw that it was Josh who had climbed behind the wheel of the rig which he was now driving up and over the top of the cave, toward us.

"Bombs away!" shouted Josh. "Lookout below!"

I had no idea that he could drive a bulldozer, and it soon became apparent that neither did he. The rig weaved and turned erratically on its path.

"Get off, you idiot! Turn off the engine!" shouted the red-faced operator. "You're gonna kill someone!"

In a matter of seconds, Josh dropped the front end and plowed into a great pile of rocks and dirt, scraping it toward us. The policeman and rig operator scrambled out of the way, shouting, "Stop! Stop!" as the debris fell into the opening above the cave. Great mounds of dust poured out of the entrance and all of us raced away as the earth rumbled.

Josh leapt from the moving bulldozer and it careened and turned over on its side. I held my breath as chaos ensued. The police officer headed straight for Josh. In the confusion, I scrambled up and over the mound of dirt and by the time the dust settled I was high in the branches of one of the tall pine trees staring down at the scene below. I watched as the police officer slapped handcuffs on Josh and led him to his car.

"I don't know where your partner took off to, but we'll find him eventually," said the policeman, scanning the area. "For now, I'm taking you into the station. You can fill me in on your buddy's address and name when we get there."

He opened the door to of the police car and shoved Josh into the back seat.

"If that other kid shows up again give me a call, Red," he said to the dazed rig operator who nodded and scratched his head.

"What the hell am I gonna tell my foreman? Shit. It's quitting time and I've got to deal with this."

The officer said, "I'm taking the kid in and calling for a tow truck. They're going to have to get that rig upright again. Son, are you ever in trouble," the policeman said, shaking his head.

I stayed as quiet as I could. Soon the cursing rig operator headed off to the company trailer. I watched the police car until I could no longer see the clouds of dust it raised on the dirt path away from the cave. Then I climbed down and checked the entrance to the cave. There still was room to enter. Josh hadn't sealed it off and I breathed a sigh of relief. I shouted, "Alec! Are you there?" No answer came back. Again I called down to him and this time I thought I could hear a faint, "Go home. Everything's fine."

I was about to climb on my bike when fear gripped me. What if Alec was trapped? Maybe the entrance to the cave wasn't as open as I had assumed. My stomach lurched at the thought of what might have happened to my friend. I climbed to Celeste's special spot and looked down at the Spi-Sea plant. Above me the Crandon Dam lay brimful and the late afternoon sun glinted off its surface. I thought I heard something in the cave below. I listened hard and heard distant rumbling, and then I thought I heard someone whistling. For an instant I believed that somehow Celeste had gotten better, that it was her voice rising up to me. I expected to hear her singing a show tune in a few seconds. The whistling faded and I knew it was only the wind swirling through the rocks below.

I crawled into the cave on my belly the way Celeste had shown me, approaching the lake from the other side. When I reached the water I saw Alec wading around the perimeter. I tossed a stone into the lake and he jumped.

I called out, "What the heck are you doing in that water?"

"Luke! You should have gone home." He waded toward me.

"The cops caught Josh. He drove the Spi-Sea bulldozer over the cliff and it's out of commission. I hope they don't come back and find us here."

"Josh? He came through?" Alec pumped his fist in the air.

"You'd have loved seeing him behind the wheel of the bulldozer."

Alec moved across the lake slowly. As he walked, the inky water swirled about him. I shuddered. I didn't think I would be able to join him in it. Who knew what lurked at the bottom?

Alec grinned at me. "I knew I could figure something out to help Celeste. Though I have to admit this place is creepy." He shuddered. "The dark here really gets to you."

Below us the earth rumbled again and I looked over my shoulder. "Alec, it's not safe for us to stay down here. That construction crew could come back. And so could the cops. And this dark, it'll get to you."

Alec shook his head. "Not a chance. It's after five and that driver is down at O'Reilly's pub. He won't be back till Monday morning I figure." His eyes glowed and I didn't like the look of them. "And even if Josh tells the cops who was here, they'll be going to your house looking for you, not here."

Suddenly Alec's body dropped a few inches below the water. He let out a yell and I thought that some creature might have grabbed him. I shined my light on his half-immersed body.

"Jesus, Alec, what the hell is going on."

"I found it, Luke. I found the spot where the lake is draining. It really is like a big bathtub."

"It could be draining from a dozen places."

He shook his head. "I thought that too. But it isn't. It's only one spot, not where we thought before either." He twisted his arms around his torso and I saw him sink a little farther down. "I'm wedging myself into this spot to see if it helps."

"Alec, you can't do this."

"Watch me."

He moved to the right a bit and then his torso sank another few inches. Alec stopped moving and I held my breath. Then he went under a few more inches so that the water was up to his chest.

"I think that's it."

"You can't stay in that water forever. Even if it works and you plug up the hole when you come out it will sink again. Don't be foolish. Let me just try bringing her some of the water. And you shouldn't stay here." I remembered how wobbly I'd become after staying only a short time.

His eyes met mine and my heart skipped a beat as I realized what he was up to. "You've got to come out of there, Alec!"

He shook his head. "Why should I? Maybe you want to join me."

"The water's rising." My voice caught in my throat. I could feel fear building in my chest. To grab him I would have to enter the water, and I couldn't bring myself to do that. It was more than the water. It was the growing dark that threatened. I trained my light on Alec and ran it over the surface. Something strange hovered above the water and I wiped my eyes trying to see more clearly.

Alec said, "I don't want to live without her, Luke. You're right about this spot. It's not easy to understand, but I can feel it." He nodded in the direction where my eyes were focused. "You feel it, don't you? There's something creepy here. I'm the only chance she has."

I licked my lips. "Stop talking crazy! There has to be something else we can do. Besides, when they pull you out the whole thing will just start draining away again. Then what?"

Alec leaned back against the wall. "As long as I do this, I'm betting things will be fine for Celeste, and that's enough for me. Beyond that, I don't care." He whooped with glee. "Would you look at that?" He pointed to where the water of the lake pooled around him. "It has no place to go anymore and it's filling up again. I only wish I could see Celeste again."

"Alec, you can't do this. You've lost your mind."

"Take care of her for me, Luke. I know how you feel about her."

I hung my head.

"It's okay. I understand."

"Can you move your legs at all?"

Alec shook his head. "The pressure is pretty strong under there."

I didn't know what to do.

Alec narrowed his gaze. "You mustn't tell anyone where I am. Especially not Celeste."

I refused to agree to his conditions. I reached in my pocket and withdrew the small jar Celeste had given to me what seemed so long ago and I unscrewed the cap.

"What the…" said Alec as a blinding flash lit the cave.

"Celeste gave it to me. She said I'd know when I needed to use it and I figure this is as good a time as any." The light grew brighter in the cave and spread out around us, reaching even the farthest corners and nooks.

"Holy shit! Would you look at that!" crowed Alec, shading his eyes from the brilliant light.

I sensed the dark scurrying at my feet, down and out of view. A large ball of brightness formed over the water and hovered over the inky lake, humming slightly like the TV did when the test pattern came on late at night. The ball sank gradually into the water and the hum diminished as the light spread beneath the surface. It was as though the lake had swallowed the sun. The water changed color from dark black to navy then to an aqua. It continued to fade, first to a pale blue, and gradually the water became crystal clear so that all that lay beneath the surface was visible. The level of the water no longer rose, nor fell. A calm fell over the cave and I could feel my pulse grow slower.

"I don't know how long that will last," I said, peering into the far recesses of the cave, then up at the ceiling.

Alec smiled contentedly at me. "It's beautiful under there. Look at the colors in the floor, in the rocks."

I couldn't share in his amazement, as I feared what might happen when I left him. I filled the now-empty jar with lake water and tucked it back inside my pocket, then I placed my flashlight beside Alec.

I said. "I'll be back as soon as I can."

"Take your time," said Alec. "I'm not going anywhere."

"Damn you, Alec. You're so stubborn and so stupid."

"Luke, don't you dare tell anyone about this."

I turned and walked out of the cave. I didn't know how long Celeste's light would be able to keep the dark at bay for him and as I walked away from the light I sensed a presence waiting to overtake the space once again. When I reached the entrance and climbed out through the small hole, the darkness at the mouth of the cave was blacker than ever and I had trouble seeing without my flashlight. Something ran over the back of my neck and a chill went down my spine. I swatted at the air and wasn't at all sure that it was my imagination that I felt an oppressiveness swirling about me. I made my way out to the evening light, which was a welcome relief.

Alec's last call to me echoed in my ears. "I can save her, Luke. I know I can. Don't deny me this chance. I'm not afraid of the dark. Fuck the dark! Come and get me dark!"

My head ached at the thought of Alec and what he was doing. I wanted Celeste to live, but not at his expense. Yet there seemed nothing I could do. He was bigger and stronger than I was and I couldn't possibly force him from his position. I gnawed at my lip and wracked my brain for an idea, for a way out of this dilemma. I had to get help, but my muddy thoughts wouldn't let me see which way to turn.

CHAPTER TWENTY-ONE

For the second time that day, I furtively entered Celeste's room, carefully avoiding the nursing station. Celeste was sitting upright in her bed and she grinned and waved at me with far more strength than she had exhibited earlier. Her hair gleamed against her hospital gown, her pink cheeks looked fresh, dewy. She looked the picture of health. Her jacks lay on her tray table, and she tossed one onto the stainless steel and chuckled.

"Would you look at that? I'm better than ever at this."

I stood at the foot of her bed and watched the sun play off her hair. The golden color drew me in and back to the time I first met her, which seemed like much more than a few weeks ago.

"Luke, it's amazing. Look at me! I can't believe I was able to come out of that, that…" her voice trailed off.

"Did they tell you what they found?"

She shrugged. "As best they know. The doctor said they thought it was like having an electrical storm in my brain, only it had lodged here." She touched her hand to her chest and I felt a pang in my own.

"For a time there we were all worried."

She nodded. Her eyes grew wide. "I felt trapped. Sometimes I could hear and see everything that was going on around me. Other times I just don't remember anything." She shook her head and shuddered. "And there was this vision that kept coming to me of a swirling cloud, of black and white, and of water. And of darkness...."

I forced a smile. "Do you have any idea when they will let you out?"

She shook her head. "They want to place me under observation. They don't understand how I recovered. Frankly, neither do I."

I sat on her bed and took her hand in mine.

"I'm better, Luke. I can feel it. They can't keep me here and I'm not going to let them. There's nothing to observe."

"Your father will have to agree to release you."

"He'll agree. One thing about my dad, he listens to me. He's afraid of me. I talked to him and he's going to see what he can do. He sounded so happy." She snorted, then leaned back and looked out the window. A few wisps of cloud painted streaks across the bright moon, which hung low on the still-bright horizon. She said, "I'm worried about Alec. It's not like him to not visit me. Unlike you who appears twice in one day."

The mention of Alec's name caused my head to jerk. I bit my tongue. Every fiber in my body screamed that I should tell Celeste what Alec was doing. I tried to form words but none came.

"I have to get back to the cave, Luke. There's some unfinished business down there for me." She narrowed her gaze and wiggled her fingers. A small rainbow appeared on the wall, then spread out over the floor. "I'm ready. I've been playing at this game for too long." She threw the jacks on the table and one of them spun wildly, then clattered to the floor.

I stooped and picked it up but the hot metal of the prongs caused me to drop it quickly on her tray. "Getting to the cave again isn't going to be easy," I said.

She held my gaze, aware of my unease. "What's going on, Luke? You look like a ghost."

I blurted, "The Spi-Sea folks are expanding, taking over most of the land above them, including the cave. They're going to bulldoze everything, level it, and build a second plant on the cleared land."

She bolted upright. "They can't do that."

"They already are."

Her eyes were wide. "The lake, the cave…if they go, I don't know what will happen."

I groaned. "We knew it. Alec and I figured you get your power there." I wished there was something I could say to comfort her, but nothing came to mind.

Celeste slid herself off the bed onto the floor and rose on wobbly legs.

"What are you doing?" I said, lending her an arm to lean on.

"I can't sit here and let them destroy that cave, not yet."

"Celeste, you can't possibly take on a construction site and the Spi-Sea folks."

"I survived this damn illness for a reason, Luke. That much is clear to me."

I looked down at my feet and avoided her eyes, but she searched mine out.

"What is it?" she implored. "You've been acting really weird ever since you came in here."

"Celeste, I have to tell you something."

"I'm not waiting around, Luke. Waiting isn't wise, it's for useless fools." She reached into a drawer and found her socks and jeans. She slipped behind a curtain to dress and I bit my lip.

"It's Alec," I said.

Celeste peered at me from behind the curtain waiting for me to continue.

"Oh God, it's Alec," I said, aware of the ticking of the clock on the wall.

"What about Alec?" she said slowly.

"He's in the cave."

She gripped the curtain in her fists and waited for me to go on.

"He went there this afternoon. So did I. The lake was losing water and he jumped in. He's convinced that your health is linked to the level of that water. Seeing you now, it seems he's right."

She moaned out loud. "Oh no, is that what's been going on!"

"He made me promise not to tell you, but I don't think he can survive long down there. It's so dark, Celeste, and that water can't be good for him. I opened one of your jars for him."

She threw aside the curtain and raced to her closet. "He can't do this. He's not the only one who will die if he stays in the cave. It's not just the water that's alive down there! My jars aren't enough, not by a long shot. Opening one will make things worse." She pulled on her sandals and tied her hair back in a ponytail. "Oh God, it's all my fault."

"He said if you couldn't live he didn't want to live either. He jumped into that water and set himself up as a drainplug. Like the little Dutch Boy."

"The crazy fool." She pointed a finger at me. "Get home with your mom and sister as soon as you can. Stay in your basement."

"What are you going to do?"

She laughed a humorless laugh. "Whatever I can."

I grabbed her by the arm. "Why are you here? It's time you told me what you know. I want to help you. So does Alec."

She licked her lips. "We don't have time."

I refused to let go and gripped tighter. Celeste sank onto the bed and I said, "You're not going anywhere until you tell me what you know. Why do you do these things? What's happening in that cave?"

"It's better if you don't ask me questions."

I could feel my hand growing hot where I held her. The heat became unbearable and I dropped her arm. "Better? For you maybe," I said, staring at my red palm. "Not for Alec, that's for sure. He could die out there in that damn place. Not for me either."

She looked pale again. My fingers had left red imprints on her skin.

"I could paralyze you right now," she said. "Is that what you want?" She raised a hand and a small lightning bolt appeared on the floor.

"That's not going to solve anything."

"Why can't you leave me alone?" The bolt disappeared and she said, "This is hard, but it's my battle not yours."

"Let me help you, Celeste. I can help, I know it. There has to be a reason, a way for us to get out of this."

She sank onto the bed and held her head in her hands. "I'm to blame. Ever since I fell to earth."

"Go on."

"I remember falling with my family in a blinding light. I was angry, lashing out at everyone and everything."

"You were an infant."

"But no ordinary infant."

"What happened?"

"I'm not sure. It's all so foggy."

"Tell me, Celeste. What do you remember?"

She pressed her fingers to her temples and I could see her shoulders shake. "I hated them all." Tears coursed down her cheeks. "It's not something I'm comfortable talking about. It's painful for me to remember any of what happened."

"Keep talking."

"Every day, Luke, every day I used to ask God if He would have me. Sometimes I asked him a hundred times a day, but He didn't answer. I've fallen as far as I can and there's no way back. That's what my father told me." She turned to me and her eyes held an ungodly glow to them. I shivered.

"But my father wasn't right. He swore I was a devil child and I used to believe him. There's no getting rid of my basic nature, so I suppose my father came to his conclusion logically. God certainly does ignore me."

"I've seen the things you do, Celeste. Your basic nature as you call it is to do good."

She held up her hand. "No. Not good. That's what I've let you see."

"Celeste, I've seen you, seen how you helped Joanie. You've helped me."

Her face was dark now. "You don't know what you're talking about. None of that matters." She pointed at her feet. "What you've seen is only a small part of me. My father thinks I'm a dark angel, from hell, but that's not true. You have to believe me. I could never fit in in hell." She laughed and the familiar silvery sound filled the room. "Hear that? It's heaven and angels' wings. How can I be a dark angel with a laugh like that?"

"I was thinking that myself."

"I'm no dark angel, and I'm no angel either. I can control the weather. I can create tornadoes, hurricanes, lightning. That's where my talents lay. One day, in the middle of a tornado I created, I saved a child I had ripped from her mother's arms. When I did that I was full of grief, full of agony. Saving a life was unbearable to me. But that doesn't mean that I won't do it. I can deny what I am to a certain degree. I've learned that."

"What are you saying, Celeste? Where do you fit in?"

She sighed. "That's what I've been trying to figure out my whole life. I'm caught between two places. When I do good I feel lousy and when I do bad I feel lousy."

The clock on the wall ticked loudly.

"So where does that leave you?"

"I can control the weather. I'm a freak of nature." She closed her eyes. "But I've never been happy with that."

"You can make it rain, hail. I've seen you do that. It's amazing."

"The weather is parlor tricks to me. I wasn't satisfied with being a weather girl." She chuckled derisively, and went on, "I'm drawn to the dark, and to the light. I seek the light and capture it as best I can, in those little jars."

I remembered all the times I had felt as though the dark itself were present when I was with her.

"I learned to reach deep down and make my heart into the whitest, purest thing I can imagine, and then I summon the dark. But it's the light that keeps me going, keeps me from succumbing to the dark." She opened her eyes and met mine. "I brought more and more light to the cave."

"In all those little jars?"

"It was wrong to do. My experiment backfired and I found the dark increasing. So I worked with it, brought more light. For days I figured I had regulated everything, brought things back to the way they were. But then I went back and saw that I hadn't corrected anything. The dark was increasing again, growing stronger and stronger." Her eyes were wide and her chin trembled. "I couldn't control anything. I never could."

I stood and held my hand out to her and she let my hand cover hers. Then with her other hand she tossed all of her jacks at once onto the stainless tray table where they careened around and spun wildly.

"You should go be with your family," she said. "I don't know if I can do any good at all for Alec. It's not safe for you to go into that cave. It's not safe for me either." She shuddered. "But that doesn't matter anymore. I have to try."

197

"Wherever you're going, I'm coming along."

"That's not a good idea. I don't know if I can do this, Luke. Trying to reset the balance is so hard. That darkness, it slams you. Last time, it was so bad, I could barely move, and then I collapsed. Oh no, I really blew it. Who knows what might happen to you if you go down there? Who knows what will happen to the world if I don't!"

Her words chilled me but didn't shake my resolve. "I'm coming with you."

Celeste scooped up the jacks and tucked them in her pocket. As we exited her room, I was aware of a drop in atmospheric pressure, almost as if air were racing down the halls toward us. My eardrums popped several times and I looked at Celeste wondering what she was up to.

"A little distraction, that's all it is," said Celeste. She pointed at the nursing station where a sudden gust of wind from an open window sent papers flying into the air. Celeste and I pressed ourselves flat against the marble corridor and slid past the station while the nurses ran after the papers that remained just out of their reach. On the way to the elevator we passed a window that rattled in the wind. Outside the clouds had turned deep gray and thunder rumbled ominously.

In the lobby I called my mother, as I knew she would be worrying about me. Outside the wind howled mightily.

"Luke, where are you? The police left here a little while ago. They want to talk to you. I told them I didn't know where you'd gone off to. What's going on?"

"I can't explain, Mom. But it's going to be all right. You have to trust me."

My mother said, "There's a storm coming. The wind is awful here. I don't want you out in it. Do you hear me?"

I looked out the window at the gathering storm and my heart raced at the thought of the fury that was about to be unleashed. I feared what Celeste might do.

"Stay inside with Joanie, in the basement, Mom. Everything will be ok." The wind in the lobby whipped the words from my mouth.

"What'd you say? I can't hear you!" yelled my mother.

"Stay inside! In the basement. I have to go. I'll talk to you soon as I can.

Tell Joanie I'll see her later."

As we leaned into the gale in the parking lot, the wind whipped Celeste's hair about her face. "Celeste, this is crazy. It's like a tornado is about to hit."

She pointed at a bicycle rack. "We'll ride to the cave. The wind will be at your back as much as I can have it there." Her words were whipped into the wind.

Soon we were pedaling madly toward the Leatherman's cave. As we rode, the rain flew sideways. It stung my arms and legs and blinded me. I could barely see the pavement and focused as best I could on Celeste's bobbing ponytail before me. The ride was far more difficult than riding in the fog behind the DDT truck. One minute the wind was at my back, the next it hit me head on. I wasn't sure which way I was going and had to stop several times to get my bearings and catch my breath.

"Keep up, Luke!" Celeste shouted back at me.

I gritted my teeth, put my head down and rode on instinct. Inside my pants pocket the jar of lake water burned against my leg, then turned cold. I put my head down and raced the clouds and the wind, raced as hard and fast as I ever had in my life, to the Leatherman's cave, to the only place that held hope for the future.

CHAPTER TWENTY-TWO

The overwhelming dark is what I remember most as we reached the cave and dismounted our bikes. Clouds blotted out the waning sun, and the dark swirled around me in great damp whorls that sucked the breath from my mouth and nose. Wind whipped at my head and I instinctively cupped my ears with my hands.

"Follow me. Fast as you can!" yelled Celeste.

We leaned into the wind and rain as huge drops assaulted us. Out of breath and exhausted from the ride and the sucking wind, I followed Celeste into the mouth of the Leatherman's abode. I waited a few seconds for my eyes to adjust to the lack of light, and in that time I lost sight of Celeste. The wind howled in my ears and my eyes were barely functioning. I felt as though the dark from outside had crowded into the cave and surrounded me. I took a few steps forward but the blackness grew thicker and more impenetrable. I held onto the sides of the rock wall and propelled myself into Celeste's lair only half-seeing.

"Celeste! Where are you?" I called, my heart beating wildly in my chest. Outside a storm raged unlike any I had ever witnessed in my life. Inside I felt as though the dark were watching me, hovering next to me. I forced myself not to think about my surroundings or what was happening and plunged forward. Celeste was gone, nowhere in sight.

I called again, "Celeste! Alec!" but only silence answered me.

My skin crawled. The dark had a presence that clung to me, the way humidity does. Cloying damp snaked over me and made me want to wipe the feeling off my arms, my legs, my face. It was not a pleasant feeling being wrapped in this dark. It was tomblike, suffocating, coiling around my chest like a boa constrictor.

I gasped for air, blinked and realized that I had moved from semi-dark to pitch blackness. I held my hand in front of my face and couldn't see a thing. My heart pounded. I didn't usually fear the dark, but I was frightened now, for this was not the familiar dark I knew, the one that had a relationship with light. This was an oppressive presence with a life of its own. I did not want to think about what that meant as the murkiness took turns crowding around me, then receding as though looking for something.

I forced myself to go forward. Eventually, drenched in sweat, I somehow reached the room that held the inky lake. I couldn't see in the pitch black, but I could tell by the smell of the water that I was in the underground chamber.

"Alec? Are you there?"

No answer.

"Celeste? Answer me!"

I heard a match being struck and then saw a soft glow of a lantern, which revealed Celeste, who kneeled on the edge of the lake trembling. Her voice was hollow, flat. "This can't be."

She held her hands to her head shaking it slowly side to side and moaning. I moved to her and followed her gaze in the thin light but I recoiled at the sight below. At our feet, at the lake's bottom, lay Alec's body. His unseeing eyes stared at us, up through the water in an eerie death gaze. The water shimmered as though it was a mirror and I wanted to wipe out the hideous reflection, wanted to reach down and shake him. Tears ran down Celeste's cheeks.

"My God," I said, gasping for air.

Celeste turned toward me. "Don't bring God into this. What kind of a God can allow things like this to happen?"

Her face was twisted, frightening. I licked my lips, trying to think of something to say or do. Celeste rose and held her hands up to the ceiling.

She gave off something as bleak and frightening as the dark and I found I could not look at her for long. Yet, no sooner would I look away than I was drawn back to her, for at her core there seemed to be a radiance that was in direct counterpoint to the bleakness. She seemed to be grappling with something, holding back the dark as well as the light from her lantern.

Her body jerked and Celeste let out the most unholy sound I have ever heard, a sound so loud that the earth beneath my knees vibrated, and my eardrums threatened to burst. She rattled the heavens with that scream. I fell to the ground and buried my head in my hands. The earth shook violently. I clawed at the dirt and prayed that I would not slip into the lake as the earth and stones beneath me buckled and opened.

Celeste shouted, "I won't accept this!"

The pressure in the cave dropped and my hair stood on end. I flattened myself against cold stone, rubbing my fingers raw trying to hold on. Lightning struck and struck again in the cave, coming closer and closer to me and to Celeste.

Rain began to fall inside. Later, I learned that the rain had fallen inside all the houses of Faith Junction that evening. In the cave, at first it fell slowly in large drops, but then it increased in intensity. The wind came next and soon it was raining sideways. I clung to a jagged piece of stone and knew we were at the heart of a terrible storm. The rain whipped and stung my eyes and I could barely make out Celeste's form though she was only a few feet away.

Celeste shouted again, "You can turn me away, but how dare you take away the life of someone good and pure. I will not stand by and watch you destroy what doesn't deserve to be destroyed."

She pointed to the ceiling of the cave and with a great crack the rough stone opened. I wiped my eyes to clear them. In the sky above, clouds whirled in a circle so black and threatening that my heart went cold at the sight.

"The Prince of Darkness has no hold on me. I renounced him years ago. The Prince of Peace will not abide my presence. If only He had it in His heart to allow me into His graces none of this would have occurred! I hold you both accountable!"

I feared that God and the devil both might appear, for that was whom she addressed. Suddenly, the water in the lake began to churn. The surface waters formed into a huge whirlpool. Round and round the water spun. The diameter grew until it encompassed the entire lake and had nowhere left to go. Out of the center of the whirlpool a funnel of water rose up. With a deafening roar the water funnel lifted up and out of the cave, sucking the contents of the lake into its core. The lake was no longer a lake, but lay empty. The darkness hovered at the edges. Above us the tornado hung in an eerie threatening sky

Alec's body lay limp on the floor of what had been Celeste's favorite pool of water. Celeste reached down and pulled him up. She cradled his head with her hands. She looked to the gloomy sky beyond the funnel cloud and then to the corners of the cave.

She shouted, "I curse both of you, light and dark! Neither of you is worth one of him. I renounce you both, for you are equally guilty!"

The earth rumbled ominously. I wanted to run but my legs would not move. Celeste smoothed back Alec's hair, and then she leaned over and kissed him gently on the lips. She raised her fist to the sky and shouted, "Take me. Take me and let him live. It's not right that he should perish. Let me die. There's no reason for me to go on. Send me where you will and stop this feuding! I was wrong, I know it. I was wrong to try to influence you, wrong to interfere with your balance!"

She fell in a heap over Alec. And then she looked up at the opening in the ceiling, up toward the dark clouds and oppressive tornado that circled above. She closed her eyes and I was aware of a pressure once again in my ears. I covered them with my hands, but this time the pressure was too much to bear. I felt one, then the other eardrum burst. Blood oozed out onto my fingertips. A bright flash of light illuminated the cave, blinding me, then a bolt of dark did the same. It was as though a battle was being fought in the cave. Celeste writhed on the floor. I concentrated hard on what was happening around me, trying to make sense of it.

A bolt of dark slithered across the floor directly toward her.

"No!" I shouted. "Get away!"

It entered her chest and she jolted upright. A bolt of lightning hit her directly in her breast and she collapsed again. Light and dark inhabited her, tore into her with a fury. Her body jerked. Her eyes flashed white then black, and her body twitched and writhed. She collapsed on the ground, her body steaming, giving off an acrid scent that left me gasping.

Something was present in the cave. Whatever it was, it terrified me even more than the sight of what had happened to Celeste. At any moment I expected the presence to take corporeal form and head for me. I wanted to run. This could not be happening. My hair felt alive with electrical impulses. I held my hands over my aching ears and made my way over to Celeste, afraid to look anywhere but at her. Her chest lay open, her heart a pulsing black and white mass that blinded me with its dazzling darkness. Evil raged around me, I was sure of it. At the same time, light shot through the cave like a laser, grazing walls and boulders.

Her words rasped in her throat. "I don't have much time, Luke. But I'm not going to give up. Not yet." She raised her fingers to the sky feebly. A storm rained down upon us the likes of which had never been seen in the last thousand years. Rivers of water flowed out of the cave down, down to the Spi-Sea plant below. The people of Faith Junction watched as their storm drains filled and the streets teemed with more runoff than any planner had ever imagined.

Still, the funnel of water that had been the lake hovered overhead in a large dark mass. The additional rains added to its size. The twister sucked up all the water in its path with the roar of a hundred lions. My ears ached and terror filled me. I clung to a rock but it was to no avail. I could feel myself being pulled upward. My grip was torn from the boulder beneath me. I gasped for air and held my breath as I tumbled up into the sky in a thick sea of water and mud. I entered the core of the tornado where I spun rapidly. Darkness blanketed me.

I awoke in a coughing fit, spitting up mud and water. I cleared dirt from my eyes and mouth and looked around. The tornado had dropped me on the promontory overlooking the Spi-Sea plant, Celeste's special spot. I hacked again. I wiped my face and watched as the tunnel of water traveled uphill where it hovered over the Crandon Dam. Slowly the tunnel sank into the already brimful dam, emptying its contents. Gradually the sky above calmed and the earth stopped shaking. Light and dark streaked across the sky then receded toward the horizon. It was over.

Beside me Celeste and Alec lay inert, covered in mud, twigs and rocks. I crawled to Celeste and felt her cold body. She was not breathing.

I heard a loud roar. The walls of the dam gave way and a sea of red-brown mud washed over the banks, sliding and destroying everything in its path. Had we not been so high we too would have been swept away. The mudslide did not stop until it had engulfed the Spi-Sea plant parking lot and half the factory. After the mud came a deafening deluge of water that had been trapped in the Crandon Dam. The water spread over the parking lot within seconds.

I gasped at the sight. The sun poked out of the clouds. I stood on wobbly legs trying to make sense of what had happened. There was no longer any darkness, that much was clear. A glittering lake lay where the plant had been.

All over town, the storm receded and left a golden glow. It was as if there were a lens across the top of the sky filtering all. People began clearing the debris from their lawns, marveling at what had occurred. Rainbows appeared in every abode.

My clothing hung in tatters, my hair was matted against my head. My ears no longer ached and I could hear once again. Beside me, Alec stirred. He vomited black water.

I jumped to my feet. My friend was back from the dead.

"Jesus, Alec, you're okay," I shouted. "You're okay!" I hugged him.

He lay back and closed his eyes. "Where am I?" he groaned.

My joy at his recovery was short-lived. Tears streamed down my face for Celeste lay on the ground lifeless. I knelt beside her and cradled her head. Her clothes were in tatters and I reached down gingerly and saw that her chest had healed over. A long scar lay at the point of entry of the bolts of light and dark.

Alec and I took turns trying to rouse her, but it was no use. I reached inside my pocket and miraculously found the small jar of lake water and unscrewed the top. I pressed the rim of the jar to her lips and let the water run a slivery course into her mouth.

"Please," I prayed, "please, let this work."

Her eyes flickered. She groaned and then spit up. Alec and I exchanged glances.

I said, "Can you get up? We should get out of here. The place is definitely not stable."

She shook her head and drew in a deep breath.

Alec stood on wobbly legs.

I leaned over and scooped up Celeste, alarmed at the lightness in my arms. "We have to get her out of here, now," I said.

But Celeste pressed her fingernails into my arm. "Wait. Not yet. I don't want to leave."

"I'm afraid of what might happen next. I want to get away from here," I said.

She shook her head. "Take me to my ship, Luke," she whispered in my ear. "I want to look out. Please."

I nodded and climbed farther up the ridge to the spot I knew she meant, to her ship. Alec walked slowly behind me.

When I reached her favorite vista, I placed Celeste gently on the ground. Below us the newly formed lake glinted in the late afternoon sun.

Celeste gasped at the sheer beauty of the scene. "Would you look at that?" She pointed to the lake. "Now that's an improvement!"

In spite of what we had been through the three of us began to laugh. The Spi-Sea plant was entombed in the watery grave of the newly formed lake and all around us the air smelled sweet and lovely. Birds swooped over the scene sending calls over the new landscape. Our enjoyment was short-lived as Celeste trembled and I grew worried.

"We should get you home and out of those wet clothes," I said.

She waved me off. "Let me stay for a bit. I can't explain how good it feels to sit here and look down at that sight. I don't have much time left, but I think things are finally all right here."

I drew in a deep breath and wondered what would happen next. Perhaps Celeste was out of the woods and we all could rest easier. The harmony of light and dark all around us was not something I was imagining. Things felt better than they had in days, weeks.

After a time I scooped Celeste up in my arms, and carried her over the boulders and debris. Alec moved slowly behind me. The sun was low in the sky and there was a noticeable coolness to the air. Celeste pressed her head into my chest wearily and when I saw how pale she had grown, I feared that she would not make it to her home. As we walked along the dirt path I saw her father's truck heading toward us. He bumped along at a furious pace and when he reached us he swung the door wide.

"Sweet Jesus," he exclaimed. Mr. Carey took his daughter from my arms and placed her in the bed of his truck. "The whole town is in a state of emergency. She's really done it this time," he said. "That was one helluva storm." He scratched his head. "Though it does seem that there isn't much damage to anyone or anything, other than the Spi-Sea Plant. That's what the radio is saying."

Alec and I climbed into the bed of the truck with Celeste stretched out on the floor between us. Mr. Carey lifted our bikes which had been unscathed into the flatbed. Then he covered Celeste with blankets, turned the vehicle around and headed back toward his farm.

As we bumped along the rutted path, a huge rainbow arched across the sky. I looked up and marveled at the colors, then I realized that there were rainbows everywhere. The glass of the front windshield reflected the sun and I could see a rainbow stretch across the cracked vinyl seat beneath Mr. Carey's massive thighs. Another small one danced across the corrugated metal flatbed at my feet. But Celeste lay lifeless beside me in the back of the truck. I glanced at Alec and neither of us would meet each other's eyes. Tears streamed down his face. An eerie stillness lay over Faith Junction and my heart railed against what I feared. If she died, where and what would any of us be without Celeste?

❦

Mr. Carey tucked Celeste into her bed with a worried look on his face. He tenderly stroked her hair, pursed his lips and said, "I suppose we've done what we can, boys. It's out of our hands now."

"She's not a devil," I told him. "You have to understand that."

I explained to him what Celeste had told me about her struggle with the dark, about how she had upset the delicate balance it had with the light. When I finished he wiped a tear from his eyes. He said, "I've been so wrong about so many things. So many years wasted." He clenched his fists and I could see his shoulders shake. "I love her so much."

"They weren't wasted," I said and I reached over and touched his arm. "Celeste's what she is and none of us can ever change that."

He shook his head sadly. "No one's to blame for any of this. But that doesn't make it any easier. If only I could have helped her, if only anyone could have."

☙❧

Alec and I rode home beneath the glorious rainbow, but there was no pot of gold or reward for us. When I reached my front lawn, I found Joanie in a tizzy on the driveway. She danced around holding Celeste's tiny jar aloft. I parked my bike in the garage and she followed me inside.

"Look, look," she said, pointing to the jar.

"I'm tired, Joanie," I said, trying to brush past her but she would not be denied.

"Look! Look now!" she said as she thrust her jar under my nose.

I glanced at the jar to appease her as quickly as possible and caught my breath. There, inside Joanie's jar, was an exquisite rainbow. It sparkled and shone no matter which way she turned the jar. I looked up at the sky, but the rainbow overhead had dissipated. We went inside where dozens of tiny rainbows danced on the walls causing Joanie to shriek with glee and my mother to come running.

As my mother pressed me to her breast, I wondered what on earth was happening to the world as I knew it. My heart ached. Without Celeste, life was not worth living. Rainbows be damned. You might as well take away the sun.

CHAPTER TWENTY-THREE

Joanie, Alec and I hung Joanie's flag on one of the first days of autumn. We headed to Lake Parrot, the colorful leaves rustling under our feet, the trees stark silhouettes in the late afternoon sun. Joanie sang loudly as she marched along the path.

"Would you look at how happy she is? It's so good to see her this way," I said to Alec as Joanie raced ahead of us. Her mood was infectious and I found myself grinning from ear to ear.

Alec smiled down at me. "She's a great kid. You're lucky to have a sister."

We broke into a run and followed Joanie as she raced along the shoreline, the three of us whooping and hollering.

"That one, that one," Joanie said, picking up speed. She had selected a tree and I craned my neck to determine which tall one caught her interest.

"Don't get too far ahead, Joan girl," I called as Alec and I ran faster to close the gap between us.

"I heard Mr. Carey isn't feeling too well," I said.

Alec nodded his head. At the mention of Celeste's father's name, Alec slowed his running. "He's having trouble walking. More than ever. That foot of his....." His voice trailed away. He looked up at the clear sky. "You really took a risk going to the cave that day, Luke."

My stomach churned. We had not talked much about the events of that day for we both could not bear to face what had occurred. Now Alec had broached the subject.

"I had to go," I said. "And what about you? Stuffing yourself into that lake." I shook my head and he cocked an eyebrow.

"I don't regret what I did, but I'll never be able to forgive myself for not being able to save her."

"What was going to happen, happened. We didn't have any choice in the matter." My words felt like straw in my mouth.

"I know you cared about her, Luke."

I nodded and we avoided each other's gaze. I didn't tell him that I needed to be near Celeste as much as I needed to breathe, and that I knew he felt the same way. He had been willing to give his life for her. Now I owed it to him to keep my feelings to myself. Mentioning my own agony would only make things worse for him. What right did I have to feel so strongly?

"There's so much I wanted to ask her," he said, "but I never got the chance."

We drew to a stop at the side of the path and I realized that neither of us could ever know enough about Celeste. I wanted her so badly. There are some people you'll wait for forever, even if they are no longer with you and never will be.

My sadness turned to anger, something that had been brewing for many days. This time I let the dark feeling take over. Alec was studying his sneakers.

I heard Joanie scream loudly. Then she screamed again and my heart raced. I looked to where she had been running ahead of us, but she was not in sight. I had lost track of her in our conversation.

I called out, "Joanie, where are you? It's okay!"

She screamed again and I listened hard trying to assess where she had gone.

"She's somewhere over that way," said Alec. He pointed to a wild blackberry thicket that framed the pines by the lake. I took off at top speed to the bushes.

"Hang on, Joan girl! I'm coming. You're gonna be fine!" I knew Joanie was in a panic by now, for she hated the unfamiliar. Her routines were what enabled her to make her way in what was a hostile environment. Most of us are not that far removed from her, but we're better at pretending we can deal with the uncertain. Her whimpers and moans grew closer as the brambles in the thicket tore at my legs, causing blood to stream from the small cuts where I did battle with the vegetation. Alec joined me and we hacked at the mesh of vines and branches.

At last I uncovered her. She lay on her back, caught beneath a bunch of wild blackberry bushes, thorns ringing her head and pricking her skull.

"Joan girl, I'm here. It's going to be all right," I said. "What on earth were you doing? Trying to tunnel your way to that tree?"

She turned her dark eyes toward me and my own began to well up. I ripped at the brambles with my bare hands. Joanie's hands bled and the sorrowful look she wore made me want to rip apart more than the bushes. Why did these things have to happen? The senselessness of the world was overwhelming at times. Again anger boiled up.

Joanie's thrashing had immersed her deeply in the thick thorny cover so that by the time we freed her all three of us were covered in brambles and thorns, bleeding from surface wounds. My eyes stung with sweat and my back ached. Joanie stood on bloody legs and then she did the most amazing thing. She smiled broadly and started to dance. In spite of the cuts trickling blood down my legs, in spite of the thorns stuck in my hands, I started to laugh, and so did Alec.

Alec joined arms with Joanie and the two of them did a silly jig. Joanie bent and retrieved her flag, then pointed at a fir beyond the brambles. The evergreen towered over the others and stood so tall I was not at all sure I would have the courage to climb it.

"That tree. Now." Joanie turned her gaze to me.

Alec smiled broadly. "She knows what she wants, doesn't she?"

I mumbled under my breath, not ready for this task as Joanie wrapped the flag around my neck. Then she leaned over and pecked me on my cheek. I felt like a knight going off to joust his peers, only my enemy was seventy-five-feet tall and full of pinecones. The kiss sent my dark feelings into hiding. A few seconds later I gladly boosted myself up into the first low branch of the pine.

"The top. The top," said Joanie.

"The top!" echoed Alec. "Excellent idea. Especially from down here."

After her last tree-climbing mishap, Joanie had promised Mom not to climb today. Alec never indulged in the activity. That left me the designated climber.

I ascended slowly as pines are not the easiest trees to scale. The sap from the bark irritated my already injured hands and the thin branches made me long for a sturdy oak. When I reached the uppermost branches, I stopped. From this point on the limbs were scrawny and I did not trust them to hold my weight. Below me were the rest of the trees and off in the distance I could see the town.

If I squinted I knew where the Spi-Sea plant would have been belching fumes. It was Wednesday and miraculously no fishy smells wafted in the air. After the storm, with no land to rebuild upon, the plant had decided to relocate. Spi-Sea sold the glimmering lake to Faith Junction and the town's fathers promptly turned it into a public recreation area. Glimmerdark Lake they called it. There were plans to turn the submerged plant, clearly visible through the transparent waters, into a scuba destination. The land abutting the lake belonged to Good Samaritan Hospital. The hospital's board of trustees erected a small chapel with a beaming white cross that perched atop the roof pointing to the sky. They named the chapel St. Celeste.

"Is everything okay?" Alec called up to me, interrupting my reverie. "Come back down if it's too difficult to tie the flag on."

I knew he was trying to be helpful, but I also knew that Joanie had her heart set on seeing her flag fly on this particular tree. Any deviation from that plan would send her into tears and an angry fit that I had no desire to witness. I wanted to spare Alec from such a show and myself from having to calm her. Most of all I wanted to get this task over and done with.

"I'm going to tie 'er up right now," I called down.

Joanie clapped her hands and began to dance at the base of the tree.

"Get ready. Get ready," I called. I slipped the ties onto the main branch of the pine and made several strong knots. No wind or storm would dislodge Celeste's creation. I leaned back to admire my work and suddenly I felt myself losing balance. My feet slipped out from under me and I tumbled down. Below me Joanie screamed frantically. I bounced from limb to limb like one of Joanie's basketballs loose on the street. The slick pine branches afforded me no grip. With all my might I grabbed at a large limb, but the branch snapped and sent me hurtling faster. For an instant I hung in the air. I summoned strength I did not have and clutched blindly at the green growth. With a jolt, I stopped my fall, my legs dangling beneath me.

Joanie's wails of fear filled the afternoon air. I called down, "I'm OK. It's nothing. I just came down a bit faster than I'd like." I looked around wondering what had spared me. I pulled myself up, then climbed slowly down to the ground.

Alec clapped me on the back. I hugged Joanie and dried her tears. "Luke fly," she said, wailing loudly. Then I pointed and she looked up to where her flag flapped in the afternoon breeze.

"Now that's a flag," I said, "and definitely one of the finest I've ever seen." Joanie hopped from foot to foot and I smiled.

After we had admired it from all angles, I said, "Let's get going," and extended a hand to Joanie who shook her head.

"Joanie's staying here," she said, jutting out her chin.

"We have to get home."

"No. Joanie, stays."

I glanced at Alec who seemed unperturbed at Joanie's recalcitrance. He smiled at her. "We can come back later on. The flag will be up there for a long time, Joan girl."

Joanie shook her head harder.

I said, "It's not safe for you to be out here alone. We have to go back together. Now."

Alec said, "We'll make sure we come back tomorrow. How's that sound? It's bound to be gorgeous in the morning. Celeste would like you to see it then, I'd bet. And you can tell her all about how you hung it."

This appealed to Joanie who finally lumbered ahead of us muttering to herself.

CR&O

Sunset found us someplace far different from Joanie's flag-hanging spot by Lake Parrot. Mr. Carey called and asked us to stop by. Since the storm that fateful night he sought us out periodically and we were happy to provide him company. Joanie, Alec, Deanna, Josh and I climbed out of my mother's car and headed to the Carey porch where Mr. Carey sat in a rocking chair puffing on a pipe.

"Goodbye, goodbye!" yelled my mother, waving long orange fingernails, her green and yellow ribbon bobbing as she blew us a kiss. My father was at home waiting for her. They would share a cup of coffee, take a walk and retire early as they had for the past few weeks, sharing quiet intimacies. I no longer feared there was something amiss between them.

Mr. Carey waved at my mother then called, "Hello, kids, make yourselves at home."

Beside him, Celeste sat in a wheelchair facing the hills to the west. Though it was a warm night, a blue and green afghan covered her lap. Since the day she had rescued Alec at the cave, she had not moved a muscle nor spoken a word. The doctors said she was in a complex vegetative mental state that no one understood.

"How's she doing, Mr. Carey?" asked Josh.

Mr. Carey shrugged. "Same as ever as far as I can tell. Those doctors don't know anything about her...never have, never will."

Josh peered into her eyes and then took a seat on the porch steps.

"I don't know what else I can do for her," Mr. Carey said, running his fingers through his hair. "I read to her, bring her those little jars she loves so much, her jacks, pictures of all of you." He nodded in our direction. "Ben sends over a vanilla cone every week and I trickle it into her mouth. I think she likes that."

Deanna sat at Celeste's feet and turned on her transistor radio. "She always liked music," said Deanna. As usual, I had trouble looking at Celeste.

Alec climbed onto the porch and lay a bunch of field flowers in Celeste's lap.

"Son, it's really not necessary for you to bring her those every day."

Alec shook his head. "It's the least I can do."

I bit my lip. Even in her current disabled state, the sight of Celeste left me weak. I would do anything, anything for that girl. I cursed heaven and hell, light and dark, for leaving her this way, for leaving me aching for her. My rage eclipsed all other feelings. I reveled in the ease with which it grew and embraced it as a lover. She may have restored the balance of light and dark in the cave, but her condition left me wallowing in moods as black as what I had encountered in her lair.

Joanie grunted. "For Celeste," she said, holding a jar out and placing it in Celeste's lap alongside the flowers. I recognized the jar as the one that held her beloved rainbow. Though I was touched by my sister's generosity, my anger prevented my expressing any feeling of good will. My mind railed at what had come to pass since the first night I found Celeste wrapped in that DDT cloud. I found a stone and threw it hard at a tree in the yard where it found its mark with an empty thwack.

"It's going to be a beautiful sunset," said Deanna.

Josh sat beside her and wrapped a protective arm around her shoulder. "I think you're right," he said. He had been subdued of late, finding companionship in the healing of Deanna. Since her hospitalization she had seen him with new eyes, much to his delight. His masturbatory talk had faded like a pair of well-washed jeans. I took no joy in the fact that there was still some happiness in the world. It infuriated me to face directly what I did not have.

Josh shot me a sly look and said, "I wonder if Susie has such nice sunsets back in California."

Susie. I shuddered at the name. She had left for fall semester a few days ago threatening me with returning with red and green pubic hair at Christmas.

Mr. Carey limped inside and retrieved a camera. "Come on, all of you, stand next to Celeste," he said, motioning for us to pose.

Alec stood and walked behind Celeste's chair. He reached deep in his pocket and withdrew a yellow ribbon. He wound the fabric through Celeste's hair and kissed the top of her head, then he stood behind her and nodded at Mr. Carey.

I wanted to scream at him. It was as though all his former anger had been bottled and poured into me. I wanted to grab him by the shoulders and shake him till he erupted in my rage.

We assembled ourselves on the porch around Celeste's wheelchair to capture the moment in time. Other than my own defiantly set jaw, the faces smiling round Celeste were young, open, with a tinge of sadness that was barely detectable in the eyes. We were stricken all of us, but we could recover. Mr. Carey snapped the picture and the flashbulb pierced the gathering dark.

The blinding light of Mr. Carey's camera left me in a contemplative mood and my anger simmered slowly.

"Sun's going down," said Mr. Carey.

We sat on the porch and watched as the orange ball sank slowly into the ridge of trees to the west. Blue, red and purple swirled across the sky painting a cloud portrait that rivaled anything I had seen on class trips to the Metropolitan Museum of Art. With a start, a chill passed over me. Though the colors were true, this was not the usual sunset. The hair on the nape of my neck stood at attention and I leaned forward as the pigments faded from bright to paler tones, spreading pale Easter eggshell hues across the watercolor sky.

I stared hard at the horizon where the sun seemed to hang on invisible wires. I blinked. There was no mistaking it. The sunset hung for an extra second and then for another. Then a band of gold rimmed the horizon, a horizon lined with a dark wire.

"Would you look at that," said Alec, pointing to the phenomenon.

"Whoa," said Josh.

Mr. Carey smiled. We all held our breath and waited.

I inclined my head to Celeste and her lips turned up slightly at the corners, though her eyes remained unseeing. "She did it," I whispered. "She's stopped the dark. Figured out the speed of it, and held it back so we have more light. She never gives up." I knew Celeste must be soaring somewhere and I longed to hear that silvery laugh, but the air held nothing but the hum of crickets. I clenched my fists.

"Well, I'll be damned," said Mr. Carey. "She'll never learn, will she?"

Moments later, the gold and black bands faded and the sun resumed its descent. The final glow entered my pores, then floated like a flame in my veins. With a dazzling flash of recognition, I understood that life was rich, full, meant for living, and a dam as large as the Crandon broke inside of me. As my anger drained away, I knew that life was in the pain, in the striving, and most of all, in the relationships we nurture and are fortunate to have.

My thoughts spiraled. The sun hung and time was suspended that night. The delicate balance between light and dark was interrupted without incident. I could feel myself grow stronger, less angry, my own balance restored. I had Celeste to thank for giving me direction, for holding her torch high and illuminating the way. The rapt faces of those gathered on the porch proved I wasn't the only one affected that way.

As my anger melted away, I was grateful to her for so much. I had loved and somewhere along the way I had crossed over to manhood. I understood that my mentally challenged sister and I had as much in common as we didn't, and that we were going to go through life together, bound by more than blood. It was my turn to go forth lighting new paths and at the same time brightening my own. I had the memory of love to guide me toward love once again. Nothing could take that away.

With a pang of regret, I could feel Celeste drifting away from me, but I knew I would never lose her entirely. I would always have that image of her rising up from a cloud of poison gas to help me.

"Come on, let's have a singalong," said Deanna.

"Excellent idea," said Mr. Carey.

As the dark gathered around us, we mocked death in the manner of the young, riotously shouting and singing until we could find no more songs to raise. No one sang louder than I, making sure to throw in some show tunes for Celeste. Under a moon dark sky, solar flares unseen by the human eye continued to erupt, uncontrollable, mysterious. I knew that we were not alone, that there was always someone there to reach out to. I understood that some things never make sense, so it is worthless to try to understand them, yet they are still important and meaningful.

"Game," said Joanie during a lull in our singing.

"Game," I said.

I stepped off the porch. Joanie did not have her ball and there was no hoop in the Carey yard, yet we played and played, faking it as the light faded to that point in time when it is neither light nor dark. We moved into a rainbow of black whose gradations were clear to me.

CR8ED

Celeste passed away quietly the next day while Mr. Carey read to her. He called to let me know, and I sat in my room for hours till the light disappeared and the dark comforted me.

A few days later, at Celeste's funeral, the rain fell in buckets while the sun shone brightly behind a gauzy curtain of clouds.

"Those are angel's tears," said Deanna, leaning into Josh after the service.

I threw an arm over Alec's shoulder and the two of us fought back our emotions.

"She's still here," said Alec. "I can feel her."

"Me too. She's so bright that no dark could ever extinguish her."

I looked up at the rain-blackened sky reassured that an exquisite balance of light and dark existed, an internal compass always pointing to true north. That didn't make Celeste's passing any easier for me, but it did comfort me nonetheless.

CR8ED

After the funeral I was helping my mother with dinner when I heard the DDT truck coming down the block. My mother glanced at me and for a second I hesitated, ready to run outside and give chase. But Celeste's face floated before me. I went to the window and slammed it down to keep the gas from entering the house.

"Why do they think it's ok to flood us all with that stuff?" asked my mother. "If it kills insects, don't they think it will be bad for us?"

"I don't know, Ma," I said, closing the last of the windows in the kitchen. "I don't know."

CR8ED

Joanie lives with us now, as my parents decided she shouldn't return to the Raritan School. My father continues to travel with his job and I accept that all is right in his and my mother's world. The storm and its consequences had an interesting affect on my mom. She took a job on the newly created Glimmerdark Lake as a tour guide on a pleasure boat named *The Celeste*, where she's a favorite of the tourists, in her orange and green pants and shirt, ponytail and yellow scarf flapping on the breezy deck. Sometimes she works a double shift, and she lets me ride for free.

Those days, I listen to Mom tell about the night that the lake appeared. She points out the wreck of the Spi-Sea plant below the shiny surface and her tangerine nails wave at the peaceful scene. She smiles and says:

"One day, thanks to a little girl who some say worked magic, a lot of things changed in Faith Junction. She taught us that everyone should always follow their dreams. They should trust in themselves and understand that sometimes when we aren't loved back in the way we want, or when we fail to achieve what we want, it doesn't matter, it doesn't minimize the depth of the feeling or the experience. Striving for our goals and caring for others is what makes us most human, and most lovable."

Many of the people on board groan when Mom says this stuff. I let my gaze go to the horizon, where the sun will soon be making its descent. And I smile. For I know Mom's right and I know that out there, on the line between sky and sea, so does Celeste.

❦THE END❧

AUTHOR'S NOTE

In 1964 it was commonplace for boys and girls to pedal close behind the DDT trucks in the poisonous fog. I know because I was one of the kids who did that. People had no idea that following the trucks could be dangerous. DDT was outlawed in 1972 after three decades of use for it was found to be an unacceptable risk to the environment, and to pose potential harm to human health.

In 1964 there was no AIDS virus, no fear of dying from contracting a deadly disease if consenting parties engaged in sexual behavior. There was, however, a fear of pregnancy, and a fear of sexually transmitted diseases, but boys and girls were reluctant to discuss sexual protection. While the characters in this book engaged in risky sexual behavior regardless of the era, when such behavior is viewed through the lens of time it is representative behavior of the mid-sixties, the beginning of the "free love" era.

In the novel, Luke's sister, Joanie, suffered from a disease called Fragile X Syndrome or Martin-Bell Syndrome, a genetic type of inherited mental retardation that was not known in 1964. The condition is much better understood now. Fragile X affects far more males than females and the symptoms are milder in females.

Printed in the United States
23877LVS00005B/196

9 781413 743081